Ann:

Here's a tip!

Stay Away From Racetracks!

J.W.

First Radio Brought You

GANG BUSTERS

Then the Movies Subjected You to

GHOST BUSTERS

Now a Daffy Publisher Provides

BLOCH BUSTERS

Eight Riotous Lefty Feep Comedy-Fantasies by America's Dean of Terror, Robert Bloch, in print for the first time in 45 years. Plus one brand-new story written just for this edition!

Prepare to be tickled by the zany side of the man who created PSYCHO . . . but beware . . .

You Could

LAUGH YOURSELF TO DEATH

OKAY, BUB, WHO'S LEFTY FEEP?

Lefty is a fast-talking racetrack tout, a comedy hero of the 1940s, who's always having close encounters of the whacko kind with crazy inventors and mad scientists and getting displaced in time and space. He's the creation of Robert Bloch, America's Dean of Terror.

BLOCH? NOW YOU'RE TALKING, CHARLIE!

Robert Bloch is one of America's best-known horror writers, who has shown his dark side in hundreds of terror tales. Here he displays his genius for buffoonery and lampoonery in stories packed with zany characters, cruel puns, raucous rhymes and other delights too seldom found in modern literature. (This is literature?)

LEFTY'S A SCREAM, HUH PAL?

He's a laugh riot of the World War II years as he heils right in the face of the Gestapo, soft-shoes with dancing mice, strikes out with bowling dwarfs, flies to Buffalo on a carpet, creates gold out of dirt, meets a semi-invisible man, and traverses time to become a movie star.

SO QUIT THE YAK, JACK, AND COOK WITH THIS BOOK

DEDICATION

This book is for

HAROLD GAUER

My frequent companion,
sometime collaborator,
and lifelong friend

Critics Are Raving
. . . Not Because They're Insane . . .
But Because They Love Lefty Feep!

Ray Bradbury:

"In a field that often takes itself much too seriously, Robert Bloch makes me laugh. Good medicine, that. I wish I had the patent!"

Fritz Leiber:

"The Lefty Feep stories are rib-tickling proof that Bloch has a sense of humor matching his sense of horror. They are as irreverently and wickedly funny as his Psycho is supremely blood-chilling. They do a Jack-the-Ripper job on the pomposity and conceit of the masters of this crazy world we're stuck with. I was introduced to Bloch by no less a person than H. P. Lovecraft, but it's Lefty who's kept the relationship blossoming sweetly.

Richard Matheson:

"Bloch has a sense of humor—which is something like saying Einstein had a head between his shoulders—the understatement of any desired year. And Bob Bloch shares that humor with us in his writing—and in his life for those among us fortunate enough to know him personally—and that is, indeed, a thing of beauty and our joy forever.

Part of Bob's munificent sharing of his sense of humor exists in these, the chronicles of Lefty Feep, that indefatigable bon vivant, that insoucient albeit somewhat accident prone gambler who seems to have an unending gift for blundering into the wrong circumstances at the right time—the right time, that is, for us the readers of these tales.

That Bloch can spin a yarn with the best of them—and better than most of the best—is a well-established literary fact. Frighten and astound us? Often. Scare the living daylights out of us? Whenever he chooses to do it. And—most delightfully—make us laugh?

Invariably. As witness the perilous antics of Lefty Feep whose observations and adventures will endure—to make future generations chortle and enjoy. Long life to Lefty and his creator. They have made the world a better—if rather more askew—place."

Richard Lupoff:

"Lefty Feep is back—what a thrill! Anyone who remembers the original stories will welcome this combination of Damon Runyon and Groucho Marx. Anyone who encounters the outrageous puns, wild wisecracks and acerbic comments on the human condition will howl with a hearty portion of pleasure and an occasional twinge of pain."

William F. Nolan:

"Whether he's writing about Lefty Feep, Norman Bates or Jack the Ripper, Robert Bloch is a supreme storyteller whose creative well never seems to run dry. He's the Court Jester of Dark Fantasy, a writer who always delivers chills and laughter!"

Richard Christian Matheson:

"Robert Bloch has done for writing what color did for paint, Nijinsky did for tights and Norman Bates did for showering with friends. He is able to levitate language and humor to a height even floating ladies rarely rise."

Harlan Ellison:

"Bloch is the mad literary equivalent of Dr. Frankenstein: He crosses Damon Runyon with Baron Munchhausen and gets a Frankincense Monster called Lefty Feep, the world's greatest liar . . . maybe. It's been too damn long that we've been without Lefty. Having him back reminds us that we've grown too stern, that we've been taking ourselves too seriously for too long.

"Decades have passed since the arbiters of taste told us the Feep stories were lightweight, that they'd never stand the test of time, and what a delight to stick our tongues out at their judgments: We have aged, but Lefty hasn't. He's still as full of ginger as Astaire, and here in the shadow of Life and the Bomb, he still reminds us that nonsense is the dearest panacea for what ails us. Welcome back, Lefty; it's great to groan along with you again."

LOST IN TIME AND SPACE WITH LEFTY FEEP

By Robert Bloch

Eight Funny And Fanciful Fables of the Forties

Plus One Brand-New Parable of Modern Times

Volume I of THE LEFTY FEEP TRILOGY

Edited by John Stanley
Cover and Sketches By Kenn Davis

Published by Creatures at Large
Pacifica California

K. D.

LOST IN TIME AND SPACE WITH LEFTY FEEP
A Creatures at Large publication
First Edition ©1987 by Robert Bloch.
 Published in the United States of America by Creatures at Large, P.O. Box 687, Pacifica CA 94044.

Bloch, Robert, 1917–
Lost in time and space with Lefty Feep.

1. Feep, Lefty (Fictitious character)—Fiction. 2. Fantastic fiction, American.
I. Stanley, John, 1940– . II. Title
PS3503.L718L67 1987 813′.54 86-71608
ISBN 0-940064-03-0 (series no.)
ISBN 0-940064-01-4 (v.1: trade ed.)
ISBN 0-940064-02-2 (v.1: deluxe ed.)

Library of Congress Catalogue Card No.: 86-071608

CONTENTS
(Without the Table)

MEET THE CREATOR . . .

ROBERT BLOCH, FROM WHOSE MIND SPRANG LEFTY FEEP

. . . AND THE CREATED

LEFTY FEEP, RIGHT AFTER HE WAS SPRUNG

Introduction to The Son of The Introduction

CHELSEA QUINN YARBRO is best known to the literary world as the creator of Count Ragoczy Saint-Germain, an eternal vampire who roves through the centuries in a series of fascinating historical fantasies which bear such titles as *Hotel Transylvania, Blood Games, Tempting Fate,* and *The Palace.*

The Count, a decent aristocrat who maintains his dignity and humanity despite his never-ending nerve-ending craving for blood, also appeared in a collection of short stories, after which he was laid to promised eternal rest. Although no future novels are planned, one can only hope the Count's creator will allow him resurrection at the soonest fall of night.

Meanwhile, Quinn (as she is best known to friends) remains active writing science-fiction, mysteries and horror. What little time she enjoys away from her smokin' computer is spent with either her horse Magick (described by her as a "thoroughbred/quarterhorse cross") or her loyal cat, Pimpernel.

She is a great admirer of Robert Bloch and his writings and knows the man on a personal basis better than many of her peers. When it came time to consider a guest introducer, I could not imagine anyone more qualified to write about Lefty Feep's creator. *—John Stanley*

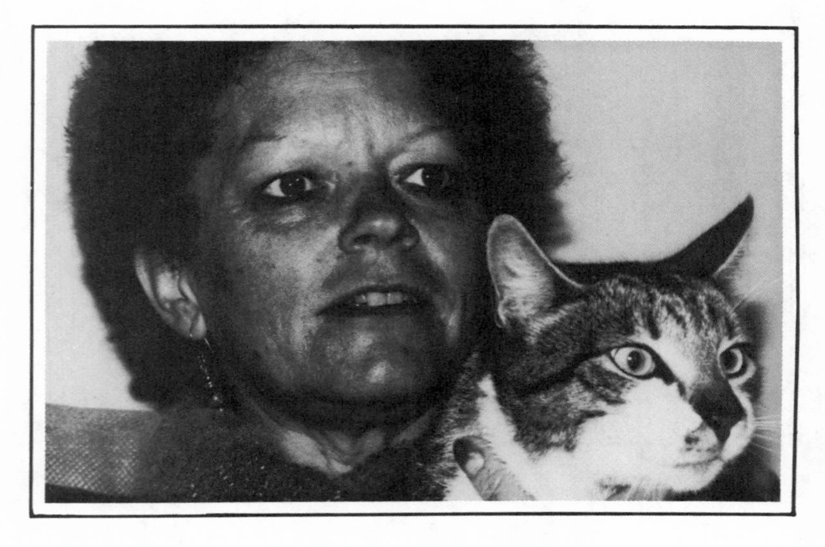

Chelsea Quinn Yarbro with a companion named Pimpernel

SON OF THE INTRODUCTION:

THE MAN WHO WROTE . . .

By Chelsea Quinn Yarbro

INEVITABLY that is how readers think about writers—as *the one who wrote* and then fill in any of the particular writer's titles. Most of the time, this is not only fine, it is desirable and complimentary, an indication the writer has managed to evoke some "reality" in the reader's mind that sticks and has a strong enough impression that the recognition continues when the book has been set aside.

However . . .

Yes, there always seems to be a however, doesn't there?

It is ironic that where a writer succeeds most effectively he or she also creates something of a bind for himself or herself, for when the stories and characters become persuasive enough to remain with the reader, the writer finds him- or herself in the shadow of his or her own work. While this happens in many other fields, no one—except perhaps actors—find themselves so colored by what they have done.

This is hardly an original observation: I am, in fact, paraphrasing a dear friend of mine who warned me about this problem years ago, based on his own experience. That dear friend is, of course, Robert Bloch, and it is my intention to tell you a little about him without the pall of any of his creations falling over us.

It would be difficult to imagine a more sincere or cordial colleague than Bob Bloch. He has always been courteous and interested in the happenings in his friends' lives, and does not limit his interest to the work, or to the good stuff. Bob is one of those rare human beings who cares for those around him, and is willing to let them know it. And lest you think this is mere introduction whipped cream, check around; ask those who have had dealings with him and you will discover that he is truly a kind man in a world where kindness is all-too-infrequently met.

When I first met Bob eighteen years ago (was it really that long ago? Yes, it was), he was attending the World Science Fiction Convention in Berkeley. In those days, a WorldCon of two thousand was considered gigantic; it filled the Claremont Hotel and two other over-flow hotels. Bob was up from Los Angeles for the occasion and, unlike some of the other venerable names, seemed to be approachable and genuinely intrigued by his readers. We had a few conversations and I came away feeling I had been given some very real help from him, as well as a boost in morale. Since I sold my first story a few months later, it is possible to say that he has a lot to answer for.

Most writers are not very good correspondents. By the time you finish throwing words around as the tools of the trade, it is difficult to change gears and dash off a letter that doesn't sound like a plot outline. Bob is a notable exception to this problem; Bob not only writes stories, novels and scripts, he also—bless his heart—writes letters and post cards. He makes a point of staying in touch. Whether it is four lines on a card or a six-page letter, Bob keeps the channels open. He makes comments on fanzines, he sends words of criticism and encouragement to newer writers, he comments on the work of those who are established. As large and diverse as his published works are, his letters go farther afield, both figuratively and literally. He is always responding with thoughtful interest.

Bob is a man of great personal warmth. He smiles when he talks. He leaves love notes to his wife on the refrigerator.

He has time for friends even when a deadline is looming. During those times of personal difficulties, he has never taken it out on those he cares about. He and Elly are the most gracious of host-and-hostesses; in their beautiful home it is impossible to feel unwelcome.

So how does this mesh with a man who writes about ultimate and exploitive materialists like Lefty Feep? Or demented serial murderers like (and I might as well get this over with) Norman Bates? Or that damned-but-happy rider of *That Hellbound Train?* What does this gentle and polite man have to do with voodoo and mayhem and murderous sacrifices, with despair and savagery and supernatural events?

What he has to do with them, how they mesh with him is that he writes about them. Being a sensitive and somewhat shy man, he is keenly aware of how easily and how deeply others can be hurt by a chance word or careless treatment. Having concerns about the society in which he lives, he extrapolates trends and fads to their most extreme manifestations. As one of the true experts on that most elusive of murderers, Jack the Ripper, Bob has spent as much or more time studying the psychology of those driven to commit such crimes as to the specifics of the crimes themselves. For Bob, the logic of madness has been one of the most effective continuing themes in his work, and one that continues to fascinate his readers.

It is a mark of his writing that he is able to tell the story through the perceptions of those characters experiencing it. Just as Norman Bates "sees" his behavior as loving, so in these tales, Bob pulls off the marvelous trick of showing you wonders through the eyes of someone who mistakes wonder for guile, who interprets the most extraordinary events in terms of a scam. You believe in Lefty Feep because the character is fully realized, and occupies his environment on his own terms, not on the terms of the writer.

That last bit is where things tend to get sticky. Difficult as it may be to understand, Lefty Feep is not an alter ego to Robert Bloch—nor is Norman Bates. Lefty Feep is a character in a series of stories, some very much rooted in their time, some of them more chronologically fluid. Lefty Feep is a sinister innocent, a small-time crook who is given gold and sees dross.

However, there is one thing Lefty Feep has in common with Bob, or rather one thing that the stories reflect, which is Bob's remarkable aptitude for making puns. In the Lefty Feep stories the quality of wit is not the same as Bob Bloch in conversation; that would not be appropriate to the work. Nevertheless, Bob is one of those writers whose close association with words results in endless games with them. He can be outrageous and/or funny and/or sly and/or erudite. He is able to make puns without getting off the subject at hand, which is much harder to pull off than it might seem. He also has the ability to pun and joke about serious subjects without trivializing the seriousness of the subjects under consideration. In fiction or in after-dinner speeches, Bob often uses humor to make his points; that is not to say that his humor is bitter or that he disguises anger with wit most of the time. Certainly there have been some instances when he has used both of the previous ploys as deftly as an epee, but generally he finds less caustic uses for his humor, which is tuned more to absurdity than to hostility.

Often writers of fiction tend to forget the working class, or those who prey on them and their industry. Somehow it is considered to be less interesting to deal with "unglamorous" types than with the glossy thoroughbreds of wealth and power. That is one trap Bob has never walked into. Bob finds richness in the machinations of grifters, in the work of pragmatic artisans, in the simplicity of those whose lives have closed in on them. He can show you all the world through those eyes and with those expectations, and without lecturing delineate his concerns through the characters who populate his fiction.

While he is not a didactic writer—few horror authors are—Bob tends to show the naive greed of Lefty Feep as amusing and perversely endearing; this man's schemes and plans endanger few people but himself. He is not in any larger sense of the word a threat. Lefty Feep is a character who wants all the goodies and yet has the most limited perspective on what might constitute goodies. Some of Lefty Feep's basic likability comes from this short-sighted avarice; much of his humor does.

Bob has a sneaky affection for these stories, and for some of his other work dealing with the small-time criminal class. It is as if he took *The Beggar's Opera,* winnowed out the false romance of the play, moved it into the 1940s and '50s and continued in the same vein. He appreciates these people, and is willing to let them live their lives as they see fit. He does not impose on them, and he does not impose on the reader. His narrative is wry without being condescending, and the events are accorded their perceived importance without any Dickensian superiority on his part as narrator.

That does not mean Bob spends his time in a badly furnished rooming house in the sleazy part of town. He writes in a large, sunny office with an extensive view of the San Fernando Valley as well as the clear sight of his swimming pool. The walls are lined with floor-to-ceiling bookshelves which are filled to overflowing. Bob's desk faces away from the window, so that when he looks up from his work he sees books, not vistas except the ones in his mind. Little interrupts him—he is a hard worker—but the occasional visits of one of his two cats, who, unlike Elly, are more than willing to cut into his thoughts when it is what they want to do.

One of the endearing things about Bob is his affection for the tyranny of his cats. He came late to being a cat-keeper and therefore learned a great deal from the furry despots. He likes them for the same reason he likes people: he likes them for being what they are. He admires the totality of the cats just as he looks for it in people, and values it in a way that is not often encountered, for he is able to accept people on their terms without compromising his own.

This understanding and acceptance is probably tied up in the nature of his work, but as to which came first, I very much doubt anyone, including Bob, could tell you. Bob is a man who takes people as they are. That does not mean he cannot be hurt or insulted. He certainly can. But he is able to perceive that the person and the insult might not always be the same thing. That gives him more leeway with his friendships and with the characters in his work than many people experience all life long.

It is never an easy thing to describe a close friend, for so much of what constitutes that closeness cannot be easily expressed in words; I find writing this introduction difficult for just that reason. There is also the problem of trying to find words to discuss art. Since fiction is done with words, it is easy to assume that the art of it can be imparted through words—which, fortunately or unfortunately, is not the case. Bob Bloch is not the kind of writer who can be easily summed up as belonging to one genre or one generation or one school of thought. He follows his interests. They, in turn, take him into strange and uncharted regions, either of the society of humanity or the human soul. As staunch as he is in friendship, he is as diverse in his interests and his development.

In his first published works, which came out while he was still in his teens and corresponding with Howard Phillips Lovecraft, his work shows some of that influence as well as a touch of Haggard and Kipling. About the only thing that can be inferred from that is that he probably liked to read Lovecraft, Haggard and Kipling. Since that time he has done a smattering of almost all the major genres of fiction with the possible exception of bodice-ripper romances. It is one of his greatest gifts, this flexibility and constant curiosity. Bob is not the kind of writer who will make you suspect that he is writing the same tale over and over again. He is constantly finding new areas of endeavor and new characters to take on the challenge of his imagination. He is willing to examine a situation in one light, and then turn it inside out and look at it from an entirely different angle. There are not many writers who can do that kind of mental back-flip; Bob does them regularly and so easily that the reader might think that there was nothing remarkable in this accomplishment, which is rather like supposing a champion acrobat is doing nothing spectacular simply because his triple somersault appears to be effortless. The operative words—in case you missed them—are *appears to be.*

Does that mean Bob is therefore one of those conversational whiz-kids who does verbal tour jetes for the sheer hell of it? Not necessary, no, but there are times when he can take off on entertaining tales punctuated with some of the most impossible puns known to the English language. Even someone like me, who generally does not like puns, stands in awe of his ability and invention. He does not use puns to attack those around them, excusing his behavior because it is supposed to be "funny."

Bob finds delight in intelligent discussions and in the companionship of his colleagues. He is willing to put himself out when he senses that this would be appreciated, and he is slow to criticize when he believes others are in error, and he withholds public judgment when matters are still unresolved. This is impressively professional conduct that few of us are able to emulate.

Whenever I think about Bob, I inevitably recall the many kindnesses he has done over the years, from the first time I met him to last week. He has never made it seem that there is any significant gaps in our ages or accomplishments, and when others have anxiously and judiciously weighed up various "brownie points" in status, Bob has not let that get in the way of his convictions or his friendships. When asked for advice, he has given it freely and without conditions. When told of misfortunes, he has been genuinely consoling. He is even willing to listen to me talk about my horse, which is saying a lot.

A few years ago Bob was the featured speaker at the Cabrillo Suspense Writers Conference, and since the San Jose Airport was en route for me, I was asked to pick him up and drive him over the hill to the Santa Cruz area where the Conference was being held. The director of the Conference knew that I would recognize Bob and said that he was sure we'd have fun catching up on the drive. He was right about that. We listened to selections from *Tosca* as we crawled over the summit on Highway 17. Bob at the time remarked that he wasn't sure he would have much to say that would interest beginning suspense and mystery writers, but that he hoped he would think of something that would make those attending think it was worthwhile.

His talk, when he delivered it after Saturday evening dinner, was considered the highpoint of the Conference, and many of those who had come there for the first time were especially delighted to have such a big name there, and one who was affable and informative at the same time. He talked for almost an hour on the transformation of *Psycho* from print to screen, and included such information as the very small amount of money he was paid for the rights and the subsequent tendency that some of the film-going community had to assume that the whole thing was Alfred Hitchcock's idea (Hitchcock himself gave full and complete credit to Bob, both in words and in print, but the reputation of that particular legend was such that there were and are those who might attribute the development of the horror story to him, except for the works of Poe).

Bob was witty and gracious in his talk, and candid in his answers to questions; he discussed what he liked about Hitchcock's treatment of the material and what he did not find satisfactory. He recalled his own move from the Mid-west to Los Angeles and the first stages of his screenwriting career, with comments about the publishing world of the same time. He never dodged a question and he never refused to answer, although he twice said that although he had heard certain complaints of some of the distinguished persons he had worked with, he had never in his dealings with them had reason to complain. For two years after his appearance at Cabrillo, those who attended regularly spoke of his presentation and of him with fondness and respect.

Bob has sometimes remarked that he thinks that the fascination with horror literature stems in part from our desire to immunize ourselves against the reality of brutality and inhumanity present all around us; by reading horror literature, we turn it into something that only happens in books, and we find explanations that remove some of the worst dread—that of random violence. It is easier to face the hideous thing under the bed that echoes back to childhood fears than to deal with the actuality of terrorists bombing department stores and airports. When we vicariously confront the ghoulie form youth which has moved from under the bed to the haunted house on the hill, we are more able to face the slaughter by the Manson Family or the PLO. Through this inoculation we find the means to render the unendurable bearable.

I do not entirely agree with him, but I do think there is a strong element of this "immunization process" in the horror audience. I'm not sure that reading Robert Bloch or Ramsey Campbell or Dennis Etchison or Stephen King or Shirley Jackson or Charles L. Grant or me, for that matter, will prepare anyone for the lasting shock of real, grotesque violence. Still, if horror literature can render such insanities less agonizing, then I suppose it is worth more than its entertainment value.

For make no doubt about it: horror is entertaining. Reading the great folk tales and fairy tales shows that human beings have loved to shudder since the first of us hunkered around a fire at night. While the stories have become more complex and the horrific elements more sophisticated, they still address the things you cannot see or control. Whether you end up wishing for a silver bullet (to put an end to the wereanimal) or a clove of garlic (to ward off the vampire) or a pyx (to make a demon vanish in a puff of smoke) or an unbroken pentagram with salt, water, metal and candle at each point (to contain the devil and all his work), the promise that there is a solution, a means to handle these terrible things, keeps the reader going to the last paragraph, just as our remote ancestors carried fire into their caves to keep warm and to make sure they did not have to share their space with things like bears and wolves.

From those distant beginnings comes the clever fellow who can overcome all kinds of powerful threats with wit rather than with brawn or magic, and these trickster figures are all through folk and fine literature. And from them comes not only the rational solution, but humor. The magicians fall on the sinister side of the line, the jokers on the dexter.

Lefty Feep is one of these jokers, and made to be as real-world as possible. Lefty is so much into the rational, the material, that he has no sense of the larger world in which he lives, and no appreciation of the ramifications of the events of his life—and as a result, he is funny. Instead of threatening, he is amusing; instead of bowing under the burder of his ignorance, his lack of understanding often becomes his greatest strength.

It takes a deft touch to pull this off, and there are many very fine writers who have attempted this without success, or who have achieved an uneasy truce with the material. For what it may be worth, I think Bob is able to do this because he is truly fond of Lefty, and does not presume to patronize him.

By now, I trust you have the sense that Bob is not the kind of man to approach a person, fictional or actual, as a mere object of study. He is too humane for that, and he is too much involved with his stories to permit himself the great distance that would make Lefty the target of derision. Bob treats Lefty with direct understanding, and he lets the character do all the things that Lefty decides he must do without cluttering up the story with asides that would remind you—the reader—that of course he, the author, was not participating, merely reporting. By his narration, Bob reinforces the environment and reality of his creation, and he constantly works to keep that environment as vivid as the characters and events that take place within it, a quality that marks all of Bob's work and gives it its strength. So this is full circle, back to the writer standing in the shadow of his or her characters. I have a last observation to add: My late mother was often troubled that I numbered Robert Bloch among my special friends. "How can you like a man like that?" she would ask, clearly very upset at the idea. "He wrote that terrible *Psycho*. How can you like someone who writes something like that?"

I would then remind her that Bob is not Norman Bates, and would often add that I was not a four-thousand-year-old male vampire, either. Since she disliked my work almost as much as she disliked Bob's, this was not an entirely satisfactory answer, but it usually ended the objection. Nothing I could say could get Bob out of Norman Bates' shadow for her, and that, perversely, speaks well for Bob's ability. His characters are able to get along just fine without him, which is the greatest success a committer of fiction can ever know.

But perhaps one word of warning is in order: You need not hesitate to shower at Bob's place, but you might very well succumb to terminal laughter over an excellent dinner there.

Berkeley, California
21 August 1986

THE INTRODUCTION

Will the Real Lefty Feep Please Rise to the Occasion?

By John Stanley

THIS BOOK EXISTS because Cheryl Ladd caught the flu. Because Pierce Brosnan and Stephanie Zimbalist were too sick to report to the set of *Remington Steele* one morning. Thank your lucky stars some stars were unlucky enough to catch some germs.

What a morning of mourning it was to be . . . but it had dawned as I donned a smile and my zoot suit/snap-brim ensemble and met a jet leaving San Francisco International. It was a cold, clear January day when I arrived in Los Angeles to Eveready myself for a battery of scintillating feature interviews for the big city newspaper that allegedly pays me to cover the entertainment scene. Journalism jack isn't much but it's a living and—being a small-town lad at heart—I like to hang out with bigshot people and rub elbows. I keep hoping some of their fame and bucks will rub off too, but so far the best thing I've picked up is llama lint and a few flakes of dandruff.

I hit the Burbank Airport all smiles because I thought I was going to hobnob with Hollywood's elite and get down low for the lowdown. Cheryl was going to tell me all about her new TV miniseries *Crossings,* hopefully with emphasis on her steamy bedroom scenes with Lee Horsley, something that needed my kind of sophisticated, in-depth reporting for its intellectual asides. Even more than that, I was hoping Brosnan and/or Zimbalist would admit in juicy, salacious terms that they were bitter rivals, jealous of each other to the point of a Hatfield-McCoy stand-off, as I had been told they were by my gossipy contact in the NBC publicity department.

But a lass was alas . . . when I arrived in beautiful downtown Hollywood at the public relations firm that was to escort me to the interviews, I was informed how the flu epidemic was decimating the ranks of movieland's finest. Angelic Cheryl was in her sick bed, with only enough strength to reach for soft-tissue Kleenexes into which to blow her lovely nose, and *Remington Steele* production had been completely cancelled. Not even the gofers would be available for interviews.

I sat for a while, wondering how to fill the time. True, the epidemic had yet to strike the beautiful Sybil Danning, but my meeting with her wasn't until tomorrow. And even a red-blooded American male can only stare at her genteel, flesh-toned artistic publicity pictures for just so long.

Let's see . . . There was always Hollywood Boulevard with its colorful primitive natives, but I didn't feel like hustling down there. The La Brea tarpits sounded like the pits. Or maybe I could catch a flick at the Chinese and compare my footprints with Humphrey Bogart's. Or size up my pectoral patterns against Sylvester Stallone's. The idea didn't have much muscle.

And then I thought of Lefty Feep.

For more than a year, this guy had been on my mind, and I was getting tired of him sitting there, his legs dangling down onto my medulla oblongata. Part of him was in my cerebral hemisphere, another part in my corpus callosium. I was beginning to feel like a clumsy oaf with two Lefty Feeps. Hey, I decided, it's time to do something about Lefty the Loiterer.

Feep is this [bleep], a racetrack tout and a lout, I used to read and heed all the time in *Fantastic Adventures,* a science-fiction/fantasy pulp magazine of the 1940s. I'm a nut about the magazine. I have this collection at home because one day I was walking past a San Francisco used bookstore and I found these bound volumes in the showcase window and I went from mild to wild and bought the lot and discovered this Feep creep in this snappy, zappy series.

I loved Feep because he was always bumping into offbeat people I wish I could beat off some day. People like silly scientists, demented doctors, husky hepcats, melodious musicians, malevolent magicians and wily warlocks. But mainly the gorgeous, cuddly, curvaceous, bubbleheaded blondes called ginches. Dames poured into their low-cut dresses, with ruby-red lips, va-va-voom legs and the kind of sway that one only associates with a hammock in a Kansas windstorm. Feep's world was where you could find dancing mice, bowling dwarfs, invisible clothing, flying carpets for an Arabian knight, the magic of Midas, and a chicken that laid Golden Eggs. (I received a golden goose in a crowd once, but never a Golden Egg.)

The stories were gasped out with a flurry of exclamation points by Lefty in the first-person present tense, emphasis on past nonsense. The language of Lefty Feep was the colloquialisms of the 1940s, when the stories were first written in the passion of literary lunacy. Stories that captured the American idiom (and idiocy) of World War II, with focus on jive-smart con men and gangland gents.

The setting was Jack's Shack, an "eats" joint that makes today's McDonald's seem like a gourmet palace built in Heaven. The guy who had to listen to Lefty, never being quick enough to escape out the door before Feep noticed him, was named Bob. Zesty Lefty was always rhyming with his timing, and coming up with pun fun to stun, hon.

You don't forget the characters in the Lefty Feep yarns, not after you hear their names: Gorilla Gabface, Magistrate Donglepootzer, Floyd Scrilch, Boogie Mann the jive musician, Gallstone the Magician, Out-of-Business Oscar, Black

Art the rug seeker, King Glimorgus the giant, and Klondike Ike the prospector. And a cast of other crazier-than-life characters straight out of a colorful gangster underworld that never was because it got rubbed out by The Godfather long before Marlon Brando started to get horse.

Yeah, I decided, sitting there in that public relations office with nothing to do, slowly realizing that thumb twirling was a fruitless pastime, it was the hour to give literary life back to Lefty Feep.

So I picked up the phone and called this hooligan named Robert Bloch.

You thought this Lefty Feep was a [bleep] creep. Wait until you meet and bleat with this Bloch bloke.

Maybe you've heard about him. He wrote a book once called *Psycho* that was directed by Alfred Hitchcock to become one of the most terrifying movies of all time, a fright classic that set whole new trends in the cinema still being

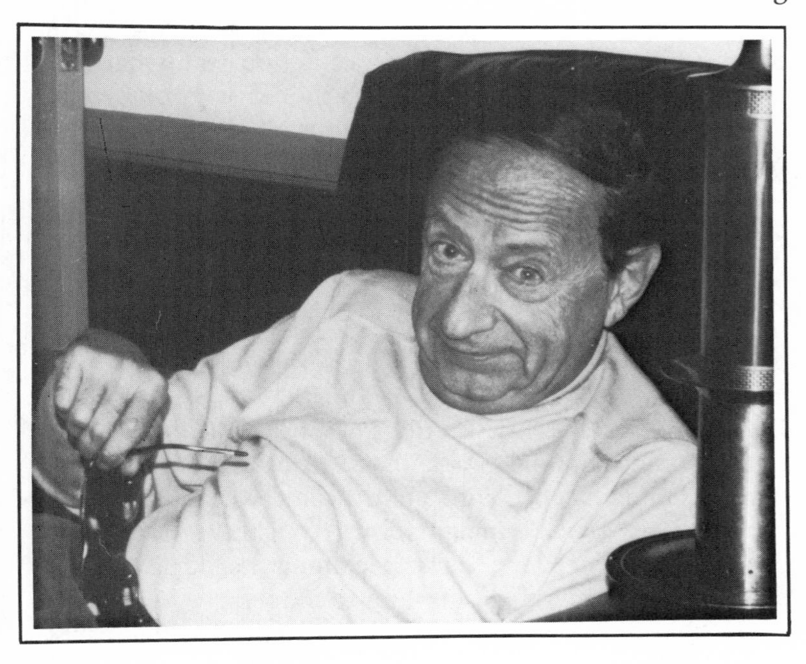

copied today . . . Not even Bloch has taken a shower since the movie came out in 1960 . . . and his wife Elly gave up on designer shower curtains years ago.

But *Psycho* is such a small part of what this mild-mannered sentimentalist has given to us insatiable readers . . . since the tender age of 17 he has been writing an unending stream of horror and fantasy short stories, almost all of which can now be found reprinted in such famous anthologies as *Out of the Mouths of Graves, Yours Truly Jack the Ripper, Atoms and Evil* and *Such Stuff as Screams Are Made Of*. Here is the tombstone territory which he has staked out like no other writer—and it's a stake he's driven home repeatedly in his vampiric yarns. In this zombie zone can be found his Enoch, his Beelzebub, his Hell-Bound Train, his Screaming People, his Cloak, his Mannikin, his Skull of the Marquis De Sade, his Opener of the Way and his House of the Hatchet.

But the bubonic Mr. Bloch has also written a spattering of mysteries, a rocketload of science-fiction, and what I like to call his coroner stones—his psychoterror books, which graphically probe into the aberrations of the human mind with the precision of a razorshape scalpel. Cutting open and laying bear its sicknesses and weaknesses. Slicing to the heart of its darkest niches. The psychotic shadow glitches you want your own mind to think clear of.

Besides the necrophilic Norman Bates of *Psycho,* Bloch's repertory of dazed, glazed and crazed people has included pyromaniac Philip Dempster in *Firebug,* strangulation-minded Dan Morley in *The Scarf,* hustling Larry Fox in *The Dead Beat,* father's-boy Charles Campbell in *The Couch* and Kali-caressing Ghopal Singh in *Terror*. All nutty putty in Bloch's hands, shaped into gnarly souls with sick, twisted imaginations. Bloch's imagination is twisted too, but with one big difference. He doesn't commit his ideas on real people, he commits them on (and to) paper.

In films and television, Bloch has also produced impact—

he's packed 'em in for producers. Film has been a natural medium for his unnatural mediums of the seance world and the other chilly characters who relentlessly stalk his stories. Whatever he writes is in a visual style and his inner ear is a reverberation chamber for inner sanctum dialogue.

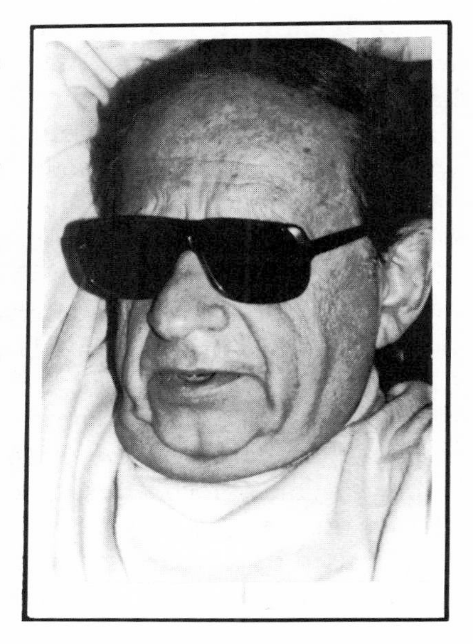

When he first settled in Hollywood in 1960 he gravitated to his first love by writing for the Alfred Hitchcock TV series, *Thriller,* and other weekly series he has long outlasted. He is responsible for three classic *Star Trek* episodes: "What Little Girls Are Made Of," "Catspaw" and "Wolf in the Fold." And he's done some quivery work for the short-lived *Journey to the Unknown* and longer-lived Rod Serling's *Night Gallery.*

In the longer screenplay format he has excelled with Gothic and baroque horrors that were largely part of the cinema of the 1960s. He created a Night Walker for Barbara Stanwyck's dreams, he put Joan Crawford in a figurative (and literal) Straitjacket, he permitted Burgess Meredith to harvest a bloody Torture Garden of humans, he manipulated Christopher Lee and Peter Cushing into the unreal estate of The House That Dripped Blood. He is the man who built the Asylum for Barbara Parkins.

Here's a writer who knows the meaning of entertainment when he splashes words on paper. Maybe Bloch isn't the greatest stylist in the world (and he'll be the first to admit it) but you'll never find Bloch dull or tedious or turgid. Not even torpid. What he is is terror torrid. A fast-flowing master at wordslay and printshock. And when he's terrifyingly brilliant, as in *Psycho* and *Night World* and *The Night of the Ripper,* he's more fun than Lefty Feep trapped in a cage filled with banana-throwing monkeys.

The first time I had met this Bloch character in his library was back in 1968, when I had been assigned by the editor of *The Castle of Frankenstein* (in its day the *Cinefantastique* of monster movie magazines) to record for all time the innermost reflections of America's Dean of Terror. That editor, Calvin T. Beck, had given me a few leading questions, phrased in a way to intimidate Bloch and force him to answer charges that maybe *Psycho* wasn't the classic everyone was calling it. But Bloch's responses (no matter how subtly derisive the pre-prepared questions) were always gentlemanly and phrased in such a witty way that it was Calvin T. Beck who came off looking second best in the subsequent two-part article.

There is no slaying wit in the literary field slier or wrier than Bloch's. He is a man with plenty of character because he is a character, plenty. He is never at a loss for a perverse twist. His mind is a veritable container for puns, amalgamated anagrams, twisted phrases and ghastly gags.

Which in a way explains how Lefty Feep sprang out of the same imagination that has created so many grisly images . . . Bloch sees the ironic side to the twisted macabre; he's always able to flip the butcher knife over and reflect on the dull edge too. And that's why so many of his horror stories have ended with a phrase that in another context would be just a cliche. In his stories these choice last words become the voice of universal laughter, deriding the forces of irony at work against us all.

The best thing that happened from those *Castle of Frankenstein* articles was our relationship. From that night forward, I remained in contact with Bob, corresponding occasionally, and enjoying his company during the 1972

SUFFERING from shattered nerves caused by constant demands from New York publishers for more horror novels and short stories, Robert Bloch often retires to his library and calms down by reading his world-famous novel PSYCHO. "Its genteel characters have a way of soothing my disturbed psyche," says Bloch.

World Science-Fiction Convention, when he and his charming wife Elly treated me as their special guest.

And there was that classic moment in 1982 when Bob consented to appear as my guest on *Creature Features,* a television program I hosted in the Bay Area for six years . . . no easy decision for Bob, since many careers had been made or broken by an appearance on that notorious program. (. . . he said with his tongue in his cheek.)

It was *the* night of nights for the host of a TV horror program; Bob's wit—like a newly honed wiggly-edged Moro *kris*—was at its sharpest, cutting into one's sides until they split. When asked why he had decided to bring Norman Bates out of the insane asylum closet in his novel *Psycho II,* Bob answered, "I thought the time was right to bring Norman back into a world that's even crazier than he is today . . ." And when I pulled the old gag of telling my audience that Bob really had the heart of a small child, in the very next second exposing a large glass container with a lamb's heart floating in fluid, Bob contributed to the old legend by adding: "I was taking a chance bringing that here tonight because if a policeman had seen me, I'd have been a victim of cardiac arrest."

So, with all these memories of Robert Bloch in mind, I decided that now was the time to approach him about the possibilities of republishing the old Lefty Feep yarns. And grabbed for the nearest phone. As usual, he was instantly accessible and bade me welcome to Lotusland, probably wondering if this Stanley guy was ever going to find a legitimate line of work. He invited me to pay a call that very day.

Now the dangerous part began. It's no easy task to find your way through the Hollywood Hills to Bob's home. His foremost abode can be most foreboding. Fellow writers have been known to be lost for as long as a week, hopelessly traversing the sinuous roads that surround his residence like some Chinese torture trap diabolically set by Fu Manchu's henchmen. It is an elusive street he lives on, and some seekers have never been heard from again. Lefty Feep would probably take a wrong sidestreet, meet a ginch in distress and promptly forget about finding Bob's. It's also a famous street, immortalized by William F. Nolan in his short story "The Pulpcon Kill," in which private shamus Nick Challis traces a prime murder-case suspect to within a few homes of Bloch's own. Homage to a home of our age.

But I followed Bob's detailed instructions carefully, and breathed a tremendous sigh of relief when I found myself safely at his doorstep. He graciously ushered me into his study, its walls lined with countless editions of *Psycho,* including many in foreign languages. Bob was at work at his manual typewriter (electrics and computers be damned!) on "Beetles," a teleplay version of one of his classic short stories from *Weird Tales.* (It was first published in December 1938.) The script was an assignment, he revealed, for George Romero's half-hour TV anthology series *Tales from the Darkside.*

Now came the sweating part there in the hills above the Sunset Strip. Like a scene of suspense from his Hollywood novel, *Star Stalker.* I asked Bob how things were progressing and he said he had decided to get as many books into print as possible in the next three years, producing new material and reediting much of the old. My heart skipped a beat. Surely "reediting much of the old" would include Lefty Feep. After all, there were 23 stories, a big hunk of material to come out of the barrel of anyone's canon, and most of them had remained unreprinted since the 1940s. Surely I had arrived too late. I envisioned Lefty Feep being caried away before my very eyes, clutched under the sweaty armpit of an ogre of the worst kind—a New York publisher.

Bob proceeded to spend the next half-hour detailing various projects. He had *that* many in the works. Two new horror novels for Tor Books . . . *Unholy Trinity,* a collection of three mystery novels from Scream Press . . . a forthcoming bibliography from a devoted professional fan, Randall Larson . . . a collaboration with Andre Norton . . . an anthology for this editor, an anthology for that editor. On and on he went, human juggernaut style, and with each new project, I shrank inside a little, knowing and fearing that sooner or later he had to tell me, "And oh yes, then there's my elaborate flamboyant colossal stupendous knock-out plan for Lefty Feep."

But he never did. And when he leaned back contentedly in his chair, no doubt imagining the piles of royalty checks that a panting mailman would have to carry to his door daily, I dared to breathe the name Lefty Feep, hoping that a reverent tone dominated my voice.

Say, said Robert Bloch, sitting up like a hounddog who's just been thrown a turkey leg, that sounds like a great idea! Exclamation point! Exclamation point!

And so this book was born, out of Bob's trust for a fledgling publisher and out of my need to share these great fantasy comedies with readers young and old. And naturally, out of a need to earn a few greenbacks, some lettuce, some kale. After all, Lefty has to have his cut too.

LEFTY FEEP is an anomaly in the career of Robert Bloch, and a legend in the annals of fantasy comedy. Because most of the stories have never been reprinted since the 1940s, many fantasy readers have only heard about them or read of them. Older readers often remember the stories with fondness, even if they can't remember their

BLOCH feverishly at work on the TV script, "Beetles." The story, Bloch reports, "really clicked for me."

specific content. People who have never read them talk them up enthusiastically. It's considered *in* to know about the existence of Lefty Feep.

While visiting the Collector's Bookstore on Vine Street in Hollywood one day, I asked for a certain issue of *Fantastic Adventures*. "Oh," said the proprietor, Malcolm Willits, "that's an edition with a Lefty Feep story." He couldn't tell you who wrote the cover story, or anything else about that issue, but he sure knew about the ubiquitous Feep. In the Hall of Fantasy, Lefty occupies a nostalgic niche, but one too-long covered with dust.

Because Bloch is best known for his tales of terror and psychological horror, I wondered what light-hearted corner of his otherwise twisted mind had enabled him to write such outlandishly wild stories. From whence sprang such buffoonery, lampoonery and tomfoolery?

Another visit to the Bloch domicile was called for, this time with literary laserprobe in hand to cut as deeply as possible into the nerve-endings of the Bloch psyche. The final answer to Writer's Bloch perhaps awaited me.

Bob ushered me once again into his library, this time taking the guest's chair and inviting me to sit behind his typewriter, which contained a page of script for "Beetles." On his desk was a letter from his good friend Harold Gauer, to whom he said he wanted to dedicate this book.

Bloch paused to explain that Gauer, former director of CARE's Midwest offices in Milwaukee and a social science analyst, had first seen the name Lefty Feep in an article in Esquire Magazine in the 1930s written by O. C. Richards, a specialist in humorous sports stories. Feep had been a terrible pitcher, whose throwing arm was so off that once one of his pitches had sailed out of the ballpark and "beaned a horse dragging a milk wagon."

STANLEY: *So, you and Gauer created this Lefty Feep as a character of your own . . .*

BLOCH: In 1936, for our own publication—a limited

(one-copy) edition entitled *Brutal: The Magazine for People.* It was a vaguely disguised ripoff of *Esquire,* which was then very popular. We satirized its features and its stories and Gauer, who had fallen in love with the name, was writing about Lefty Feep, a somewhat degenerate character. Later on, we decided to expand our efforts and we wrote a novel in collaboration with no mind of having it published. Because obviously it was unpublishable.

BLOCH seriously studies Lefty Feep, California style.

JS: *Obviously . . . That would be* In the Land of the Sky Blue Ointments.

BLOCH: And this gave Gauer an opportunity to use Lefty as a somewhat drink-sodden author.

JS: *Like those who had created him?*

BLOCH: Not really. Gauer was far from a drinker and at that time far from full-fledged authorship. [Later, Gauer would write and publish *How to Win in Politics* and the novel *Bury Me Not.*] But Feep didn't distinguish himself particularly in this little effort. He had no personality, he was still little more than a name.

This was the 1930s, and as it has been rumored, everybody was broke, including us. We had no money to provide amusements so we invented our own. Gauer and a friend devised, by very clever and careful calculation, a baseball game played with an ordinary deck of cards, each card in the deck having a different value. And we used the name Lefty Feep to identify a player on one of the teams. That kept him alive in *my* consciousness. And when the time came to do the stories for *Fantastic Adventures,* I resurrected the name and placed it on a totally different type of character.

JS: *The style you used in the Feep stories has been compared to that of Damon Runyon, whose colorful underworld characters were used in* Guys and Dolls. *Was Runyon a favorite of yours? Had you read some of his short stories?*

BLOCH: I had read a great deal of Runyon's work, yes. But I was not a fan of his. At times I've imitated quite a few writers in pastiches . . . I wasn't particularly offering a homage, it was just a matter of utilizing a style because it seemed incongruously appropriate to the subject matter.

I had been reading enough science-fiction and fantasy to realize nobody had ever attempted that style in the genre. So I said, "Why not." It's a strange way of going about things but it may make the stories a little more distinctive if they're told in contemporary vernacular or what passes for contemporary vernacular.

I gradually added the rhyming slang and the puns on my own, and at that time, Damon Runyon, being alive, did not turn over in his grave.

JS: *After you had begun the series, didn't pulp magazines run imitations of the Feep stories?*

BLOCH: Feep may have pointed a new direction. Actually, my first experiments in that style were not Lefty Feep stories per se. At that time *Unknown Worlds* had published my first attempt at humor, "A Good Knight's Work." I wrote in that style and later on wrote a sequel, "The Eager Dragon," for *Weird Tales*. The title means nothing today but at that time Disney had just released a feature film, *The Reluctant Dragon,* so there was a relevancy then. ["A Good Knight's Work" and "The Eager Dragon" were collected in *Dragons and Nightmares,* published in 1968 by Mirage Press.]

Then along came the invitation to do something in the humorous line for *Fantastic Adventures*. I had the style and I had a name and that was all I had.

JS: *Today, so many people talk about the Feep stories, even if they haven't read them. Was there strong reader response when the stories first appeared?*

BLOCH: If there was, I never heard about it.

JS: *What did the editor, Raymond A. Palmer, tell you after he read the first story?*

BLOCH: "Send another." That's all he said.

JS: *He didn't say, "Gee, Bob, that was a marvelous story"?*

BLOCH: That's the kind of thing that causes writers to ask for more money. Editors never told you about reader response. The only magazine that gave any indication was *Weird Tales* because it had a letter column that ranked the stories in the previous edition. This was the only way one ever learned of such things.

JS: *So, when you wrote the first Lefty Feep story,* "Time Wounds All Heels" [April 1942], *you just thought you were writing another short story . . .*

BLOCH: I thought I was just writing another short story but Palmer wanted more. He and his successor, Howard Browne, never gave me any editorial comment. I saw them quite frequently in Chicago but in all our personal confrontations we never discussed Lefty Feep. They just kept on taking the stories. They never increased my word rate. For that matter, Lefty never had a cover story in all of his adventures.

JS: *For quite a while the magazine was printing a Lefty Feep adventure every month. How long did it take to write a Feep yarn? Was it a week's work for you?*

BLOCH: I would say usually so. I was writing other stories and I was working full-time at the Gustav Marx Advertising Agency in Milwaukee. And raising a small daughter.

JS: *Did you do all your writing at night?*

BLOCH: No, I never worked at night. I had a special arrangement with the Marx agency. As copywriter I would place the ad layouts on one side of the typewriter, and my own material on the other. And when the agency pile went down or disappeared, I would stick my own stuff in the typewriter. That's how I did it for eleven years. Advertising copy or short stories—it was all fantasy.

JS: *How much did the magazine pay you?*

HUNDREDS of editions of Bloch's 1959 novel PSYCHO, many of them in foreign languages, line the shelves of the library in his Hollywood Hills home.

BLOCH: One cent a word. And believe me, those stories were definitely worth it. I've heard vague rumors on the grapevine through the years of writers who got a cent and a half a word or two cents a word but I never found out through personal experience.

JS: *Did the ideas come pretty fast for Lefty Feep? Are you the kind who just sits down and starts writing?*

BLOCH: I never sit down and start to work on anything without an outline. Everything I write is plotted before I begin, whether it's a novel, a short story, a teleplay, a screenplay, or a response to a creditor.

I'd spend half a day devising a Feep plot once I had an initial idea and a theme . . . and a punchline. Because I start from the back with my play on words or whatever it may be. I always have my ending in mind. Then I work towards it, formulating a plot that will make it pay off. Finally I type up an outline, usually one page, single-spaced.

JS: *Some secondary characters are recurring in the stories. There's Jack, who runs Jack's Shack, although we never do learn much about him, except that he deserves to be ranked with Madeleine Smith, the Borgias and other great poisoners. Did you keep a glossary of notes to yourself about the gallery of characters?*

BLOCH: Many Lefty Feep characters were borrowed from the baseball games Gauer and I played or from that immortal novel, *In the Land of the Sky Blue Ointments*. By this time I was quite familiar with the nomenclature and all I had to do was attach some kind of characterization.

The one that horrified me, though, was the victim of an editorial change. Not on the part of Raymond Palmer but on the part of either Colonel William Ziff or B. G. Davis, the publishers of *Fantastic Adventures*. I had a character named Gorilla Goldfarb and they were so afraid of being accused of ethnic bias that without telling me they changed the name to Gorilla Gabface, which meant nothing. But they were very leery of antagonizing anyone. They should have been in

BLOCH, wondering how the reappearance of Lefty Feep will affect his future career as a writer, philosophically contemplates his next career move.

television. [In one of the magazine stories, the name "Goldfarb" accidentally pops up in place of "Gabface"—a proofreading oversight.]

JS: *When you visited the offices of Ziff-Davis, what was the atmosphere like?*

BLOCH: In those days Ziff-Davis published a tremendous number of magazines. *Popular Photography, Popular Pornography, Popular Child Molesting*—almost any hobby was given a magazine. *Amazing Stories* and *Fantastic Adventures* were pretty low on the totem pole. My editors had these little cubicles filled with manuscripts and confusion and this made no particular impression on me whatsoever. Yet Palmer and Browne made a success of the magazines.

JS: *It's been suggested that the Lefty Feep stories were well received because they were escapism, published during the war years, a time history has recorded as pretty grim. How was your own personal life at that time? You had a full-time job, you were selling to the magazines. Were those happy years . . . or struggling years?*

BLOCH: In retrospect, those were grim, unhappy years. My first wife had turberculosis of the bone which had not been properly diagnosed. She was physically handicapped and I had a good deal to do with the raising of a young daughter along with my writing and work . . . and while a fair (for that time) income was coming in, it was also going out to physicians. I never reached a point where I could own a car, but all of our doctors did.

So, between worrying about my wife's illness, my daughter's welfare or what was going to happen next—would I be suddenly drafted and taken away from them, leaving them without any means of support?—I was not exactly in a euphoric state. But somehow the worse things got, the more I was inclined to write humor. As a result, whether I did this as an escape or as a counterbalance, it helped to carry me through. Whenever life becomes a little bit rough, it's best to cultivate a sense of humor. Look what it did for Pagliacci . . .

JS: *Did the Lefty Feep stories die off because the war had ended and editorial needs were changing, or did you lose interest in writing about the character?*

BLOCH: I had lost interest in two things. One: the character. Two: the cent-a-word payment. I began to get into markets that were more lucrative and by that time I was ready to branch out. I'd written my first novel *[The Scarf, 1947]*, I'd had a radio series of my own *[Stay Tuned for Terror, 1945)* and I was interested in getting into the mystery-suspense field. I didn't think there was a great future in doing Lefty Feep. I had reached the saturation point both psychically and financially.

JS: *The last Feep story of the 1940s* ["Tree's a Crowd"] *was in July 1946. Then you did one final Feep story for* Fantastic Adventures *in July 1950* ["The End of Your Rope"]. *That was a gap of four years.*

BLOCH: That was due to a direct request on the part of Howard Browne, who had taken over editorship of the magazine.

JS: *Was Howard Browne a Lefty Feep fan?*

BLOCH: None of these people ever expressed feelings for Lefty Feep. Not until years later, when they were safely out of their roles as editors. Talk is cheap; paying higher rates is expensive.

JS: *So, when Lefty Feep was laid to rest you didn't feel any nostalgic pangs or overwhelming wave of remorse.*

BLOCH: None whatsoever. I never considered myself to be a writer of series. I didn't identify with Lefty, heaven knows. He was practically the antithesis of my own persona in every respect. Except for his attitude toward blondes.

JS: *You never really described Lefty Feep in the stories. Did you have an image in your mind as you wrote?*

BLOCH: None whatsoever. A couple of artist friends from California, Albert and Florence Magorian, who worked for

Fantastic Adventures, pictured me as Lefty Feep in some of the illustrations for the stories. Without my glasses. It was an in-joke. I will say the clothing in the illustrations approximated the sort of thing I used to wear: gaudy stripes and loud colors. I looked like a racetrack tout, but I never went to the racetrack. In fact, I never saw the front end of a horse until I got out of advertising.

JS: *So, the stories have gone unreprinted all these years, except for a few rare exceptions. Do you feel this is a good time for the stories to go back into print?*

BLOCH: Yes, because they're safely removed from the contemporary scene and they now read like historical fiction. There are so many things in them that are not part and parcel of today's readers' experience. They have a certain novelty value.

JS: *Some of the stories have names or descriptions that might be construed today as racial slurs. The phrase "Jap" appears now and again. Are you going to change those things in the text?*

BLOCH: Once I start removing anachronisms, where do I stop? The word "Jap" was in use at a time when we were dealing with a military enemy. Rewriting turns history to hypocrisy. I'm inclined to believe that on the whole these stories will have to stand as period pieces; any obvious explanatory tinkering will cause them to fall apart.

I don't believe that because we are in an age when we no longer exploit ethnic distinctions that we've got to change the title to *Uncle Tom's Condo.* And besides, if I had to rewrite them in terms of making them more comprehensible, I'd have to make them more literate too.

JS: *Occasionally there is a name reference which will probably mean nothing to today's readers. Do you think the book should have footnotes?*

BLOCH: In featherweight yarns like these, such interruptions are fatal because they pull the reader back to "reality." I'd rather chance an instant's puzzlement than interfere with the mood and tempo of the story. So I'm in favor of letting the material stand.

When an archeologist uncovers a Sumerian tomb dating from a little-known period of ancient history, he welcomes translation of any cuneiform or ideographic messages which might offer some clue to the lost lifestyle of the distant past, and for that purpose he has no choice but to interpret what little is available. But if a sociologist wants to recreate the reality of our own society fifty years ago, he doesn't have to turn to Marvel Comic books for that purpose—or to Lefty Feep stories.

To me, it's dangerously close to taking the whole thing too seriously. Over-analysis and over-explanation can result in a backlash of overkill. We're not offering a college course in Lefty Feep I (3 credits).

JS: *I still think it would be enlightening to hear some of your thoughts about these stories, some of which you haven't read for more than forty years. So let's save any pertinent comments or insightful asides to run at the end of each story.* After Words, *you might call it.*

BLOCH: You may recall that in one of the stories ["Gather Round the Flowing Bowler"] I mention the magistrate Hiawatha Donglepootzer. A famous case involved a medical malpractice suit in which a man accused a surgeon of partially castrating him by mistake. As Exhibit A in evidence, he offered his amputated left testicle, preserved in a jar. One day the Judge was unable to locate the missing organ until a zealous bailiff discovered it tucked away under the judge's bench. Whereupon he announced to the Judge—as I now do to you—"The ball is in your court."

The very first Lefty Feep story ever, in which our racetrack lout, with a Rip Van Winkle in his eye, is bowled over by some dwarf stars of the alley who have only moments to spare. A striking narrative!

TIME WOUNDS ALL HEELS

I DROPPED into Jack's Shack the other night for a slice of tongue—some of it in a sandwich and some from between Jack's lips. The place was pretty crowded, but I managed to find a booth as Jack glided over to take my order.

"What'll it be?" he asked. Then—"Well I'll be damned!" said Jack.

"Probably," I observed.

But Jack didn't hear me. He was staring at the tall, thin man who elbowed his way toward the booth.

I stared, too. There was nothing remarkable about the gentleman's thin, somewhat dour face, but his suit was enough to attract anyone's attention. It isn't often that you see a horse-blanket walking.

"See that guy?" Jack whispered, hurriedly. "He's a number for you. Used to be an upper bracket in the rackets."

"He looks it," I confided. "Is he dangerous?"

"No. Reformed, completely reformed. Ever since he divorced his third wife he's led a simple life, playing the races. But I never expected to see him in here—he hasn't been around for months. Wait—I'll see if I can steer him into your booth. You'll enjoy it—he's the biggest liar in seven states."

"What seven?" I asked, in some curiosity. But Jack was signalling the glum-faced man in the checkered suit.

"Hello, Lefty! Where in blazes have you been?"

"Everywhere, and up to my neck," said the stranger. "But make with the menu because at the moment I arrive by express from hunger." "Sit here," Jack suggested, indicating my booth. "This guy is a friend of mine."

Lefty favored me with a long look.

"Is he a righto or a wrongo?" he asked.

"He's a writer," said Jack. "Bob, I want you to meet a friend of mine—Lefty Feep."

"A pleasure," I said.

Lefty sat down without a word and grabbed the menu from Jack's hands.

"Shoot the steak to me, Jack," he said. "Also I will have bean soup, clam chowder, a double order mashed potatoes, peas, carrots, roast chicken, a ham on rye, baked beans, an order of waffles, asparagus, pork tenderloin, scrambled eggs, coffee, apple pie, ice cream and watermelon."

"You kidding?"

"No—eating. Now bring it here, but fast. My stomach is empty so long I think it's haunted."

Jack shrugged and moved away, muttering the incredible order under his breath.

Lefty Feep turned to me suddenly with a scowl.

"Vitamins!" he grated. "Vitamins!"

"You need them?" I asked.

"I hate vitamins," said Lefty. "Give me food any time."

"What's the matter? Been on a diet?"

"You speak a mean truth, all right. For a week now I partake of nothing but vitamins. I am going pill-wacky." Lefty sighed heavily. "B'-bugs," he mumbled. "D-dizzy."

"Doctor's orders?" I inquired.

"No. Restaurant orders. It's all I can get. Will you live in a burg where nobody nibbles anything but pills?"

"What town is this you're speaking of?"

"New York."

"But there's plenty of food in New York—" I began.

"There is and there isn't," said Lefty, darkly brooding. "There is now but there will be ain't."

"I don't get it."

"I figure you don't. Nobody will. I can make with the explanations but it is not such a thing as anyone will believe and I do not wish to get the reputation of a guy who sniffs snow."

"You're no drug addict," I said. "Come on, spill it."

Lefty Feep looked at me again with a wry smile. He shrugged.

"You ask for it," he said. "It is a story that will make your hair curdle and your blood stand on end."

"Shoot," I urged.

He shot.

LAST WEEK (began Lefty Feep) I am coming back from Buffalo where I wager a few pennies on the bow-wows. My pooch comes in and I make collections, so I drive back very happy. It is the first time I make money by going to the dogs. More and over, I know I have five rancho grandos waiting for me in Manhattan, where I place another bet with a personality name of Gorilla Gabface.

This Gorilla Gabface is a number I dearly love to hate. He is a big noise in the rackets, and I do not care to have dealings with such riff and raff. Our association is just sentimental, because he and I once work our way through reform school together selling alky.

But while I straighten out, Gorilla merely gets more and more unscrupulous in his business deals, until he is left with not one single scruple at all. I do all right, but he is always poking fun at me, saying the only gold I will ever see will be in a halo, while he has enough gold for a complete set of teeth.

So I am very hepped over winning this little wager, like I say, and I start driving back thinking about how I will hand him the old razz and he will hand me the old cash and it will be a very fair exchange.

Along about noon a.m. I find myself in the mountain country, and I am so happy I start to yodel while I drive. In fact, I even open the car window a trifle to sniff some air, which is unusual for me, because I have a theory that air is not so healthy on guys if it is too fresh. But the hills are very pretty, and the road has more curves than a Minsky stripper, and the sun is shining, and the birds are singing, and it is just one great big popular song if you know what I mean. I feel like a character on the Alka-Seltzer Barn Dance.

I am too happy to notice where I'm going, so it is no wonder at all that I snap out of it to find myself off on a side road going up a hill.

I figure on turning around when I reach the top, so I keep driving up and over. But the hill does not seem to have any top to it—I just keep on twisting and turning, and all the time the road is getting dustier and smaller, and the woods on each side are as thick as thieves, you should pardon the expression. It is so uncivilized, I do not even spot a gas station. For that matter, I no longer see any farm houses or catalogue cabins. I wonder about this more than slightly, but keep on driving. The air is blue up there, and so am I, because I figure I am lost for sure unless I get a chance to turn around.

Then all at once I come to a level grade that goes off for quite a space into a little valley between the hills. I am just ready to wheel around when I notice the sign.

It is on the side of the road just ahead, standing on a stick between some rocks. I am curious to see what kind of advertising goes over here in the provinces, so I pull up and read it. It says:

PICNIC TODAY
DIMINUTIVE SOCIETY OF
THE CATSKILL MOUNTAINS

FREE ENTERTAINMENT AND REFRESHMENTS
STRANGERS WELCOME

I suddenly realize I am panging from hunger, not gobbling groceries yet today. And here is free refreshments, so what can I lose? I never hear of the Diminutive Society of the Catskill Mountains before, but I figure they never heard of me either, so we're even.

Before you can say Jack Dempsey, I make up my mind to drive on in, which I do. The road is just a little trail now, but I can manage if I go slow between the rocks.

All at once I look up at the sky, because I hear thunder. The sky is still blue, and the sun is shining, so I figure I make a mistake. But no, I get a little further, and the thunder is louder.

Then I round the last bend in the road and come out on an open space, and I see what is making with the thunder. There is an outdoor bowling alley, so help me, and the noise is from the balls rolling along the rocks.

But that is not what makes me turn off the ignition and sit there like somebody stuffs a watermelon in my mouth. I am staring at the bowlers.

Now I am a personality who gets around considerable for many's the year. I have the pleasure of placing my peepers on a lot of screwy spectacles, including pink elephants. But never do I see a wormier-looking sight than this.

Because the bowlers at this picnic are a bunch of dwarfs. So help me, there are a couple dozen of them, little shorty guys in nightcaps and ski suits, all running around like fugitives from Walt Disney.

This baffles me but plenty. Because the sign says this is a picnic for the Diminutive Society, and instead of seeing Diminutives, there are these dwarfs.

Finally I figure it is some kind of circus brawl or publicity stunt, though I don't notice any Pathe newsreel cameras. What I do notice is the nice collection of beer kegs off on one side.

KENN
DAVIS

I sit there and watch the pint-size personalities knock off the tenpins for some minutes. And then, all of a sudden, I hear a scratching at the side of the car. "Aha, termites!" I say to myself.

But when I open the door I do not see any termite. Instead, the smallest guy in the world is standing on the running board, trying to reach the door handle.

He has a long gray beard on his face and a short beer in his hand. "Welcome, stranger," he pipes up, in no voice at all. "Welcome to the Diminutive Society of the Catskills." I do not altogether understand this, but what he says next shows me his heart is in the right place. "Have a drink," he says.

So I climb out and take the mug from him. The beer is plenty good, and has more kick than a chorus girl with her costume on fire. "Little man, what now?" I ask.

He grins through his chin-spinach. "What gives out here?" I inquire. "Make with the explanations."

He shrugs. "We do not entertain visitors very often, I fear," he pipes. "I fail to comprehend your meaning."

By this time a whole crowd of shorty guys are standing around watching and poking each other. I begin to feel like I was back in school the time I am 16 and in the third grade. Most of these babies could pick my pocket without using a stepladder.

So I turn around to the head squeaker again and try to make him understand, because I can see from what he says that he can't be any too bright.

"Listen, quaint-face," I say, politely. "Where's Snow-White?"

This does not go over. Evidently these jerks cannot even understand English.

"I mean, what's the score? Which one of you is Dopey? What is this—a convention of Midget Auto Racers?"

The head little guy smiles again. "You don't seem to understand at all," he tells me. "This is the annual picnic of the Diminutive Society of the Catskill Mountains. It is the one occasion each year when we venture forth from our homes to celebrate our ownership of these hills. We bowl, we drink, we make merry from sunup to sundown. It is a long time, as I say, since the last stranger's arrival. May we welcome you?"

I don't get it at all. There is something screwy about this whole setup. The way these little guys dress, and talk, and giggle. But what have I got to lose? They are too small to hurt me, and I don't see any equalizers in the mob. They are kind of drunk and out for a good time so why shouldn't I stick around for a few drinks and a few laughs? Maybe it is the mountain air that does it, or maybe it is the first beer on an empty stomach. Anyhow, I shake hands with the head midget and say, "Thanks, Shorty. How's for a little bowling?"

So then it begins. I take a turn at the alleys and I take a turn at the beers. These small fry have special bowling balls to fit their hands—about the size of tennis balls and not much heavier. I fling them two at a time, to be fair.

These small fry also have special beer mugs to fit their mouths. So I drink three or four at a time, also to be fair.

Pretty soon I turn out to be not only fair but also quite stinkaroo. These local yokels brew a mean beer, and before I notice it I am quite dizzy. The dwarfs do not seem to notice, either, but keep right on setting up the pins and the drinks, and I keep right on knocking them down.

I am a nasty hand at the old strike-and-spare, even though the ground is rough, and they stand around cheering me on while I polish off one bowler after another, also one beer after another.

Perhaps I am telling this kind of confused—but that's the way I get, all right.

It only seems like minutes, but it must be hours, when I glance over my shoulder and see the old sun is going down. The dwarfs also seem to keep track of the time, because all of a sudden they quiet down and get ready to take a last drink. Nothing will do but for me to drink with them. And on account of there being two dozen of them, I have a lot of drinking to do.

The head shorty keeps staring at me and nudging his pals while he watches me inhale the brew. "Verily, he has a greater capacity than Master Van Winkle," he giggles.

The name seems to penetrate the speckled fog in my noggin for a minute. "What's this about Van Winkle?" I ask.

But the sun is very low and red, and it is dark all around, and I see the dwarfs suddenly start running across the bowling lawn and into the shadows. The head shorty runs after them. "We must leave you, stranger," he calls over his shoulder. "Pleasant dreams."

I start to run after him, but all at once I stumble on the grass and everything starts going round and round—ten little red suns juggle themselves in my head, and the ground comes up and I am out.

Just before I close my eyes I manage to holler after the last little runt again. "Who is this Van Winkle?" I gasp.

I cannot be sure, because I am going down for the third time, but I think I hear his voice come from far away. "Why, Master Rip Van Winkle, of course," whispers the dwarf.

I open my mouth to say something, but the only thing coming out is a snore.

When I open my beautiful baby blue eyes again, it is daylight. At first I do not remember where I am, but then it all comes back in a hurry and I realize I pass out and probably sleep the night here.

I raise up on one elbow to see if my little friends are around, but there are no signs. In fact, to make it funny, there is not even any bowling lawn, or tenpins, or tennis-size bowling bowls. To make it not so funny, there is no beer keg, either—and I have a thirst, but strong.

Maybe it is all a dream, I figure. Then I turn my head and I begin to pray it is a dream.

Because I am now staring at the car, parked off to one side. And what I see is not altogether a sight for sore eyes like mine.

Yesterday I leave a nice new coupe standing there. Today I find a jalopy you couldn't trade in on a pair of roller skates. It is covered with rust an inch thick; the tires are down, and the windows are out.

I get up in a hurry because it is all clear to me now. These dwarfs I drink with are nothing but a gang of car thieves. They slip me a Mickey Finn and steal my coupe, leaving me this broken-down wheelbarrow just to be quaint. No wonder they treat me so well—they're nothing but a bunch of Dead End Kids in whiskers!

I run over to the wreck and wrench open the door. It not only opens but comes off in my hand.

Then I reach inside, and all at once something flies out and hits me in the face. A couple of bats—so help me!

I stare down at the cobwebs on the seat. Then I go around in front and stare again. This time I nearly fall down.

Because I see my license plates on this jalopy!

There is something wrong here. This is my car, all right—but . . . But? I reach up to scratch my chin. My hand never gets there. It tangles up in something soft, like a fur coat. My hand is tangled in a beard. A white beard. *My* beard! At least it is growing on me, so it must be my beard, though I do not want such a thing. No, I do not want such a thing as this beard at all, because it is all messed up with burrs and thistles.

I look down at my clothes and that is the last straw. You could even say that is the last shred. Because there isn't much left of my clothes except shreds. My trousers have got French cuffs made of rags. The moths have been holding a convention on my knees. My coat and vest look like something a goat would eat for dessert.

I am not sitting in the hot seat at the moment, but I am still plenty shocked.

Here I am, lost in the mountains, with an old car and a new beard. It is enough to make a guy holler—so I do. I kind of lose my head and run around yelling for the dwarfs to come out and make with the explanations. I guess I am off the beam for several moments, just screeching there, when I hear a sound.

It is a buzzing sound, and it gets louder. All at once I look up and see a plane. The plane circles around, comes lower, and taxis down right in the open space where the bowling green should be.

I just gawk. It is a new model plane, very small; all silvery and shining. What makes me gawk is the fact it lands in just about a minute, and it only taxis maybe a hundred feet. I do not have much time to gawk, because a guy climbs out of the door and steps over to me. "Anything wrong?" he asks me.

"Yeah," I reply. "You are." And he is.

He is wearing a pretty funny getup himself—a pair of overalls with long sleeves and lapels on top. Instead of a hat he has a kind of basin on his head that looks like a helmet with antennae sticking up.

"Who are you?" I say, kind of sad. "And if you tell me you're Flash Gordon, you can lock me up."

He just grins. "My name is Grant," he says. "Special investigator for the government. What might your name be?"

"It might be Old Man Moses, from the looks of things," I tell him. "But it isn't. I'm on my way to New York, but I run into a little difficulty."

"You mean to say an old man like you intends to walk all the way to New York?" he says. "No wonder you are yelling. Would you like a lift?—I'll be hitting New York in about half an hour."

"I'm with you, brother," I say. So we hop in the plane. I do not look back at the car again, and for some reason I do not wish to look down at myself, either. Still and all I have to make a crack. "Who are you calling an old man?" I yap.

He grins again. "Why you, of course. You're every bit of 60, aren't you? And with a beard, too—I do not see one of those things in years."

This shuts me up as we take off. "You are quite a hot

sketch yourself," I tell him. "What are you doing with that thundermug on your head?"

Grant looks at me like I am stir-simple. "Why, that's the radio control helmet for the plane, of course. Don't you know planes are operated by radio adjustment?" he asks, turning the antennae on top of the basin and making the plane rise. "Say, how far in the backwoods do you come from?"

"Brother, I wish I knew," I answer.

"You know, there's something funny about you," he goes on. "Those clothes you're wearing—they aren't exactly 1962 cut."

"1962?" I yell.

Grant gives me a long look. "Of course. Don't tell me you don't know what date it is?"

"Why, April 30th, 1942," I snap back.

He begins to laugh. Somehow I do not like to hear him laugh because I am not on the Bob Hope program at the time. "This is April 28th, 1962," he tells me. "You are just 20 years and 363 days off. Or maybe you're further off than that."

"I think so myself," I say. "Because I lay me down to sleep just last night, and if it is not 1942 at the time, I am robbed when I buy a newspaper."

"Are you kidding me?" asks this Grant.

"Somebody is kidding somebody," I tell him. "All I know is I hoist a few beers with a gang of dwarfs on a picnic and fall asleep. When I wake up my car is rusty, my suit is a ragpicker's delight, and I have long white whiskers. Which is hard to figure out, because I am really a young guy with a sporty car and a nifty checkered suit. And if I'm not the guy who has the beard, then who the hell am I?"

"You sound like Rip Van Winkle to me," laughs Grant.

I pick up my ears. "Rip Van Winkle!" I yell. "That's the bozo the head dwarf mentions to me just before I hit the hay. Who is he?"

So this Grant guy tells me a story about some jerk who

lives way back when and gets lost in the mountains like I do. He meets up with a troupe of Singer's Midgets or somebody and starts bowling and drinking. They slip him some knock-out drops and he goes out for the count. In fact, he has such a hangover he sleeps for twenty years. At least that is the line he hands his wife when he gets back home. "That sounds like me, all right," I decide. "So I do a twenty-year stretch on the grass. Well, there are worse places. But I see where I am plenty behind on current events. What do you hear from the mob?"

This Grant guy doesn't know whether to take me seriously or not. "You actually claim an experience like Rip Van Winkle's?"

"I do not make up such a line just to explain to my wife," I say. "Because at the moment I do not have a wife, only alimony expenses. And after twenty years I wager I do not even have to pay alimony. But make with the news broadcast, buddy. What goes on in the world? Who wings the Series last year? Are they still running the nags at Saratoga and wherever? Is Joe Louis still boxing champion? Give out with important stuff like that."

Grant's face falls about a foot. "I'm afraid the world isn't in such good shape," he tells me.

"You mean the New Deal isn't cleaned up *yet*?" I ask.

"No, not exactly. Things are a lot better now, nationally and internationally, I suppose. You'll find plenty of new customs and fashions current, and a lot of inventions and improvements over your time. But one problem still remains. And it's a problem that's baffling me in my work right now."

I ask him what it is.

"Crime," he tells me. "Bootlegging. Right now I'm investigating the biggest bootlegging racket this country has ever seen."

"What's the matter, is Prohibition in again?" I ask.

"Prohibition? Oh—no, it's not liquor that's being bootlegged. It's vitamins."

"Vitamins? You mean that alphabet stuff—like A, B, C, D? I never go for such articles personally. Give me a beefsteak rare any time."

"You don't understand at all," Grant tells me. "Vitamins are food now. Today we eat only vitamin pills. Scientific research has perfected vitamin sources of energy and nourishment during the past years, largely as a result of crop shortages and famine following the Second World War. Now everyone takes a daily ration of vitamins. It's improving the stamina of the world's population. But lately large stores of synthetic vitamin capsules are being stolen—hijacked, you'd call it—from the government warehouses. Women and children are starving again in a world where we have no place for hunger and want any more. Some organized group of vandals is stealing capsules and bootlegging them to merchants. And since all vitamin production is centered in New York, and most of the capsules are stored there before distribution, the situation is grave. For weeks now, millions of capsules disappear daily. And people go hungry.

"I am on my way back to New York from Cleveland. My clues there prove to be false leads. But unless I can crack this mess soon, it's all up with me." Grant admits this sourly.

"I am an old alky runner myself," I tell him. "Maybe when I get into town I will look up some of the old mob and see if there are any leads. If so, I will give you a buzz. How about the phone number?"

"Use the private shortwave system," he says. "You'll find sending sets wherever you go. But you're not leaving me—I want to hear more about this Rip Van Winkle yarn."

"I have business in the city. But urgent. I will contact you later," I promise.

He doesn't answer. He is fiddling with his headpiece again, making a landing. Because before I realize it, we are already over New York. I look out. The burg is not much changed. The buildings look a little taller, but I still see the Empire State

Building and Radio City, and I think I spot Minsky's as we circle down.

We land just outside Flushing, in another little field. The air around us is filled with little silver specks—more planes. In fact, we come down in a place that says:

PLANES PARKED—50 CENTS
OVERNIGHT HANGARS—75 CENTS
MOTOR TUNEUP—ONE DOLLAR

And a guy comes running out to wipe off the windshield. I duck out of the seat in a hurry, and head for the gate. There is a subway entrance about a block away.

"Hey, wait for me!" yells this Grant guy. "I want to talk to you."

"See you later," I call back. "I may be a little slow getting there, but I still got a five-grand bet to collect from Gorilla Gabface."

There is a lot I could tell. About the rocket subway they put in instead of the old one—all new improvements, except that I still have to stand up. About the screwy way they dress, in these overalls with the lapels, and about the new type cars I see downtown that operate with these radio controls but still try to get every pedestrian who steps off the sidwalk. I notice television movie houses, too, and I kind of get to wondering what happens to the old-fashioned strip-tease, but I do not have time to find out.

Because, like I tell this Grant, I am on my way to see Gorilla Gabface. In 1942 he hangs out behind a pool hall on Second Avenue, and I figure it is an even chance he is still there, because Gorilla is not the kind of character who gets around much. In fact, he is very lazy and hardly ever moves from his chair except to kick his wife.

So I get off the subway and start walking. The streets look no better; in fact, twenty years age them the way they age me.

On the subway, persons look at me kind of peculiar and

I am undoubtedly a sight, but here on Second Avenue I look quite natural—because the street is full of broken-down bums.

I get to thinking about that. I am a broken-down old bum myself, now, and I hardly know what to do. But I figure once I get my hands on that five grand I will shave and dress and look around for some odds on the dogs or nags, and get back on my feet.

Still and all, it is not pleasant to hike along. Because there are a lot of sad-looking people on the street, sitting in front of their houses. Kids crying, and women with shawls around their heads, and guys sitting with their heads in their hands.

Pretty soon I come to a long line of guys standing in front of a store. They are mumbling and double-talking under their breath. Up at the head of the line they are pushing and rattling the door to the joint, which is locked.

All at once a guy sticks his head out of the window upstairs. "Go away," he says. "Go away, all of you. Government orders. We can't sell any capsules today—vitamin shortage."

Guys in the line let out a moan. "What about my family?" one yells. "My old lady and the baby have nothing to eat for three days now, except a few capsules of C and half an ounce of E."

"I'm sorry," says the guy in the window. "You know how it is. I'm not responsible."

"We got to eat," says the fellow in the line. "It's those damned hijackers! Why don't they catch them?"

Most of the men turn away. I walk on. All at once I notice a little rat-face personality sneaking up to one of the guys in the line.

"You want some capsules, buddy?" he whispers. "I got some here—nice fresh stuff. A to Z, anything you want, if you'll keep your mouth shut."

The guy looks at Rat-face kind of funny, but he says, "I

suppose I have to. My folks are hungry. How much for a two-day supply of general rations?"

Rat-face smiles. "Ten bucks," he says.

"Ten bucks? Why, that's robbery—these capsules are only 80 cents at a regular store!" says the guy.

Rat-face smiles again. "Regular store hasn't got any," he whispers. "You know that. Ten bucks, buddy. You're lucky to get it."

The guy hands him the money and gets a little tube. I don't wait to see any more, but I know Rat-face is going down the line now. I understand what this guy Grant tells me on the plane, about the vitamin shortage. It's just like bootlegging—only with a difference. Because, you see, these people *need* food. They must have it. And to hijack this stuff and then sell it—well, I don't go for it, that's all. Maybe I am getting soft in my old age.

Anyhow, I do not think about it any more, because I arrive at Gorilla's pool hall and walk in. The joint looks just the same, and it is just as empty out front. There is only one guy sitting there—a new guy to me. He has a red face with a lot of warts growing on it, and there is a dead cigarette butt in his mouth. A collar ad boy.

"Hello, character," I greet him. "Is Gorilla around?"

Warty gives me a slow look. "He might be. Who's looking for him?"

"Tell him Lefty Feep wants to see him. It's about five grand."

"You got five grand?"

"I'm going to get five grand from him," I correct.

He gives me the old leer and sneer. But I stare right back, and finally he climbs off the stool and goes into the rear room. He returns in a couple of minutes.

"Go right in," he says.

So I toddle back and open the door.

"Well, pappy?" says a voice.

I see a big fat guy sitting at a table. He has a bald noggin and a couple spare chins, but mostly he is all jaw from the neck up and all arms from the neck down. He looks like King Kong with a bad shave.

"Pardon me, curly," I state. "Where could I find Gorilla Gabface?"

"In hell," says the fat guy at the table. "He's dead for eighteen years. Come to think of it, you don't look far from dead yourself, pappy."

"Don't call me pappy!" I snap. "Or I will let the air out of your chins, you overgrown walrus."

Then the fat guy gets up from the table and I see he is about ten feet tall, or maybe six and a half anyhow. Part of him is muscle and the rest is meanness, so when he laughs I am not fooled, and when he sticks out his mitt I do not clasp it in any fraternity grip. "Who are you and what do you want?" he asks, moving around toward me.

"I am Lefty Feep, and Gorilla Gabface owes me five Gs on the dog-races," I repeat, stubborn. Only my feet are not stubborn, because they back me to the door.

"Well, I am Gorilla's nephew and I am running this show now for many's the year. I do not ever hear my uncle mention your name, and he certainly never mentions owing anyone five pennies, let alone five grand. So my advice to you, Feep, is to get out of here before I strangle you in your whiskers, you old sponge!"

"I take it you do not wish to pay me?" I inquire, just to make sure.

The fat guy reaches out across the floor with one hand, which wraps around my neck. "No," he says, lifting me off the floor and shaking me like a used bar-rag. "Though I can see you have a good use for five thousand dollars, if only to pay hospital expenses after I get through beating you up."

This is not exactly good news to me, and it is even less good when he smacks me one on the side of the head. I am just hanging there helpless while the fat guy draws back for another clout, when all at once he drops me to the floor.

Another guy comes in behind me, and he attracts the fat guy's attention. I lie there on the floor looking up and I see the newcomer is none other than Rat-face, the slug that was selling bootleg vitamin capsules to the citizens in front of the market. He is so excited he does not even notice me, and nearly steps on my face while I am lying there. "It's going great, Boss!" he yells to the fat guy. "I sell three hundred bucks of pills in the last hour. The rest of the mob is covering the district. We are running out of stock."

Rat-face is still talking when Wart-face comes in from the front room. He has an acetylene torch in one hand. "The boys are ready to tunnel through to the Government warehouse again this evening," he says. "Shall I send the trucks over?"

Fat guy looks at the two of them kind of funny. "You birds talk too much," he says. "Here," he says to Rat-face. "Go back out and tell the mob to stop selling for today. We don't want to flood the market all at once." Then he turns to Wart-face. "Get down to the warehouse. The boys are tunneling through from the building alongside. But leave this torch with me. I think I got to use it. Now—powder!"

The two guys back out of the room without even noticing me. I am lying on the floor listening to the birdies from that crack on the head, but I am also thinking. If these guys are the ones Grant is after, they have been running this bootleg vitamin racket from this place. One gang must be tunneling through to steal Government supplies, and the other gang goes out and sells the pills. And this fat guy is the brain.

So there I am, locked in a room with Gorilla's nephew. I am sixty years old, I have no equalizer, and he is a pretty tough customer.

What he has to say to me is not encouraging, either. He stands over me and looks down with a very nasty grin. "I am sorry about you, pappy," he says. "I only intend to beat you up and send you to a hospital. But now you hear a little too much, so I guess your next stop is the morgue."

I think in high gear. "Have a heart," I tell him. "I am an old-timer myself. I know your late uncle, in fact I am associated with him, you might say. I just do a twenty-year stretch, but I am an uptown boy. I can help you plenty."

Fat guy stands right over me and laughs some more. "No use, pappy," he says. "You old-fashioned gangsters are all through. We don't use rods and rattlers any more. This is big business. I am bucking the Federal Government myself, and winning. Why, we got eighty million vitamin food capsules stored away under this joint, and we're tunneling through tonight for another thirty million. I got a hundred guys out organized to cover bootleg territories. It's big business. We got a dozen cities at our mercy. Do you think I am some cheesy little punk in back of a poolroom like my late uncle? Not for a minute—this is big-time stuff and you has-beens are no good."

"But give me a chance—I know a few tricks," I plead.

He turns on the laugh again. "Not on your life," he chuckles. "And speaking of your life, here goes."

So he reaches down for the acetylene torch and the interview is over.

Fifteen minutes later, after I locate this guy Grant by shortwave from a cigar store on the corner, he arrives and claps the cuffs on the fat guy. Also his men surround the pool hall and snag Rat-face and his pals when they drift in from time to time.

They also capture, I hear later, all the mob down at the tunnel job, and they find the stores of capsules in a big cellar warehouse hidden downstairs.

So all in all it turns out to be a good thing for this guy Grant. And also for me, when I learn the Government is paying a five-grand reward for turning up the vitamin racketeers.

Two days later the money comes through. Meanwhile, I pal around with Grant and eat vitamins in restaurants. That is why I get so sick of them.

In fact, on the third day I am sitting in a hamburger stand making faces while I gulp down my third order of the dizzy beef pills with a ketchup drop on the side. Grant is with me, and he says, "Well, what are you going to do with the reward—go into business for yourself?"

That is when I get mad. "No," I tell him. "I am not cut out from this day and age, I see that. I am too old to start in again, I do not like the class of people that run the rackets nowadays, and besides, I do not see any strip shows in progress at all. More and over, these vitamin pills ruin my digestion and I have not even got an excuse to carry a toothpick. I think maybe I am better off back in 1942."

"Too bad," Grant tells me. "Those days are gone forever."

But I do not hear him. I am staring at a calendar on the wall. "April 29th!" I holler. "Listen, do you or do you not tell me I sleep for twenty years and 360 days? And do I or do I not spend four more days here? That makes tomorrow April 30th again!"

"So what?" asks Grant.

"So that means tomorrow is the annual picnic of the Diminutive Society of the Catskill Mountains. Hop into that plane of yours—we're going to see those dwarfs and give them a little proposition."

Which is just what we do. Grant lets me off near the top of the mountains the next morning. I go up and find the dwarfs bowling as usual. They are surprised to see me, and kind of embarrassed, till I get the head shorty off.

I ask him if he has got anything to drink that will send me back to where I was. He plays smart and says no. Then I tell him that fun is fun, and a gag is a gag, but I want to go back and am ready to pay for the trip.

This gets him interested, and he asks what the deal is. I tell him. He gets excited and calls a conference. Well, to make a long story short, they get together with me and the head shorty goes off and mixes up a fresh drink. Not beer, but something else. I promise not to mention it. Then I take care of my end of the bargain and drink the stuff.

It puts me out right away. And when I wake up everything is O.K. It is morning and when I hike down the mountain I find out that it is May 1st, 1942.

I wire ahead for some funds, and rush into town. The first place I head for is here, because after eating nothing but vitamins for four days, I am plenty hungry.

LEFTY FEEP concluded his story with a profound sigh. It was followed by a snort from over my shoulder.

Jack stood there with the tray of food. "What did I tell you?" he asked me. "Did you ever hear such a line in your life?"

Feep bridled. "What's wrong with my story, I would like to know?" he asked.

Jack snorted again. "Everything. But even if I believed it—which I don't—there are just a few things that puzzle me. To begin with, I thought you were at the mercy of that fat guy in the back room of the pool hall. He was going to kill you with an acetylene torch, wasn't he? In fact, you were lying there on the floor and he was standing over you. And yet you say that fifteen minutes later you walked out free and left him there to be captured."

"Oh, that," said Lefty Feep. "That is very simple. Like I said, this guy thinks he is so smart, and that old-timers do not know any clever tricks. But I have one trick up my sleeve he does not know. It is a very ordinary trick today and much used in the rackets—but I suppose he never hears of it in 1962. I am lying there on the floor, he reaches down for the torch, but I grab it first. He shoves his foot down on my arm, but then I pull this old-fashioned trick on him, like I say. I merely turn on the torch and give him the hot-foot. And if you do not think a hot-foot with a torch is effective, you are crazy."

Jack turned crimson. "All right, I give up," he sighed.

"But just one thing more. About that deal you made with the dwarfs."

"What about it?"

"Well, certainly you didn't just offer them money. They have no use for money."

Feep smiled. "Of course not, Bob. But I use the money to make the deal. I buy something the dwarfs will really go for. That is what I tell the head shorty to make him go through with it. I tell him I will give his little pals something they can use at their picnics from now on."

"And what is that?"

"A modern bowling alley. Sure—I tell him I contract to build a bowling alley right on top of the mountain, so they can organize a league and get into the tournaments. In fact, next year I am going back there again and play them myself. Maybe you would like to get on the team?"

"Come on," said Jack to me. "Let's you and I get out of here."

We left the table, but Feep didn't see us go. He was tearing apart the roast chicken with the famished look of a man who has eaten nothing but pills for four days.

AFTER WORDS

STANLEY: *That's a very clever title for the first Lefty Feep story.*

BLOCH: I must hasten to correct you. I am not the originator of the term "Time Wounds All Heels." It had been around as a catchphrase for at least a dozen years beforehand, but uncredited. Perhaps Goodman Ace created it on his radio show, *Easy Aces*. But it had never been used as a title to my knowledge, so I appropriated it.

JS: *This first story seems to be inspired by Rip Van Winkle. Had you re-read Washington Irving's story?*

BLOCH: I may have . . . I have no direct recollection. I probably would have, just to refresh my memory.

JS: *One unusual thing is the serious theme about food shortages caused by crop losses and the famine following the beginning of World War II. Usually the Feep stories don't have a serious bone in their (anti)bodies.*

BLOCH: I was referring pretty directly to what was then on every citizen's mind: The rationing system, the food coupons which limited the amount you could buy of meat, sugar and other major foods. And vitamins, of course, became quite popular. Up to that time they had not played so great a part in supplementing anyone's diet.

JS: *There are no internal rhymes in this first story.*

BLOCH: I started to put those things in later just to amuse myself. They're certainly not Runyonesque. Runyon gave picturesque names to his characters and let it go at that. But the British rhyming slang had always intrigued me and now there was another influence in radio. The so-called hep-cat musician characters were coming in; people like Jerry Colonna, who was Bob Hope's stooge. As a result, one would hear what was supposedly the musician's rhyming argot on comedy shows.

JS: *Hep to the jive.*

BLOCH: Umm hum. I probably introduced it for that reason.

JS: *You get more into the hep-jive lingo talk in the third story,* "The Pied Piper Fights the Gestapo." *But first comes something else . . . the second story . . .*

The sequel to "Time Wounds All Heels," *in which the intrepid Lefty Feep lives in the fast lane of bowling to learn that it never rains but on his pores. A story of the gutter.*

GATHER 'ROUND THE FLOWING BOWLER

I WAS SITTING in my usual seat at Jack's Shack the other night when I was startled out of it. I literally began to rise and show the shine on my trousers.

"Hey, there!" I called.

A gangling figure paused midway between tables and veered rapidly in the direction of my booth. With a melancholy grin, Mr. Lefty Feep sidled over and extended a dripping hand.

"You been carrying a herring?" I inquired. "Your hand is wet."

"I am all wet," said Lefty Feep. "And I like it."

It was true. Lefty Feep was all wet. For the first time I permitted my gaze to run along the rainbow of his suit. Feep was wearing a box-shoulder Navajo blanket pattern of such blinding hue that at first I thought somebody had spilled spaghetti on him.

But it was not spaghetti that poured from his lapels and cuffs. It was water. Lefty Feep was soaked to the skin.

"Have you been out in the rain?" I ventured.

"You win the $64 dollar question," said Feep. "I am strolling in a storm this last hour. Outside it is mostly moistly."

"But you'll ruin your clothes," I said—as if it were possible to ruin that atrocious costume.

"So I buy another suit," Feep grinned, sitting down. "You will pardon me if I seem to drip."

"I never knew you liked water."

"I am extremely fond of water—for external use only. Why, it is water that brings me my fortune this last year."

"Your fortune?" I echoed. Then I regretted it.

For the last time I'd met Lefty Feep he was introduced to me as the biggest liar in seven states. The story he told then more than qualified him for that honor. It dealt, as I remember, with Mr. Feep's accidental visit to the bowling dwarfs of the Catskill Mountains. Feep claimed to have followed the footsteps of Rip Van Winkle by drinking the dwarf's brew and sleeping twenty years into the future. He explained his return by claiming he'd bribed the dwarfs to send him back—by building for them a regulation bowling alley on the mountain top. When Feep had unfolded this slightly incredible saga there had been a curious glint in his eye. I saw it now, as I mentioned his fortune.

"Fortune?" he murmured. "Friend, I have adventures in the last annum that will make your blood run from zero below. I have experiences that will make icebergs out of your corpuscles. Doubtless you wish to catch the details?"

"No," I grated.

"Well, if you insist—" said Lefty Feep.

AT FIRST (began Feep) I think I am lucky last year when I do not run into pneumonia. Then something worse happens to me—I run into Gorilla Gabface.

Gorilla Gabface, I believe I mention before, is quite a lusty shout in the old rackets, and he and I are what you might call unfriendly enemies for many the year. We are always making sociable wagers on who will win the pennant, or what bank will be held up next, and such matters of sporting interest.

Gorilla hangs out in a poolroom night and day. In fact, I never know him to leave this cue casino in all his unnatural life. I even state the fact that he would not stick his neck out the door if there was a ten-pound cheese on the sidewalk. And this should be quite a temptation, because he is a rat.

So I am quite naturally confused when I see him this night walking down the old stem. He is bouncing along like a bed check, and almost runs me off the sidewalk.

"What crooked parole board lets you out?" I naturally inquire.

He blinks at me and sticks out his paw. I do not take it, because there is a ring on my own hand which I value.

"I am on my way to the bowling alleys," he cracks.

I just stare. "Bowling alleys? I never hear you are a sports-lover."

He gives a laugh. "There is a lot those big floppy ears of yours never hear, Feep. But it may interest you to know that I am now manager and owner of none other than Yank Albino, the world's champion pin-punisher. Tonight we are holding an exhibition match with Ed Knight, and I am on my way down to take charge of the box office receipts." He laughs, and several persons look around to see if a hyena is loose. "I am making myself some pin money, you might say."

What I might say I say under my breath. It grieves me extremely to see this Gorilla muscling in on something like the bowling game, which is a line I am personally fond of. I figure it a nice clean sport, and do not approve of putting vaseline on bowling balls, or plugging up the finger-holes with corks, or otherwise bollixing the works. But if Gorilla Gabface is operating, it will sooner or later be too bad for the bowling game. How he gets hold of a champion like Yank Albino I do not figure out. So I ask him.

"Simple," he says. "Albino owes me a number of years on a little bet, so I take over his contract and he will work it out. Right now I am figuring a few neat deals. You know," he says, "the bowling game is so clean it hurts me to look at it. Give me a few months with this champion and I will put over so many angles that it will take a cross-eyed accountant ten years to untangle the mess." And he laughs again, causing several people to run home and hide under their beds.

But I do not say anything, and when he asks me if I want to come along and place my peepers on the exhibition matches, I make with the feet to the bowling alleys and take a seat.

This Yank Albino is indeed a sweet bowler, and when I grab a place in the crowd watching, I am soon exhibiting my pleasure by uttering such sounds as "Wow!" and "Atta baby!"

All at once I hear a voice at my side contradicting me in such a manner as "Boo! Take him away! He stinks!"

This more than surprises me, particularly since the voice comes out of the mouth of a very pretty ginch. This ginch is just a little thing with long 18-karat hair, but she has a very loud voice, and she keeps up with her "Boo! Throw him out!" even when I stare at her. So naturally I inquire, "Why, ginch, do you make like a censor? Is it the bowling, or do you have a grudge against Yank Albino?"

She gives me a stare and then she starts to bawl. "Boo hoo!" she yammers. "Yank Albino is my fiance. Boo hoo!"

Naturally I do not catch, and tell her so. If Yank Albino is her fiance she should be happy to scramble with such a champion instead of hollering out in public that he is a menace to the nose.

"You do not understand," she tells me. "I don't want people to like Yank's bowling. Because if he becomes unpopular, then maybe his manager will break his contract. I want this to happen, because I know his manager is no better than a thug, and he has got Yank tied up on account of debts and is making some crooked plans for him. I tell Yank this, but he won't believe me, and he refuses to bowl badly. I don't know what to do."

"Leave it to me," I advise. "I have a few ideas I wish to talk over with Mr. Gabface."

She gives a little jump. "Oh, you know Yank's manager, too?" she asks.

I wink. "I know him like a book," I tell her. "Even better, because I am not acquainted with any books except racing. I think I have me an idea which will make you happy and me money."

"What is it?" she pipes, cheering up a little and giving me a smile that would go good in advertising love seats anywhere.

"I think I can find a bowler to beat your Yank Albino," I say. "In fact, I will wager with Gorilla that I find such a character. Then when he beats Yank I will win the bet and Gorilla will get mad and release his contract."

"You are crazy," sobs the ginch. "Nobody can beat my Yank."

I smile.

Then I run down to the box office and catch Gorilla Gabface. I tell him what I tell the ginch, or at least part of it—that I am willing to lay a grand on a bowling match against Yank Albino if I can provide another champion.

"Who is he?" asks Gabface. "Albino already beats every bowler in all leagues."

"My man is none other than the Masked Marvel," I tell him.

"You are making a bad bet," chuckles Gabface.

I dig into my pocket. "Here is the alphabet for you—one G that says my Masked Marvel will beat Yank Albino in an exhibition match, any date after April 30th."

"Why after April 30th?" he asks.

"I got to go get him," I answer. "He lives outside the city. Way outside."

"How about May 1st?" says Gabface. "We got a date open."

"Pretty quick, but it's okay with me," I agree.

Gabface takes the money and laughs again. "I still say that no human being can beat Yank Albino," he gurgles.

I answer, but under my breath. "I do not say he would be a human being," I whisper.

DRUNK AND EARLY on the morning of April 30th, I slip out of my pajamas and into a Manhattan. I grab me a flask and make for the car, heading up the Hudson Valley and cutting west.

From time to time I take a slug from the flask, because I am looking forward to a rough time.

Pretty soon I am in Catskill country, on my fourth side road, and I figure I might as well be as high as the scenery.

The old bus clunks along pretty steady, but I am doing the shivering. Particularly when I get off the last side road, which is so deserted there aren't even any hot-dog stands.

I am driving all alone up steep hills covered with trees so they look like a bunch of Smith Brothers' faces without a shave. To make the resemblance complete, it is so quiet you can hear a cough drop.

Then it isn't so quiet any more. Far off in the distance there is a low, rumbling sound—like Gorilla Gabface makes after a heavy meal.

I climb higher, it gets darker, and the noise is louder. In spite of myself I begin making like a goose with the flesh. Here I am, all alone in the Catskills, without any weapon but my flask.

By the time I rise over the top of the highest hill, the rumbling is strictly from thunder. A minute later I know I have arrived. Because there is the sign on the rocks at the end of the deserted road.

ANNUAL PICNIC
THE DIMINUTIVE SOCIETY
OF THE CATSKILL MOUNTAINS

I am back with the dwarfs I meet last year, and, sure enough, up ahead is the open-air bowling alley I build for them. The rumbling comes from inside, so I park the car and go over.

This takes some time, because my feet want to go the other way. You see, I do not wish to remember my last meeting with these half-pints, when they slip me the old double cross and I wake up twenty years too late for the current World Series.

But I have my scheme to collect a thousand government etchings of old George Washington, and I know what I must do.

So I do it. I walk inside.

There on the alleys are about twenty of these extremely small fry that call themselves The Diminutive Society of the Catskill Mountains, although what they really are is dwarfs. Some of them are bowling and the rest are glassing around a beer barrel.

I almost run out again when I see the beer, because it is this stuff that knocks me out for the long count last time. But I take a deep breath and go up to them.

"Hello slobs, what you hear from the mob?" I ask politely.

The whole crew looks up. They have to look up to see me, because they are only three feet tall, and besides, most of them have beards growing right into their eyes.

"Why, it's Lefty Feep!" cackles the head shorty, who I remember from before. "Back to visit us again!"

They get very excited and start dancing around me like I was a Maypole. Some of them are thanking me for the bowling alley, and the head shorty tells me that the new alleys work very good, and that they are using a couple field mice for pinboys.

"Have a drink," says the head shorty, holding up a tanker.

But this time I play smart. "Not on your life," I tell him. "This is the stuff that rips Van Winkle. Me, I am sticking to my little flask this trip. I just drop in to see how you boys are getting along."

Well, they do not seem offended, but get back to bowling again, and I take a couple turns at the alley myself.

It is a regulation alley, you understand—I send up a gang to build it myself, because the dwarfs only come out once a year on April 30th, and there is nothing around on other days to make the workmen suspicious. The dwarfs always go in for lawn bowling and nine-pins before, but I am glad to see that they understand the new alley very well.

I keep my eye particuarly on the head shorty. He is a little guy, like the others, and he has a long white beard that hangs down to his knees, but this does not interfere with his bowling. This personality just runs up one strike after another, even though he stands wrong and his arms are so long I am afraid he bruises his knuckles because they scrape along the alley. But he strikes and drinks and drinks and strikes, and I know I find what I am looking for.

I sit tight, and after a while the dwarfs get tight. They spend more time around their beer barrel than they do on the alley, and pretty soon I signal the head shorty to come over and sit down with me.

"I wish to ask you a few questions, shrimp," I inform him. So he leaves the beer barrel polka and sits on my lap, confidental like.

"Now, my little Charlie McCarthy, I offer a proposition for you. How would you like to make some money?" I ask.

He just blinks.

"Big money," I tell him. "A fortune."

"What is money?" he asks.

"Cash. Dollars. Hay. Mazuma. Laughing lettuce."

"Squire Feep, you jest."

"I just what?" Then I catch on. This midget is so far back in the woods he does not even know what money is. So I explain. Then he shakes his head. His beard bobs around like a dust mop.

"What do I want with money?" he asks. "I do not visit the face of the earth save once a year, on April 30th. And then it is only to bowl and drink, as is our ancient custom."

"That's just the point," I tell him. "You can make a lot of money bowling the way you do. And then you won't have to live in a hole in the ground. You can live in a swell dump in town. You can visit the Stork Club. Why, you can even go to a barber! A clean shave will make a new man of you.

"Besides, I never do figure out why you dwarfs are not around except on this one day, April 30th. Can't you live above ground the rest of the year? Or do you just figure rents are too high?"

"No," he tells me. "I can live above ground. But it's so much nicer down below. All that nice dirt to dig and eat."

"You sound like a columnist," I tell him. "But seriously now, how about coming back to town and bowling for me? I'll manage you and we'll clean up. I can arrange a little exhibition match for you tomorrow night. All you got to do is get up and sling a few balls."

"Tomorrow night? Never!" squeaks Shorty. "I tell you, we of the Catskills must not bowl save on one day alone. If we transgress, dire things transpire."

"Cut the double talk," I tell him. "This is your big chance."

"I must refuse, Squire Feep," Shorty pipes. And he wiggles off my knee.

So there I sit, thinking about my lost G. There is nothing to do but pull out my flask.

I do. And then the idea hits me.

Why not? That's what the head shorty does to me the last time I visit him. Turnabout is fair play. I drink his beer and pass out. What if he drinks my whiskey?

I amble over to the keg. The dwarfs are singing now in voices that would not please Walt Disney, but I do not mind.

I just stand there and tug at my flask, making happy faces. And sure enough, pretty soon the head shorty sees me and his eyes begin glowing.

"What are you drinking, Squire Feep?" he asks me.

"Just a little beer of my own," I tell him. "Have a slug?"

He takes one. Pretty soon his nose begins glowing.

"Methinks it powerful strong," he tells me.

"Have another."

He does. We sit down in the corner and I let him play spin the bottle.

Meanwhile, outside it is getting dark. The dwarfs begin bowling again, and the rumbling gets louder and louder, drowning out the way my little shorty pal is burping.

Then I see the dwarfs looking over their shoulders at the sunset, and they begin scurrying out of the bowling alley pretty quick. I know they are going back to their caves on the inside of the hill. It is all over.

It is all over with the head shorty, too. Because he is lying under the seat. I cover him with my coat and nobody notices he is missing. The dwarfs say goodnight, and leave.

So I sit there alone in the twilight with the empty flask. It is very quiet now on the mountain. In fact, I hear only one sound, like a dive bomber calling its mate.

It is the head dwarf, snoring under my seat.

"Come on," I whisper, carrying him out the door and into the car. "Little man, you have a busy day."

It is a very busy day indeed, that 1st of May. When the dwarf wakes up in my room about lunchtime I can see that he does not want any.

"Where am I?" he groaned.

"In my dump, pal," I inform him.

"Why is my beard in my mouth?" he asks.

"There is no beard in your mouth. What you have is merely a slight hangover." I do not tell him that I Mickey Finnish him, but he can guess.

"It is another day!" he squawks, climbing out of the

bureau drawer which I park him in for a bed the night before. "Squire Feep, you are a false friend! Now I am stranded on upper earth for a year!"

"Calm down," I advise. "It isn't going to hurt you any. A little fresh air and sunshine will do you good."

"Fresh air!" he squeaks. "Sunshine? Never!" He begins to dance up and down, tearing at his beard. "Take me back to my cave!"

"You've got a bowling match tonight," I tell him. "And there'll be lots of nice beer, too."

"I'm hungry. I want some dirt!" he yells.

"How about some nice scrambled eggs?"

"Fie upon eggs! Bring me some nourishing dirt—I need humus!"

Well, what can I do but humor him? So I go downstairs and borrow a vacuum cleaner and let my small feathered friend get at the bag. For dessert he finishes up a little pocket fuzz I find in my overcoat.

"Fine," he says. "Now, Squire Feep, if you'll take me back to the mountains, I can get along very well for the next 364 days until the Diminutive Society comes out again."

"Not on your life," I remind him. "You're going to bowl tonight. Not only that," I say, pulling out a little black mask, "but you're going to wear this over your puss because you are now the Masked Marvel."

"Never, never, never!" says the dwarf. "My name is Timothy."

"I will call you Tiny Tim for short, then. But you are still the Masked Marvel and you bowl tonight."

This does not please Tiny Tim at all. I am none too pleased myself, because the doorbell rings and I have to answer it.

There is the little blonde ginch who is engaged to Yank Albino.

"Oh, Mr. Feep!" she says. "I'm so worried, I have to stop by and see if everything is all set for tonight."

"It is," I tell her. "In fact, I have the Masked Marvel right here with me now."

Which is true. Because Tiny Tim sticks his head out from between my knees and stares up at her.

"Is this the Masked Marvel?" asks the blonde ginch, with a little shriek. "Why, he's so little and old—"

And then she lets out a real shriek, because Tiny Tim leaps up in the air and begins yanking on her curls.

"Gold!" he yells. "Gold!"

"That's hair, you dope," I tell him, pulling him down.

"Then what is that creature?" he asks.

"A ginch."

"What?"

"A broad, a dish, a babe—a woman."

"Woman? What is that?"

"I have not time to go into the matter with you now," I say.

But the blonde giggles. "You mean your little friend never sees a woman before?" she asks.

"He is a very backward personality," I explain. "In fact, he is a hermit from the Catskill Mountains."

"You want to eat some dirt?" Tiny Tim asks her.

The blonde giggles again.

"I think he's cute," she says. And pats him on the head.

Tiny Tim lets go with a smile. Then he blushes. "I like her. Your hair is gold. I like gold," he tells me. Then he makes a grab for her finger. "Gold!" he hollers, tugging at her ring.

"Mustn't touch!" I say, politely bopping him one on the old orange.

"Eccentric, isn't he?" says the blonde ginch. "I hope he knows how to bowl. He *must* beat Yank tonight."

"Will you be there?" asks Tiny Tim.

"Certainly," she says.

Tiny Tim turns to me. "Very well, then. I shall bowl. I shall beat this Yank of yours if you wish me to."

I wink at the ginch, because this is a big load off my mind.

"Give me a nice dirt supper," squeals Tiny Tim. "I'll show you some bowling you've never seen in your life!"

It turns out he isn't kidding.

WHEN WE GET to the bowling alleys that night, Gorilla Gabface is waiting at the door.

"So there you are, Feep," he greets me. "I do not figure you will even turn up after that foolish bet you make. In fact," he sneers, "I already send word to Yank Albino to start exhibition stunts so the crowd will get something for its money. Which is more than you will get for your money, Feep, because I never see anyone in top form like Yank tonight. He has more strikes than an eight-day clock."

"Well, here is somebody to fix his clock for him," I announce, and push Tiny Tim out from behind me.

He does not look any too good to me, wearing that old-fashioned pair of square-cut shorts the dwarfs caper around in. More and over, he is standing with his knuckles touching the pavement and his beard hanging down between. There is a lot of caked earth on his beard, too, because he insists on having mud-pies for dessert at supper. Besides, his mask is on crooked, and you can't see his face under the hair.

Gorilla Gabface stares. "What is this, a trained monkey?" he yaps. "I do not realize you make your money with a hand organ before, Feep."

"This is the Masked Marvel," I tell him. "Which you will find out as soon as we get on the alleys. Kindly move your fat figure along, Gorilla—I want that thousand smackers."

We go inside—Tiny Tim, the blonde ginch, and myself. Halfway down the aisle the dwarf nudges me.

"I forget!" he whispers. "This is not April 30th. I cannot bowl. It is against the Catskill laws."

"Quit stalling," I whisper.

"But I mean it, Squire Feep. Something dreadful happens if we bowl on any other than the permitted day. That's why we only appear on April 30th. On all other days something terrible occurs. For your own sake—"

Then the ginch takes over. She gives him the old eye and begins to play with his beard. "You'll do it for me, won't you, Tiny Tim? You must do it."

He turns very red. "Yes, but—"

"Never mind," I crack. "Get hold of a ball and let fly."

Meanwhile I get hold of his whiskers and drag him out there before the crowd of yahoos in the audience.

They begin to laugh the minute they see him. Gorilla is still introducing the Masked Marvel, and when they see this dopey-looking dwarf stumble out they let out a howl.

But after that first ball they howl from astonishment.

To make a short story shorter, Tiny Tim knocks down no less than 240 pins in a row, in less than seven minutes.

He keeps four alleys busy—he does not bother with rules—just picks up a ball and hurls it whenever he sees ten pins together. Yank Albino stands there with his mouth open, and so does Gabface, and everyone in the crowd. For that matter, I am breathing through my tonsils myself.

The crowd howls and the balls rumble, and the dwarf bowls. And then maybe I am cuckoo, but it seems to me the rumbling is getting louder. It *is* getting louder. It sounds like thunder. It *is* thunder.

Because something hits me on the tip of the nose just then.

Water.

The thunder gets louder, I look up, and I see an extremely strange thing.

It is raining in the bowling alley!

Yes, right there inside, under the roof, rain is pouring down from the ceiling. And now the thunder is louder than ever, and I can even see a flicker of lightning.

The crowd sees it too. They set up a murmur, but it is better for them if they set up umbrellas, because in a minute the rain turns into a downpour.

Yank Albino and Gorilla Gabface run around making with amazement. But the dwarf is so excited he does not even notice—just keeps right on tossing balls down the four alleys, one after another. And now, every time he makes a strike there is more thunder, and a big streak of lightning to keep score.

People are screaming and pointing at the ceiling, and the alley is getting wet so that the balls float down. Pretty soon the pins are bobbing around on top of the water, and the dwarf's legs are wet to the knees. He is almost doing the Australian crawl every time he lets go with a ball.

Then the old panic comes on and the crowd is screaming and trying to head for the door—and Gabface runs out like he hears they discover gold in the next room.

"Hey—stop!" I call to the dwarf. Now I realize what he means when he says something dreadful happens if he bowls. Because drowning is dreadful, and that is what we are all liable to do here. The water is rising, and now there is more lightning. But the dwarf does not stop. He cannot hear me over the thunder and shouting.

I see I have to yank him off the floor, so I wade down and by this time he is up to his waist and swimming in a pool. But he manages to hurl one last ball—and that does it.

A streak of lightning bangs down from the roof, all the lights go out, and the side of the bowling alley caves in. It is struck.

I get to the dwarf just as he is going down for the third time.

And that is when the cops get to me.

"WHAT DO you mean, disorderly conduct?" asks Magistrate Donglepootzer.

We are lined up in front of him in night court about an hour later—me, the blonde ginch, and Tiny Tim.

The cop that brings us in looks at Magistrate Donglepootzer and shrugs. "These people are the ones I find creating a disturbance in a bowling alley," he says.

"A disturbance? What kind of disturbance?"

"Well, this little runt here is bowling and the wall comes down."

"That sounds pretty serious," says the Magistrate, frowning. "You mean he knocks the wall down with a bowling ball? Doesn't look like he has the strength."

"Not exactly," says the cop, turning red a little. "He bowls and lightning knocks the wall down."

"Oh, lightning. Then it turns out that a storm is responsible for the damage, and not this man. So why arrest him?"

"He started the storm, Your Honor," pipes the cop, kind of embarrassed.

"What kind of talk is this? People don't start storms, you know. And come to think of it, it isn't raining at all outside."

"I know, Your Honor. It's only raining inside this bowling alley."

Magistrate Donglepootzer stares at the cop for a long time. "Do you mean to stand there and tell me that it is raining inside a bowling alley?" he repeats, in a nasty voice.

"I know it's hard to believe, Your Honor, but that's the way it is. I nearly drown trying to arrest these people."

Donglepootzer stares again. "I wish you would drown!" he groans. "Drown dead! Telling me that it's storming inside a bowling alley and a wall falls down—and then arresting these innocent bystanders for disorderly conduct!"

"But this guy starts the storm," protests the cop. "I see it myself. He bowls and it rains."

Donglepootzer turns red again. "Are you trying to drive me crazy?" he says.

"Yes, Your Honor," says the cop.

"Shut up!" yells Donglepootzer. "I can't stand this. You're trying to tell me this midget with the moss on his face starts storms in bowling alleys. What about the mask on his face, then? Isn't he a burglar, too? And I suppose the woman is his gun moll. And that stupid-looking oaf next to her is undoubtedly an accomplice, perhaps an umbrella salesman."

When he says the part about the stupid-looking oaf he points to me. I resent this, because pointing is not nice.

"Speak up!" he yells at Tiny Tim, all of a sudden. "Maybe you can explain this mad story?"

"It's true, Squire," pipes Tiny Tim. "But I am not responsible. Squire Feep here drags me out of my cave and makes me eat dirt all day—otherwise, I'd still be happy up in the hills with the other dwarfs instead of making thunderstorms in bowling alleys."

Donglepootzer pulls out a handkerchief and wipes his forehead. Then he talks, in a sort of strangled voice. "That last sentence is perhaps the most remarkable one I shall ever hear," he chokes. "Before I break you," and he points at the cop, "and before I turn all of you maniacs over to the court psychiatrist, I should like you to repeat one statement. Do you or do you not start a thunderstorm in a bowling alley?"

"I do," says Tiny Tim.

Donglepootzer groans. "No, no," he whispers. "I can't believe it. I won't believe it! All of you—come with me."

"Where are you taking us?" asks the blonde ginch.

"Downstairs," says Donglepootzer. "Downstairs. There is a recreation gymnasium here in the station for police officers. I believe it has a bowling alley attached to the premises. You are going to bowl for me, my little friend. I want you to show me exactly what you do before I see a psychiatrist myself."

"You will not enjoy it," says Tiny Tim, pulling at his beard.

And when we get to the alley, Magistrate Donglepootzer does not enjoy it a small bit.

While the cop watches, he gives Tiny Tim a ball. I act as pinboy. And Tiny Tim lets go.

At first everything is fine. Donglepootzer cannot believe the way he knocks the pins over.

Then I hear a rumbling.

"How about stopping?" I ask.

Donglepootzer shakes his head. "I must see this," he groans.

I shrug. Tiny Tim bowls. Thunder growls.

Well, what's the use? All I can state is that ten minutes later Donglepootzer is trying to dog-paddle his way out of the alley when a bolt of lightning uncorks from the ceiling and the police gymnasium roof caves in like an eggshell.

"Help!" yells the blonde ginch.

"Blub-blub," gurgles the dwarf, going under water.

"Holy Smokes!" bawls the cop.

"Six months for disorderly conduct," groans Magistrate Donglepootzer.

IT IS LUCKY for me that Tiny Tim and I end up in the same cell that night. It is also lucky for me that the dwarf is in good appetite. Otherwise he can never swallow all the dirt he does, to say nothing of about three pounds of cement.

But he manages. It is nearly six a.m. when he finally gets a hole big enough at the bottom of the side of the cell and wriggles out.

He crawls down the hall to the turnkey's office and manages to sneak the keys off the desk. Then he crawls back.

I unlock the cell and we do a fast and furious powder. This powder does not end until we are in the car and heading out of town.

Before I go, I stop for only one thing. I call up Gorilla Gabface on the phone and get him out of bed.

"About that thousand bucks," I tell him, "I still claim my Masked Marvel wins and you owe me."

"I owe you nothing, Feep!" growls Gabface. Then he laughs. *"Because the match is called on account of rain!"*

I let out a few harsh names, but I can do nothing—except get out of town before the heat is on.

Which I do.

We reach the Catskills that afternoon. I dump Tiny Tim out of the back seat.

"Well, now what?" he asks me.

"Help me with these canned goods," I tell him. "Bring them inside your private bowling alley here. I need something to eat these next 363 days."

"You are staying here?" he asks.

"Where else? The heat is on in town for me, and you can't go back to your little pals until next April 30th. We might as well live here together. Then neither one of us gets into trouble. We are all alone here in the alley on top of the mountain, and I hope we stay that way."

We do.

There is not much worth telling about that year. I am not cut out for the hermit life, being an uptown boy, but after I teach Tiny Tim how to deal a few hands of pinochle, we get along all right. Besides, I keep him in bowling practice.

Every once in a while I slip down the mountain into town to catch up with this and that. I find out from the local bladder's sports section that Gorilla Gabface takes his Yank Albino on a tour all over the country, and is cleaning up.

I just smile, because I figure out a plan. I smile and keep track of the days, and finally the time comes.

One morning I grab Tiny Tim by the beard to wake him up, as usual. Only this time I have a scissors in my other hand. And in two snips the beard is off.

"What is this?" he bawls. "Squire Feep, what are you doing?"

"I am shaving you," I tell him. "But close. So hold still."

He does not hold still, but I shave him.

"What is the meaning of this?" he squeaks, feeling his chin.

"It means that you are now Tiny Tim, the Boy Bowler," I say. "Let me put on this hair dye, now."

Which I do, holding him down until I finish and he is a little clean-shaven guy with black hair.

"Boy Bowler?" he gasps.

"Certainly," I tell him. "You do not think I spend my time this year with you because I love your company. I prefer to be a hermit with somebody like Lana Turner. But I am going to get my money back from this Gorilla Gabface before you go back to the hills for good, and so I figure out this scheme.

"Today is April 27th. We drive to Milwaukee and arrive there on the 29th. I wire ahead and arrange a match between the Boy Bowler and Yank Albino—because the papers tell me he will be playing exhibition games there. And I make another bet with Gorilla, only this time I collect, rain or no rain. Then we fly back here in time for the 30th and you can join your pals, the Catskill Mountain Junior G-Men, or whatever they are."

Tiny Tim listens to this and scratches the place where his beard should be. "Methinks it sounds reasonable," he decides. "But it rains when I bowl."

"Just leave that part to me," I say. "I have it all figured out this time."

Which I have. Only it is not figured out the way I care to tell him about. Because I tell him it is the 27th when I know it is the 28th. So we will arrive in Milwaukee on the 30th and hold the match.

Of course, the 30th is the one day a year when it will not rain if the dwarf bowls.

That is not such a hot trick on Tiny Tim, I know—but I need the money and after all, I spend a year in hiding. I figure that the next year will be easier on him, now that he knows pinochle. Besides, when I clean up, I will not only buy him a bushel of the best dirt, but also some fancy milorganite from Milwaukee.

So we make the drive. A thousand miles between the

Catskills and Wisconsin is not too easy, but I am so happy at figuring things out, I do not mind.

In Buffalo I wire ahead to Gorilla Gabface that I find a new champion bowler and want another match with Yank Albino.

"Play it up big," I state. "My boy is only seven years old and a marvel. But five grand says he beats Yank Albino."

I get an answer waiting for me in Cleveland. It is OK, bet and all.

And so, on April 30th, at 8 o'clock, we pull up in front of the Milwaukee alleys, Tiny Tim and I.

It is a beautiful spring day, and I cannot help but wonder how the dwarfs are enjoying it back in the Catskills. Only I do not speak to Tiny Tim about this, because he will not understand and just get sore.

So far everything is under control. I buy clothes on the way, and now Tiny Tim the Boy Bowler is wearing a little knicker suit and a moppet's hat. He is disguised perfectly, as I shave him again, close.

Gorilla is waiting in the office, and when he sees Tiny Tim he doesn't tumble.

"Feep, you pick up the oddest characters," he chuckles. "First a fugitive from a miniature golf course, and now a school boy. Of course it's tremendous publicity stunt stuff, but why you want to plunk away five grand, I don't know."

"I am making five grand," I tell him. "And besides, this is no school boy, but a genuine Quiz Kid. Come on, let's get started."

Gabface steps close to me. "Just a minute, Feep," he says. "If there's anything phony about this kid, you're going to catch plenty. Because unless Yank Albino makes a good showing tonight, I'm dropping his contract and taking another man. Bowling officials are here to look him over. So just remember—if you cross me you can mark the 29th of April as your unlucky day."

"The *what*?" I gasp.

"The 29th of April, dope! Today."

I go green around the gills. I realize I make a terrible mistake in keeping track of days back there in the Catskills. I think I am kidding the dwarf about the dates, but I really kid myself. Today is the 29th—and it looks like thunderstorms ahead!

But it is too late to say anything.

Because a bald-headed man sticks his head in. "Come on, all set?" he yells. "You should see the crowd out there—boy, we're packing them in. Bet you a hundred there's 2000 people."

"This is Better O'Brien, the promoter," Gabface introduces. "Better, meet Lefty Feep and the Boy Bowler."

Tiny Tim keeps plenty quiet. He thinks it's all right and I have a scheme. He should only know!

"Go on out there, Tim," I tell him, gulping. "Everything is all set."

Set is right. The dwarf marches out, with his arms dangling. This Better O'Brien person laughs.

"Some champion you dig up, Feep," he chuckles. "Hear you put five grand on him to win out tonight. Wish I had a piece of that myself. Why, that little kid couldn't lift a ball, let alone beat Yank Albino. Gorilla has a sure thing betting against you."

All I do is groan.

"You wouldn't want to make another wager on him, would you, Feep?" says O'Brien.

I groan again. Because outside in the alleys I hear a rumbling that tells me the match is starting. And the rumbling is getting louder. Like thunder.

"Frankly," O'Brien keeps up, "I think your man is all wet."

I groan again and walk into the alleys with O'Brien. What else can I do? I am a drowning man without a straw.

To make a long story short, I guess you know what happens on that Milwaukee alley on the 29th of April. All I

K.
D.

can say is that after the storm I pay Gorilla Gabface five grand, he bounces Yank Albino off his contract, Yank Albino makes up with his blonde ginch, and me—me, I'm spending two hours pumping water out of Tiny Tim the dwarf, who nearly drowns.

The alley is flooded, and this time lightning hits the top of the building outside. In the excitement I wade down into the water and shrink a brand-new suit.

Then I hop a plane with Tiny Tim and get him back to the Catskills the next day and turn him loose with the other dwarfs. This time I do not stay to bowl, but come right back into town. And so here I am with my fortune.

LEFTY FEEP finished his story and shook the water from his hair as he looked at me.

I stared back.

"That's a pretty hard story to swallow," I commented.

He just grinned.

"Not that I don't believe you about the dwarf and all," I told him. "But that other stuff—about making your fortune. I thought you said it stormed in Milwaukee and you had to pay Gorilla Gabface five thousand dollars. Where does your fortune come in?"

"Do I forget?" asked Feep. "Do I forget to tell you why I like rain?"

"You didn't."

"It is all very simple, Bob. You remember I mention a personality name of Better O'Brien the promoter who talks with me before we go into the alleys?"

"Yes."

"Well, I make a fortune from Better O'Brien. The idea comes like a flash while we stand there. I know I lose five thousand to Gorilla because of what will happen, so I turn around and bet O'Brien ten thousand. It looks like a sure thing to him and he takes it up."

"You mean you bet O'Brien ten thousand dollars that your dwarf would win at bowling?" I asked.

"Of course not," grinned Lefty Feep. "I merely bet him ten thousand dollars that it is going to rain all over his brand new suit in ten minutes."

AFTER WORDS

STANLEY: *The second story is a true sequel in that it returns to the Catskills and to the same bowlers from* "Time Wounds All Heels." *In later stories you had recurring characters, but not situations.*

BLOCH: I remember nothing about this story. It was so long ago.

JS: *That crazy judge . . . Danglepatzer.*

BLOCH: Donglepootzer. Hiawatha Donglepootzer. A very famous character. I had to come up with a ridiculous name. A name created at the typewriter. Longfellow's poem, *Hiawatha,* came to mind. I think it was Shakespeare who wrote a poem called *Donglepootzer.*

JS: *You created another name, The Masked Marvel, which a year later was used as the title for a 12-chapter Republic serial. You should sue for royalties. If you could just remember the slightest detail about this story . . .*

BLOCH: My mind is a total blank, I'm happy to say. But then, as I recall, this story has no details.

JS: *This next story should jar your memory. It's a real gas . . .*

Alive with jive, hep with pep, living off the fad of the band, Lefty Feep has a swing fling when he meets a mean king of clarinet deep in debt whose musical pipe is ripe, whose note-worthy bent gives glint to a new dancing prancing—the Rodent Waltz.

THE PIED PIPER FIGHTS THE GESTAPO

WHEN I WALKED into Jack's Shack I saw Lefty Feep sitting at his usual booth. With the suit he was wearing, it was impossible not to see him. Even a blind man would have found Feep at once—if he couldn't see the suit, its color was so loud he'd hear it.

Feep was waving his arms at Jack as I approached. He turned and gave me a nod of recognition, then continued to place his order.

"Make please with the cheese," he demanded. "But snappy."

"You want some snappy cheese?" Jack inquired.

"I do not care what kind of teeth the cheese is using," Feep asserted. "Just so there is plenty of it. Let it be long and strong. Let it be mean and green. Let it be old with mould. But bring me lots of plenty in a fast hurry."

Jack scribbled his order and shuffled away. Lefty Feep turned and I saw his beady eyes were unstrung.

"Cheese," he whispered reverently. "Limburger with real limbs! Thick brick! I love it. Swiss is bliss. Cheddar is better. Camembert is the nerts!"

I stared.

"What's the matter?" I asked. "You sound like a cross between Ogden Nash and Mickey Mouse. Since when did you develop such a passion for cheese?"

"It is not all for me," Feep explained. "I take some of it to a friend of mine."

"Are you hanging around with a bunch of rats?"

Feep shook his head. "I do not see Gorilla Gabface for weeks," he declared.

"Then what in the world—" I began, but didn't finish. For Jack returned, bearing an enormous platter loaded with concentrated nose-torture.

"Ah!" sniffed my companion. "The breeze of cheese! What a stiff whiff!"

The whiff was almost too stiff for me. But Feep inhaled ecstatically.

"It brings memories," he exclaimed.

"It brings suffocation," I corrected.

Feep picked up a hunk of Roquefort and began to nibble eagerly. All over the cafe, patrons were hastily retreating to tables near the open door. Feep smiled as he saw them go.

"We are alone," he grinned. "Maybe now I can tell you the reason I am so partial to this cow-candy."

"Go ahead," I urged. "But your reason must smell better than your cheese. And if there are as many holes in your story as there are in your limburger—"

Feep waved his Parmesan at me indignantly. Then he bent forward.

"Hold your nose," he muttered. "And I will give you a blow-by-blow description which I guarantee is not to be sneezed at."

IT ALL STARTS (said Feep) two months ago when I suffer an accident one night. It seems I get my fingers stuck around the handle of a slot machine at a very embarrassing moment—in fact, it is the moment when a couple of bloodhounds break down the door of the joint.

They invite everybody to play cops and robbers with them and take a little ride in the city taxi downstairs.

Which we do. Of course, when the patrol wagon arrives down at night court, I am bailed out at once. I think nothing of it and am just getting ready to go, when a little guy rushes up to me and grabs my hand. I recognize him at once for a personality named Boogie Mann.

"I am so grateful to you," he shouts. "How can I ever thank you?"

"What did I do?" I asked, lightly, but politely.

"I hear you give your seat in the patrol wagon to an old tomato who is standing there," he says.

"That's right. So what?"

"She is my mother," says Boogie Mann, and tears of gratitude come into his eyes.

"You are a gentleman and a scholar," he tells me. "Giving a seat in the paddy wagon to my dear old mother."

"It is nothing," I assure him. "She looks like she is too high to stand up anyway."

We walk out of the court together, and all the time this Boogie Mann is thanking me, I am looking him up and down. You see, I never have much to do with such a personality before, because this article happens to be a swing-band fan—what they call a "hep-cat." And I personally have nothing at all to do with swing, not being a hangman. So here and to fore, I steer clear of Boogie Mann and his unusual brand of swing-talk and his dizzy enthusiasm for juke symphonies.

When we get outside, Boogie grabs my shoulder by the padding and hangs on.

"Feep," he says, "I must reward you for what you do tonight. I am going to let you in on a big deal."

"The last time I am let in on a big deal," I answer, "I am holding a full house and the other guy turns up four kings."

"This is terrific," Boogie insists. "I will give you the chance to make a fortune. A fortune. Do you like money?"

Well, this question is easy to answer. I do, and then ask him one.

"What's the angle?" I inquire.

"How would you like to be the agent for the hottest swing musician in the world?" he asks.

"Who is it—Nero and his fiddle?" I crack. But he doesn't bend.

"No, this is the genuine jive," he tells me. "A hep Joe from Buffalo. A walkie-talkie from Milwaukee. Strictly a mutt from Connecticut."

"Who is he, where is he, and how come I get a chance to be ten per center for such a wonder man?"

"That is easy," Boogie tells me. "He is a refugee and nobody discovers him yet. He is playing in a little joint called the Barrel House way down the street, and nobody suspects that he plays the warmest licorice-stick in the business."

"Licorice-stick?"

"Clarinet, of course."

"A refugee, huh?"

"That is right," says Boogie. "The whole band is made up of refugees. Hot Mickey is the leader."

"Hot Mickey?"

"Sure. The outfit bills as *Hot Mickey and His Five Finns.*"

"Do tell."

"They are not Finns, though—most of them are German refugees. But they ride with a solid slide. They groove. They send."

"But can they play?"

"Play?" yells Boogie. "Wait until you hear the way they dig it out of the dugout! The fella on the slush pump is terrific, the guy who handles the gutbucket can really slap doghouse, and they've got an alligator who really can keep the plumbing humming."

I ask for an explanation, and I find out that Boogie refers

to a trombone player, a jerk with a bass viol, and a saxophone snorter.

By this time Boogie is so excited he is dragging me down the street.

"No contract," he yells. "He can get this guy for next to nothing. Take him uptown. I guarantee once you get him in for an audition, any band in the country will offer him half a G a week to start. He's playing for peanuts here—it's the chance of a lifetime! Wait until you see what he does to a crowd. Here we are—just step into the silo."

"What silo?"

"The place where they keep the corn. The dance-hall."

Sure enough. We are standing in front of a little rat-race track called the Barrel House. Before I can make up my mind, he drags me inside.

It is nothing but a made-over barn, with a bar and a lot of tables instead of stables. A gang of jitterbugs are shagging all over the floor, and up on the platform sits this Hot Mickey and his refugees. They look like refugees from a bathtub to me.

In fact, I never see such a mangy collection of human beings outside of a Turkish Bath on the day after New Year's Eve. They look like they are dying, and they sound like it, too.

Because they are playing a brand of noise I never hear in all my life, and I once work in a steel foundry for a year. But these cookies are hammering and yammering on horns and trumpets and drums, and they are blasting so loud you would think somebody was building a subway.

But the crowd loves it. The place is packed, and everybody is prancing around with their fingers in the air, and sometimes their skirts. I do not need to take a second squint to see that there really are a lot of finks who go for this kind of bazoo.

Boogie drags me over to a table and leers.

"Listen," he chirps, beaming all over. "Come on and

listen," he urges, making me take my fingers out of my ears. "Hear that baby pounding the tusks."

"What?"

"Punching ivory," says Boogie.

"Huh?"

"Playing the piano."

"Oh."

"Scar me, Daddy, eight to the mar," he yells, or something like it. "Feep, I want you should pipe that clarinet."

Me, I do not know a clarinet from a ocarina; in fact, where music is concerned I cannot tell a bass from a hole in a piccolo. But I look for the guy who is playing most loud and proud, and I spot who he refers to.

He is a tall, thin drip tooting on a tall, thin horn. He stands up when he plays, and the rest of the band follows. When I try hard I can hear his clarinet honking way up above the other noise, and it has plenty of rhythm.

In fact, the whole crowd hears it, because they do not wish to stop dancing at all. Whenever a number finishes, they clap their pinkies together so hard and long that the band must keep right on playing.

"See?" whispers Boogie. "What do I tell you? He's a natural. He's hep to the step." Boogie jerks his finger at the mob. "Look—even the bartenders have to dance."

This is a fact. I notice them myself. Also I find my own feet jumping up and down a little. It is really rhythm.

"Pipe that!" grunts Boogie, all of a sudden. He points to the floor. I see a little mouse run out of its hole in the woodwork and scamper up and down in time with the music.

"It takes a real hep-cat to catch mice," Boogie tells me. "Now come on up to the stand and tell this guy you want to be his agent. Tell him you'll line up an audition with a big-time band for him. Take it easy, because he is plenty timid and he doesn't know the score yet, being new in this country."

So when the number is over and the crowd finally finishes

clapping and sits down, we slide over to the stand. First Boogie introduces me to the leader.

"Come on, ick, meet the stick," he says. "This is Hot Mickey. Mickey, my pal here would like to talk to your clarinet player."

"Huh," grunts the fat leader. "Is he safe?"

"Strictly a square from Delaware," Boogie tells him. He drags me over to the skinny clarinet man. "They're all nervous about meeting strangers," he whispers. "Afraid of spies on their trail, or something. These refugees have a pretty tough time getting out of Europe. So take it easy."

Then he pushes me up on the platform and grabs the skinny man by the arm.

"Herr Pfeiffer," he says, "I want you should meet your new agent, Lefty Feep."

The skinny guy looks up. He has big, deep eyes, with a light in them like burning reefers. It is a very powerful stare, and when we shake hands I find out he has a very powerful grip.

"Agent?" he says. "I do not need an agent. I have here a good job, I am in this fine orchestra playing, so why in the world should I an agent want?"

This double-talk turns out to be a kind of German accent, but I just pass it off and do what Boogie tells me.

"How would you like to earn big money in a real band?" I brace him. "I can get you a job where you'll be famous overnight."

Pfeiffer shakes his head very fast.

"I do not wish to famous become," he says. "I have on my trail enemies, and I do not wish publoosity." He shakes his long curly hair again.

Then Boogie and I really go to work on him. It takes an hour between dances, but to make a long story, he finally agrees to show up tomorrow, on his night off, for an audition.

So Boogie and I leave, very happy, while he is playing the

last number for the evening. When we go out the door, the crowd is making like crazy all over the floor.

"He's a sensation," Boogie yells. "Broadway will love him! Think of the radio—movies—ouch!"

The last word comes from him when he nearly trips going out the door. He stumbles over a gang of mice that are waltzing around in the hall.

"We can at least sell him to Walt Disney," I decide.

But it is not Walt Disney I sell Pfeiffer to the next day. Boogie and I go down and arrange an audition with none other than *Lou Martini and His Cocktail Cavaliers*. They are playing in a big hotel, in what they call the Tiger Room.

Boogie handles all the details. I learn that the way a player auditions is to show up for a regular dance performance and sit in with the rest of the orchestra, to see if his noise fits in with the blasting. And Boogie gives this Lou Martini a terrific buildup about how good Pfeiffer is. From the way he describes his tooting you'd think Pfeiffer is the angel Gabriel instead of a broken-down refugee. But Martini says all right, he'll give him a chance, let him come around tonight with his clarinet for the dinner dance hour. Only Martini warns us that Pfeiffer better be good, because the Tiger Room only caters to the cream of society, and bad music will make them curdle.

So out we go, very steamed up, and I take Pfeiffer up to my place and tell him the good news. Pfeiffer doesn't seem any too pleased—in fact, you would think he has a date to be hung in the Tiger Room. Those big eyes of his get misty and he runs his skinny fingers through the mop on his head.

"*Ach,* this playing I do not like the idea of, Mr. Feep," he grunts. "My music is safer to play a stable in, but on a dance floor not."

"You're terrific," Boogie tells him. "You know all the numbers Martini uses anyway. Besides, you have your own style, and all you do is hot licks, not score-work."

"Perhaps the licks too hot will be for this band," Pfeiffer mourns.

"The crowd will go wild over you," Boogie promises.

"That is what I am afraid of," says Pfeiffer. "Besides, there are on my trail now certain men I do not wish to find me."

"What's the matter, you owe money on that clarinet?" Boogie asks him.

"*Nein*. The instrument, I make it myself a long time ago," Pfeiffer says, "and it is not a clarinet."

"I wonder about that," Boogie tells him. "It does not resemble an American instrument at all, but it sounds like one."

Pfeiffer smiles.

"I can make it sound like many things," he answers. "But I do not make it sound tonight. Positive!"

Well, I see a great opportunity slipping away, so I stick in my oar.

"You have to play, Pfeiffer," I argue. "It's the chance of a lifetime. A young punk like you ought to have a big future."

"You are wrong," he says. "I am not so young and not so punk, and I have a great past. But if the men on my trail up to me catch, I will have no future left at all."

"How will they know?" I tell him. "All you do is sit in on a few numbers with a big band. Nobody will even notice you."

I'm wrong. I find it out that night.

We finally argue Pfeiffer into keeping his date, and at eight in the evening we breeze into the Tiger Room and take him up to Lou Martini, who gives him a seat with the band.

Then Boogie and I sit down at a table and order a couple hamburgers while we wait for the dancing to start. I gander around and I am impressed. The Tiger Room is strictly uptown—some of the customers have as many as six chins, and most of the guys are wearing tuxedos nearly as good as the waiters have. There are a lot of old society tomatoes and a whole gang of debutramps. I begin to worry a little about whether this Pfeiffer is as good as we think he is—because from the looks of this mob they don't go for anything but the best. If they dance, they got to have at least St. Vitus leading the orchestra.

And there is skinny Pfeiffer up on the platform with his old clarinet, wearing the kind of suit they put on window dummies when they want to burn them. His big round eyes are rolling, and he looks frightened and nervous. He keeps staring out at the tables like he was afraid of seeing a ghost, or his mother-in-law.

Then I see they are ready to start. Just before Martini goes out to lead the band, he stops over at our table and throws down a sheaf of papers.

"This is our stock contract," he tells me. "If your man is any good tonight, we'll sign it."

Then Pfeiffer blows, and Boogie and I sit there, biting our nails without ketchup when we see Martini raise his stick.

The music begins. Couples get up from all the tables and begin to break down their arches. They jiggle along, and I look at Pfeiffer and see he is playing kind of soft behind the band. So far, so good.

There is another number, and this one is a little on the torrid side, so I know pretty soon Pfeiffer will have a chance to let out some blasts on his kazoo. Sure enough, comes the second chorus and Pfeiffer begins to let go with those high notes. They shriek out plenty loud, and the rest of the band lets him carry the tune. He has to carry it, the way he is mangling same, but everybody seems to like it. The dancers wiggle a little harder, and when it is over they all push their paws together. Pfeiffer is plenty red in the face, but Martini calls for another number and off they go.

This time he must pick out a special, because it is almost all clarinet. There are some drums, but what you hear is that awful squeaking. It runs up and down my spine like I have frogs down my neck. But these hep-cats are crazy for it. They begin to truck all over the place, and Pfeiffer stands up and blows away.

"Look at that man send!" Boogie shouts.

But I am not looking at that man. I am looking at something else.

We are sitting at a table near the wall, and I happen to glance down when I see it. There is something crawling out of the woodwork, and I recognize it right away. It is a mouse. A big, black mouse. And behind it is another mouse. And another.

I turn away, not believing my peepers, and then I see something else running between two tables. Grey mice. Three or four of them, scampering out onto the dance floor. I turn to the bandstand and I see a couple more, jitterbugging out from underneath.

"Jumping jive!" yells Boogie. "Look twice at the mice!"

And all at once the floor seems to be full of them. They are running and squeaking between the dancers. Some of the society tomatoes notice them for the first time and begin to let out little squeaks themselves, pointing down at their feet.

Martini turns around to see what the matter is and he is so astonished he nearly drops his stick. Then he waves at Pfeiffer. But Pfeiffer doesn't pay any attention. He is blowing his clarinet, and like Boogie says, he is out of this world. His eyes are shut, his face is red, and all he can do is squeal out that high note of his.

And the mice run out, dozens of them, from all over the place. Some of the men are trying to kick them, and a couple of the jitter girls climb up on chairs and go right on dancing while they scream to take them away. A waiter is crossing the floor, running very fast, and he trips over a brown rat.

Everybody is squawking and running at once. By this time mice are climbing up on the tables and grabbing at food, and I see one fat bozo going crazy with the giggles because a mouse crawls into his tuxedo and tickles him.

Boogie runs up to the bandstand and helps Martini grab the clarinet away from Pfeiffer. Meanwhile, I am very interested watching a young tomato at the next table who

D.

seems to get a mouse caught in her bustle. She is doing a very torrid rumba even after the music stops.

So the next thing I know is when Martini grabs me by the collar and pushes me out of my chair. He has Pfeiffer's neck in his other hand, and he is sort of kicking Boogie along with his feet in a mild sort of way. Also he is saying things that I do not wish to repeat.

"But what about our contract?" I ask, as he moves us along to the door. "What about our contract?"

"Take a look," Martini gurgles, between curses.

I look back at the table and all I see is a pile of mice scampering around a few strips of paper. They eat our contract for us! And something tells me Martini is not going to make out another one. In fact, he confirms this suspicion when he throws us down the stairs of the Tiger Room.

"Get out and stay out," he shouts. "You rats will bring a bunch of mice into my place!"

"Aw, shut your trap!" yells Boogie, which is not the right thing to say, because Martini turns very red and throws a small chair after us.

It happens to hit me on the head, so the last words I hear come from Martini when he yells after us:

"I'll teach you—trying to put the Pied Piper in my orchestra!"

When I come to, I am sitting in the alley, and somebody is pouring water over my noggin like I am some kind of potted plant. I look up and see Pfeiffer.

"Where is Boogie?" I ask, strictly from confusion.

"I do not know, Herr Feep. He says he wants to make a grab far."

"Grab far? You mean, a get-away?"

"Yes. *Ach,* he runs very fast, that Herr Boogie."

I stand up, and when I do I remember everything. I stare a long stare at this skinny guy with the wild mop of hair, the big bulging eyes, and the funny clarinet.

"What is this Martini yells about you being the Pied Piper?" I get out, finally.

Pfeiffer's eyes turn down and he does a slow shrug. Then he sighs.

"I might as well confess," he whispers. "It is true. That is why tonight I do not wish the music to make. Because when I play, little mice and rats come out. In the stable where it is dark, the customers do not notice take, but when I play upstairs right away they smell a mouse. It is just what I am afraid of."

I listen, but all the while I am wrecking my brains to remember what I hear about this Pied Piper. I catch the gossip when I am a brat in school, I guess. Some burg over in Germany gets filled with rats—even before the Nazis arrive. And instead of calling the exterminator, they hire this guy with the pipe to swing out a few tunes. He plays and the rodents follow him and get drowned. Then he comes back and turns in a bill, but the rats are gone and they try to stall him off on a cash settlement. So he plays again and all their moppets run after his music like jitterbugs and dance away forever.

I ask him about this story, and Pfeiffer shakes his head.

"It is a lie," he hollers, waving his arms. "It is a dirty black lie; propaganda. It is true I go to Brunswick, to Hamelin where the rat-plague is. It is bad, that plague. Across the Volga the rats swim, from Asia they come, brown rats. To Prussia they march, like an army on its stomach traveling. Because they eat everything. Food, merchandise, poultry, flowers, seeds. At buildings they gnaw, at the pipes and walls and the foundations even. Fires they start by gnawing matches. Floods they commence by gnawing dams. In Hamelin there are more rats than people.

"And in Hamelin they hire me the rats to kill. I have my pipe and my music which I learn from traveling in India where they charm serpents. So for the rats a concert I arrange and they follow me to the river and drown dead. This is true.

"But it is a lie that I take away children! It is a lie made up to spoil my business. Now they only mouse-traps use and I am—how you call it?—a bum. It gets so bad I must a job in an orchestra take, playing my pipe like a clarinet. Still, the music I make enchants the rats, so I get from many theatres and cafes on my behind thrown out.

"Then come the Nazis, and because of what I do must from Germany run like a rat myself. What happens after that you know."

Pfeiffer shakes his head. I pat him on the shoulder.

"Why don't you spill this before?" I tell him. "You got a fortune in that pipe of yours and you don't know it! Why, you could set yourself up as a rat-remover and put the exterminator companies out of business!"

"*Nein*. You forget—they are still on my trail, those Nazis, because of what I try to do before I leave. That is why to Pfeiffer I change my name—it is German for Piper. Publoosity would be deadly fatal. The Gestapo wants to take me back. Up to now I sleep in the basement under the Barrel House because I am afraid. Down there the rats and mice protect me. But now I will be caught and they will—how you say so?—bake for me my goose."

"Nuts to that," I console him. "We got no Gestapo over here. The government cleans out fifth columnists. You got nothing to worry about. Just put that in your pipe and play it."

Pfeiffer smiles a little.

"You are kind, Herr Feep."

"Come home with me," I tell him. "I'll figure an angle for you. A guy with your talent—a regular rat Stokowski—you won't have any trouble."

We start off down the side street. I am still talking to Pfeiffer and I pay no attention to the car that pulls up alongside the curb ahead. I just give Pfeiffer the old juice.

"I got a million ideas for you," I am saying. "Maybe not

playing in a swing band, but other places. Hold it—I've got it—I see the light!"

But it is not the light I see.

It is the dark. Because when I say this I suddenly feel something hard smack me across the back of the head. A big hand reaches out and grabs me, and just as I turn around, I get it in the hat-rack again, and everything goes blankety-blank. For the second time that night I am down and out.

And when I wake up I am higher than ever in my life. Twenty thousand feet, to be exact.

I am in a plane, and so is Pfeiffer. We are lying on the seat of the rear compartment, and in the seat ahead a pilot is giving out with the old push and pull.

I sit up, and that is all I can do. Because Pfeiffer and I have our hands and legs tied together in Boy Scout knots.

Only one look at our pilot tells me he is very far from being a Boy Scout. He is a big side of meat with shoulders like a wrestler, and his head is shaved, even though his face isn't. He is wearing a pilot's outfit, but there is a little round badge on his sleeve. Pfeiffer looks at it and shudders.

"Ach!" he whispers. "Gestapo!"

Sure enough, I spot the swastika. I give Pfeiffer a nudge.

"What gives?" I ask.

"Just what I am afraid of. They catch up to me, as I know they will. They drag us into the car and take us to some place where this plane in a secret hangar is kept. Now they fly us back to Germany."

I raise my head.

"But feel how cold it is. We're heading north. And look down there—we're over land, not water."

Pfeiffer shakes his head.

"We are probably to Canada going first. To another secret hangar. We make the trip in installments, and I am worried only about the last payment."

The pilot never looks around. It is getting very frigid in

the plane, and steam comes out of our yaps when Pfeiffer and I whisper. I squirm closer to him.

"I don't get this," I remark. "Just what is it you do in Germany that makes the Gestapo so hot to catch you?"

"I may as well tell you now," Pfeiffer decides. "I play for the rats."

"So what?"

"You don't understand. I play for the rats over the underground—the secret radio broadcasts against the Nazis. Music I make for them to come out, music I make for them to appear in every city. So they will jaundice bring, and typhus, and the plague. There is a rat for every man, you know—a population of millions. And I play oh so sweetly for the rats, to make them happy, to make them hungry. I play music that is with appetite filled, so they will eat. They will eat under buildings and bite away the foundations. They will destroy docks and warehouses and railroad bridges. They will make sabotage and the machinery up-ge-shcrew."

"I get it."

"So does the Gestapo. Every night I play, hidden away, over the wireless. And every night they hunt for me and my broadcasting set. Because the rats and mice come out and eat. Finally—how you say it?—the heat is upon me. I must smuggle myself from the country out. And now, even here, they have orders to find me and bring me back. So now they do. *Achoo!*"

This last remark is a loud sneeze. It is very cold, and Pfeiffer is shivering. So am I, but not from cold. I merely have to look at the bullet-headed pilot to start shivering.

"You really can get the rats to go on a rampage with your music?" I whisper.

"That is so. Music has charms—*Achoo!*"

I sit there thinking about the screwy pickle I am in, but not for long. Because the pickle develops warts very soon. We start going down. The plane noses over and I look out and see us rushing into blackness. No lights, no nothing.

At first I think we are cracking up, but the pilot is still sitting very calm. Then all at once I see a flare shoot out, and it hangs in the air while we land.

We taxi along some dirt almost into a clump of trees, and some patches of snow.

"Canada, all right," I whisper to Pfeiffer, while the pilot gets out. "Must be another hideout."

This turns out to be a good guess. Because the pilot comes around to the rear door, opens it up, and cuts our feet loose. For the first time I get a full look at his bearded puss, and it is a face that only Karloff's mother could love.

"Raus!" he says, kindly dragging Pfeiffer and me out by the neck. "To the cabin—march!"

And he pulls us along the ground toward a little cabin standing there all alone in the wilderness. The door is open and we go inside, Pfeiffer sneezing his way ahead of me.

And he pulls us along the ground toward a small cabin standing there all alone in the wilderness. The door is open and we go inside, Pfeiffer sneezing his way ahead of me.

Now I do not like the buzzard with the beard, but I will take him for a cellmate any time instead of the personality waiting for us inside the cabin.

He is sitting at a little table, and when we come marching in, he waves us to a seat with a smile and a big black Luger.

He is an old character, but his age does not make him any more harmless than a lot of other old things, such as tigers. He has a big beak of a nose which he points at us like he does the Luger, and behind the schnozz are two red eyes that go through me and come out of the back of my head.

"So," he says to the beard. "You bring guests, *hein?"*

"Ja," snaps the beard, lifting a hand like he wanted to leave the room. *"Heil Hitler."* And he stands at attention.

"Good, good. This is Pfeiffer. And the other garbage?"

I do not know who he is referring to, but I can guess.What he calls me is appropriate, because I look like I am down in the dumps.

The beard starts to wag.

"I wish to report that I make contact with the man Pfeiffer and his companion tonight at nine o'clock, in the sedan. No trouble picking them up. I bring them with me to the plane and here we are."

"Good, good." The beak is smiling. "Go outside to the tanks and refuel at once. You must leave immediately and deliver our guests to the proper authorities."

The beard smiles and heils, then ducks out to refuel the plane. Meanwhile, the beak gives us the old eye.

"Sit down," he says, gesturing with the gun in a way that is too careless to suit me. "You seem cold, Pfeiffer."

Pfeiffer is sniffling and shivering again.

"Yes," he whispers.

The beak smiles. "Too bad you are so cold, but it will not be for long. Soon your journey will be over, and then I am sure they will make it hot enough for you."

This does not strike either me or Pfeiffer as so funny.

But the beak laughs.

"Yes, they are waiting anxiously for you, Pfeiffer. The Pied Piper is quite a catch, even for the Gestapo. It is well worth the risk we are taking to maintain a plane service when we can handle such passengers as yourselves." He grins very wide. "You are going for a ride."

"Achoo!" says Pfeiffer.

"Gesundheit," says the beak, very polite.

I study the situation. There is nothing in the old cabin but the table, some chairs and a couple bunks. Nothing to throw or hide behind. And the beak has a Luger. In a couple minutes we will be back on the plane, headed for Germany. I wish very sincerely to get my hands on that gun—but my hands are tied. I begin to feel a trifle depressed.

And Pfeiffer just sits there and sneezes. He has a terrific cold.

The beak notices it. "It is too bad I cannot light a fire," he remarks. "But sparks fly up from a chimney, and this is Canada. One must be very careful, you understand."

Pfeiffer shakes his head. And then a kind of gleam comes into his eye.

"Perhaps I can make myself warm," he suggests. "If you do not mind, I will my pipe play the time to pass."

The beak chuckles.

"A serenade? *Wunderschon!* It is not every man who can hear the Pied Piper play."

Pfeiffer reaches into his coat with his bound hands. And the beak's Luger follows every move, in case Pfeiffer springs a gat or something. But nothing comes out except the clarinet from inside the overcoat pocket. It is pretty beat-up, but Pfeiffer puts it up to his lips and lets out a blat. The squeaking starts.

The beak doesn't care. Out here in the wilderness there is nobody to hear. So Pfeiffer begins to dig in. He smiles a little and wrestles with the cold pipe. It doesn't seem to work right, somehow. The cold air makes the notes lower. And Pfeiffer's cold does something to his breathing, so that the tones are all screwy. They carry a long wail, a sort of echo from far away.

Somehow it is all kind of impressive—Pfeiffer sitting there tied up in this cabin in the woods at night, with a guy pointing a gun at his head—playing like one of those statues of Pan, or whatever they call him. His long fingers tug at the pipe and his lips pucker up, and the big squeals run up and down the air.

Now the door opens and the beard comes in. The plane is refueled and he is ready. He sits down for a minute when he hears Pfeiffer tooting away. He tries to get the beak's attention, but the beak is watching Pfeiffer.

And then I hear it. Far away. That rustling sound. That padding sound. It seems to be coming nearer, getting louder. More like a clumping noise. It sort of moves in rhythm to the piping. I look around, quick, but I don't see anything.

From the look in Pfeiffer's eyes, I know he hears it too. And all at once he pulls out the stops and gets loud on the clarinet. He rides to town. And over it comes the running sound, nearer and nearer.

Then the beak gets it too. He stands up all at once.

"Stop that!" he yells. But it is too late. All of a sudden there is a cracking sound, the walls of the cabin start to bend in, and the side of the door breaks down with a crash.

Pfeiffer's tune blares out louder, and there is a hell-splitting bang. The table spins into the corner.

"Himmel!" gasps the beak, turning around to face the door.

This is my chance. I throw myself across the room and grab the gun out of his hands. The beard falls down when the door topples over on him.

"Come on, Pfeiffer!" I advise him. For a minute or two there is nothing but confusion when the cabin is filled with what Pfeiffer calls on his pipes.

Then we are running down the trail, keeping the gun in the beak's ribs, and climbing in the plane. In three minutes we are off, making the beak pilot the ship.

"SO THERE IS not much more to tell. When we return, we hand the beak over to the FBI, along with the plane. They get all the details on this Gestapo ring from the beak, and that is that.

"Naturally, Pfeiffer is a hero. I guess he will be doing sound effects for Walt Disney pretty soon. But right now he is working with the Coordinator of Information's office. You know, the babies that broadcast short-wave radio to the Axis.

"He is doing just what he does back in Germany—playing request numbers for the mice over there. He is trying to get the mice to revolt by using his pipe over the radio. Maybe he can get a bunch of them to tunnel under Berchtesgarden and kill Hitler. Perhaps the mice will get that rat.

"So that is why I come in here and order all this cheese. I take some down to the headquarters where the Pied Piper makes his broadcasts from, and feed it to the mice and rats that sneak into the studio when he starts to play.

"It is better to feed them than bump them off, because they do us such a good turn."

Lefty Feep sat back and folded his hands.

"Does this answer your questions?" he asked.

I stared him straight in the eye. "Listen, Feep. When you started this wild story of yours, I warned you. About holes in the story, wasn't it? And there is something you haven't managed to explain. Thought you'd get away with it—but I've caught you."

"To what do you refer, Bob?" asked Feep, pleasantly.

"To that little matter of Pfeiffer playing in the cabin. You said he did something which caused an awful commotion; started some kind of row that you took advantage of in overpowering the Gestapo men and escaping."

"Of course," Feeped answered me. "I can set you straight on that."

"Just a minute." I raised my hand. "I think I know what you're going to tell me. You're going to tell me that Pfeiffer played his pipe and a lot of mice started to tunnel under the cabin and eat away the foundations so that the door fell in. And I tell you right now, I won't believe it!"

"You don't have to believe it," Feep grinned. "That is not what happens. Pfeiffer has such an idea when he starts to play, but it is lucky for us that he also has a bad cold."

"What's that got to do with breaking the door down?" I snapped.

"I tell you before, Pfeiffer has a bad cold and it makes his music sound different."

"I know that," I replied. "And I also know that you won't find mice running around in the wilds of Canada."

"Sure," Feep agreed. "It is not mice that break down the cabin door. Pfeiffer plays music for a mouse to come, but his cold causes a slight mistake. And he does not get a mouse."

"What does he get to break the door down?"
"A moose," said Lefty Feep.

AFTER WORDS

JS: *This is one of my favorite Lefty Feep yarns because it was the story where you really seemed to find the fullblown style for the series. And you've got one of those beautiful last-liners for which you're famous. One of the terrible-great all-time puns. It's so awful-hilarious, I winced twice.*

BLOCH: Well, the interesting thing about all of these stories, I suppose, is that they were written by someone completely sober, who wasn't on anything.

JS: *You wouldn't think that, reading the stories.*

BLOCH: I'm like Harlan Ellison, you know. I have a natural high I live on and never have to resort to artificial stimulants.

JS: *You get into this whole lingo thing with the jazz world, with the jive-talking musicians.*

BLOCH: Those hep-jive terms were common words in those days. I invented what wasn't commonplace.

JS: *Here's where you began to play with the rhymes. You're really having a ball with all those cheeses.*

BLOCH: This was the Jerry Colonna sort of thing. "Greetings, Gate, let's celebrate." That kind of business. He was Hope's chief stooge in the 1940s and a former musician in his own right. A clarinet player with a leading jazz orchestra.

JS: *The next story is about a nerd. Named Floyd. Floyd Slurch.*

BLOCH: Scrilch. Floyd Scrilch. Yes, I remember now, the average man . . .

In which our racetrack tout, the haunter of the park, has his ginch benched when he meets an unsound 90-pound meekling and wishes he had formed an ad hock committee. A story with a buyer-and-cellar ending.

THE WEIRD DOOM OF FLOYD SCRILCH

I HAD ALMOST finished with my meal over at Jack's Shack. In fact, I was halfway through my last cup of coffee and my first bicarbonate of soda. Shaking the gravy off my newspaper, I unfolded it and began to read.

Suddenly a hand descended and brushed the pages aside. I looked up into the startled face of Lefty Feep. His wildly rolling eyes were staring at the discarded paper with a look of intense loathing.

"Remove it away," he grated. "Grab loose from that!"

I raised my eyebrows as he lowered his hips into a seat.

"What's the matter, Feep?" I asked. "Does the sight of the news upset you so much?"

"News?" echoed the eccentric Mr. Feep. "It is not the news which upsets me at all. It is the advertisements that drain the rosy color from my handsome face. I cannot bear to look at them."

For the first time I foresaw that I was going to get into an argument with my friend.

"So you're just another highbrow, eh?" I said. "Just another one of those know-it-alls who run around pointing their fingers at the advertising business. Don't you realize what advertising has done for this country? How it has revolutionized business, brought new and better products forward to the average consumer, given ethics to commerce? Advertising today is more than a profession—it's an art, and a science. The American public owes a debt of gratitude to advertising for—"

"Yeow!" yelled Lefty Feep, quite suddenly. His hands covered his ears as he rocked back and forth in his seat. In a moment he regained composure and leaned forward.

"Please," he whispered. "Pretty please, with ketchup on it. Do not mention that word to me. It gives my dimples goose-pimples."

"Why?" I asked. "What harm has ad—all right, what harm has commercial display ever done to you?"

"Not a bit," Feep answered. "It is not because of myself that I ache and shake. I am merely thinking of what advertising does to poor Floyd Scrilch."

"Floyd Scrilch?"

"Perhaps I better tell you about Floyd Scrilch from the beginning," said Lefty Feep. "It will teach you a lesson."

"I'm sorry, Feep," I said. "But I've got to be going. Heavy date. Some other time, perhaps?"

"Well," Feep shrugged. "If you insist."

He pulled me back into my seat and held me there firmly. Then, plunging his elbows into the butter plates, he began.

WHEN I FIRST meet up with this Floyd Scrilch (narrated Feep), I do not pay any great attention to him. He is that kind of personality. A nobody from nowhere. Strictly a dud. When he walks into a room it is just like somebody else walks out. You don't even know he's there even after you look at him. His face is as empty as a Jap's promise. He never opens his mouth between meals. He is so shy he never looks in the mirror when he shaves. He is what the psychologists call an introtwerp, if you follow me.

He hangs out around the poolroom, and also around the elbows. His clothes are a model of what the well-dressed scarecrow doesn't wear. Also he is very puny. In fact, he is so thin that when he has a toothpick in his mouth it looks like he is hiding behind a tree. One glance at him and you know he cannot lick his weight in wild flowers. One day I am standing in the pool parlor when he weighs himself and I see he only tips the scales at 84 pounds. Not stripped, either, because the poolroom is crowded.

That is the first time I have anything to do with Floyd Scrilch. He notices I am watching him, and he turns around and hands me a sick smile.

"I do not seem to be so healthy," he gets out.

"At least you won't be taken by the draft," I console him.

"I always get pneumonia from drafts anyway," he sighs.

"Why don't you visit a croaker?" I inquire.

"A what?"

"An undertaker's understudy. A pulse-promoter. A doctor."

He shakes his head.

"No use," he tells me. "All the doctors give me up for dead long ago. The last medico who examines me says my lungs look like a couple of tea-bags and my heart only beats to mark the hour."

I feel sorry for this weak but meek little guy, and I want to pat him on the shoulder, only I am afraid he will collapse.

But Gorilla Gabface does not share my sentiments. He is watching this Floyd Scrilch hang around his poolroom for the last week, and just now he waddles over to where Scrilch is standing and grabs him by the collar, which rips.

"Listen, jerk,'" says Gabface. "You got a job?"

Scrilch shakes his head.

"No," he mumbles. "Nobody will hire me."

"You got any money?" Gabface sneers, shaking Scrilch up and down like a dice-box until his teeth roll sevens.

"No money," Scrilch chatters.

Gabface grunts.

"That is the way I figure it, too," he says. "And I do not

wish for my poolroom to become a Rescue Mission. So I fear I shall invite you to get the blazes out of here."

Gabface sort of emphasizes his remarks by picking Scrilch off the floor and tossing him through the door. He lands someplace out on the curb, and when I run out to see what happens he is still bouncing. I catch him on the third bounce and pick him up again.

"That is a mean thing to do," I console him. "Gorilla Gabface is no better than a skunk in wolf's clothing. If I am you I go back in and give him a good beating."

Scrilch sighs.

"I cannot beat up an eggnog, let along a big ape like that," he tells me. "But I only wish I can peel his orange for him some day. Only it is no use, I guess. I am just a rundown weakling. Nobody ever worries about me. I got no friends, no girl, no job. I just as soon go home and put my head in the oven, only the gas company turns it off on me."

Then I get an idea. I have a newspaper in my hand, fanning Scrilch with it to bring him around, and I happen to glance at the page. And I see the advertisement.

It is a big muscle-building ad. I grab Scrilch by the hair.

"Listen to this!" I holler.

"Nuts!" says Joe Stronghorse in the ad. *"In seven days you can have a body like mine!"*

"You wouldn't think to look at me that I am just a 92-pound weakling. Yet I have no muscles painted on. I am just a nobody, but my body is as good as anybody's. You can possess the same muscular strength.

"Let me tell you how you can add three inches to your biceps, eight inches to your calves, sixteen inches to your chest—or bust!

"No complicated exercises! No harsh laxatives! Earn big easy money at home growing hair on your chest in your spare time!

"Send for my exercise system today! A free tiger-skin included with every order! I will build you a powerful body

in three weeks, or your muscles refunded. This course guarantees a powerful physique. It will even make your breath stronger!"

Anyhow, it reads something like that. And when I spill this to Floyd Scrilch his eyes light up. He looks at the picture of Joe Stronghorse and a grin spills down his chin.

"Say," he whispers. "Do you think it will work for me?"

"All you got to do is tear out this coupon," I tell him.

"I'll do it!" he shouts. "Yes sir, I'll do it!"

Then his face falls. "Can I ask you one favor, Mr. Feep?" he gulps.

"Sure. What is it?"

"Will you please tear out the coupon for me? I'm too weak to do it myself."

SO THAT is how Floyd Scrilch answers his first advertisement. I forget about him in a couple of weeks, because I do not see him at the poolroom any more.

I am playing a little game on the first table one afternoon about a month later when an elephant flies over my head.

I do not notice this at first, but then I hear the elephant trumpeting, so I look up and see that it is none other than Gorilla Gabface. He is flying through the air and traveling very fast. He does not even stop to go out the door, but plows right through the plate-glass window. Then he sits down very carefully on the sidewalk and pulls splinters out of his ears.

I turn around to the back and duck very quick, because two other personalities are doing a nonstop flight my way. They land up against the wall and pause for a nap.

And I hear a big booming voice say, "Any other goon want a trip to the moon?"

The rest of the mob just stands there very quiet indeed while a broad-shouldered little guy walks out from between them. I take a good look and then another. Because I recognize none other than Floyd Scrilch.

But he is plenty changed. He has big arms and a broad

chest and looks like he weighs 170 in muscles alone. He walks over to me and yells, "Hello, Feep—glad to see you! Put 'er there."

"Ouch!" I remark, shaking hands. He has a grip like a politician.

"I want to thank you for what you do for me," he says. "Ever since I mail that coupon, I feel like a new man. Once I get those lessons they do wonders for me. A month ago, if I want to tear a telephone book in half, I have to do it one page at a time. Today I can tear a telephone booth in half."

He slaps me on the back and I cave in.

"Now that I settle with this Gorilla person, I feel like celebrating. How about coming along with me for a little drink?"

"O.K.," I tell him. "But aren't you hard up for money?"

He laughs.

"Not since I answer the advertisement," he tells me.

"The muscle ad?"

"No. The other one. About entering the big $5000 prize contest. I enter it and win."

Sure enough, when we get outside I notice Floyd Scrilch is wearing a new English burlap drape suit, and he leads me over to a big car with actual new tires on it.

We go over to Daddy's Tavern, where you always find about eight to the bar, and have a drink on Scrilch's new success.

"It is a funny thing," he tells me. "Ever since you point out that ad to me, I study advertisements and answer them. And every ad I answer works out for me."

"How do you mean?"

"Well, take like this ad about raising a truck garden at home. My neighbors send for some seeds a long time ago and try it out, and they tell me nothing comes up. Me, I send in just ten days ago and already my garden is full of carrots and tomatoes and peas and radishes and such articles. It is like magic.

"Then, just for fun, I send in for another ad which tells about getting rid of unsightly pores. And now look at me. Go ahead, look at my face."

I stare at him real close. Sure enough, there is not a pore on his face. The skin is closed up tight all over.

"You see?" he tells me. "I got no more pores than an empty bottle. I got a hunch I am going places with these advertisements. For some reason they just work out right for me."

I have to leave just then, because I have a heavy freight date. And when I duck out, I do not see Floyd Scrilch again for weeks.

This is because I am all the time riding these heavy freight dates. I happen to be mixed up with a torrid tomato. I call her Pearl, because her old man is a bad oyster.

I am not a personality who usually makes like a wolf after the little red riding hoods, but this dame has me dizzier than a Joe Louis left. I am almost on the point of hanging a ring on her finger, even if it means she will then be leading me by a ring through my nose. We do the old dine-and-dance routine every night, and she has old Lefty Feep's name down in the Number One spot on her hit parade. We are closer together than the Gold Dust Twins—and prettier, too.

So when she calls up one night and asks me to take her out, I give her the nod, quick.

"Will you take me down to the Sunset Roof?" she asks. "I hear there is a new piano player there that can really barrelhouse the boogie in a lowdown doggy way."

She is just crazy for music and culture like this, see?

Well, the Sunset Roof is very high in its class and also in its price, but who am I to refuse Pearl anything her little ticker desires?

So I tell her sure, and pick her up after dinner, and take her down to the Sunset Roof. I bring her a lovely orchard to wear on her dress, and I hire a taxi, and I pay the stiff cover charge without a squawk, and I give her the old routine, so by the time we sit down at the table she is practically in my lap. She is givng me the gaze—you know, the old "we-can-buy-our-furniture-on-the-installment-plan" look, and I am going for it three ways. Hook, line and sinker.

Then the floor show starts, and the slush melts all of a sudden. Because that piano player she is so crazy to hear wheels out his infant grand and begins to polish ivory.

"Listen to that man play!" squeals Pearl. So I listen. He is really a gee with the keys, and everybody is quiet while he meddles the pedals under a blue light all alone.

When he chalks up his numbers, there is a lot of palm-pounding, and then lights go on, and Pearl yaps, "Isn't he just like Eddy Duchin?" So I take a squint at the face and shake my head fast.

Because this piano player is not like Eddy Duchin. He is not like Rachmaninoff, either. But he is exactly like my old friend Floyd Scrilch.

In fact, he is Floyd Scrilch, in a tuxedo. He spots me when he is coming off the floor, and runs over.

"Well, it is Lefty Feep!" he gurgles. "And with a charming companion." He bows like a movie extra.

So I make with the introductions and he drops his creases in a chair at our table.

I cannot resist asking him the natural question, which I do.

"What are you doing here?" I get out. "Since when do you manicure a keyboard?"

He turns and gives me a big smile.

"A month ago I am ignorant of music," he admits. "The only notes I can read are the ones I get from my creditors. I think A sharp is a card player and A flat is some place you live in. Then I pick up this magazine and read the ad. '*They Laugh When I Sit Down at the Piano.*' It tells how you can learn to play in ten easy lessons, or five hard ones. So I mail the coupon, get my lessons, and right away I am so good I figure I can get a job. So I come up here and they hire me. It is sensational, no?"

He talks to me, but he looks at Pearl. She giggles. "Why, Mr. Scrilch, you must be a virtuoso."

"Never mind my private life," he tells her, with an enchanting leer. "And why be so formal? Just call me Floydie." His eyes light up like pay-off numbers on a pinball machine.

"You just answer the ad and get what you want, huh?" I ask.

But Floyd Scrilch is not paying any attention to me. He is too busy casting the old goo-goo glance at Pearl.

"What?" he mumbles.

"I say what you got in your hand?" I inquire.

"Why, Pearl's arm," he tells me. And he has. "Pearl," he whispers. "A lovely name. Pearl, you are too good to cast yourself before swine."

This sounds like a dirty crack of some kind, but Pearl just giggles and wiggles, and I see the handwriting on the wall. Also on the check.

"Shall we waddle out of here?" I ask her.

"No, I want to stay. Floydie here says we're going to have lots of fun," she simpers.

So that is the way it is. Floyd Scrilch sits there in his tuxedo, with his big broad shoulders waving and his hair slicked down, handling my tomato like she comes from his own vine.

I get up to go. I should be sore, but for some reason I am more interested in how he does it. In fact, I have a little suspicion when I see his hair. I cannot resist bending down and whispering to him before I exit.

"Tell me the truth, Scrilch," I mutter. "Do you also answer one of these ads which tell you to buy hair tonic that makes you irresistible to women?"

He grins.

"You guess it, Feep," he admits. "I just mail the coupon

and in comes the stuff to put on my hair, and now wherever my hair goes, women get in it."

I shrug and sneak off. I make up my mind right then and there to forget Pearl and this guy Scrilch.

But this is not so easy to do. Because how can you forget a guy with hair three feet long?

That is the way Floyd Scrilch's hair is when I bump into him on the street a few weeks later.

He is running down the block wearing a purple nightgown, and a big shock of long bushy hair is tangled all over his dome.

In fact, he bumps into me and I get a mouthful of the stuff. I chew a while and then let go and Scrilch recognizes me.

"Don't tell me," I say. "You figure you have falling hair so you send in for a hair restorer and this is what happens."

"Right," he says. "It almost worries me, the way these ads come true. I begin to think they overdo things for me a little."

"But why the purple nightgown?" I ask.

"This is no nightgown," he comes back. "That is a smock."

"Smock?"

"Sure. All artists wear smocks."

"Since when are you artistic?"

"Since I get this long hair. It gives me the idea. All guys with long hair are artists. So I happen to be looking through a magazine and I see this ad.

"'*Be an Artist!*' it says. And there is a picture of an animal down below it. '*Get Out Your Easel and Draw This Weasel!*' it states. And it says that the guy who draws the best weasel gets a free art course from this school, by mail. Now me, I think a palette is something you have in your mouth, and a brush is something you have with the law. But I draw, and I win the course, and every lesson works out. In fact, I am way ahead of the lessons. I get some oil paints and start to work three weeks ago. I quit my job at the Sunset Roof and take up painting in a big way.

"Last week I have about twenty paintings done. And the big art critic, Vincent van Gouge, happens to drop into my place and—"

"Wait a minute," I cut in. "Since when do guys like art critics come to see you? You are not so popular as that."

Scrilch smiles.

"I am since I answer that ad about *'Be the Life of the Party'!*" he tells me. "I win friends and influence people all over the place. So they are always running around to see me. Anyway, this van Gouge drops in, takes one look at my paintings, and tells me I got to have an opening."

"You tell me he is an art critic," I object. "So why does he give you advice like a doctor?"

"You don't understand. He means an opening—an exhibition of my paintings. In fact, he gets up some sponsors, and today I have twenty paintings hanging down in the art gallery up the street. So I put on my smock and go down there now to the big reception. I am going to be famous. I answer the right ads."

By this time I am a little dizzy. In fact, I am so dizzy I decide to go down to the art gallery with Scrilch and see what this is all about.

On the way down I ask him about Pearl. He does not even remember her name.

"I am so popular," he babbles. "Like the ads say, I have friends and invitations galore."

I just groan.

When we get to the art gallery I groan again. Because I see Scrilch's paintings.

There are twenty of them, all right, and they look like two sets of ten nights in a barroom. Never in my life do I see such screwy drawings, and I am a fellow who goes in a lot of phone booths.

But there is a big gang of society people walking around

and making bleats over the things. Mainly they stand around a big painting at the end. It is a study of two goldfish with skis on, waiting for a streetcar at the North Pole during a thunder shower. Anyhow, that is the way it looks to me.

But not to the society crowd.

"Look!" yaps one old babe. "It reminds me of Picasso in his blue period."

"Blue, lady?" I tell her. "He must be ready for suicide."

The old babe sniffs and trucks away from there.

I turn to Scrilch.

"What kind of stuff is this?" I ask. I point to another picture. "How about that one? It looks like a kangaroo walking a tightrope over a garbage dump with Mayor La Guardia in its pouch reading a newspaper."

"You do not understand," Scrilch shrugs. "This is all surrealism."

"You and your sewer realism," I sniff. "If you ask me, the only things you can draw is your pay and your breath."

Scrilch puts his finger to his lips.

"Not so loud," he tells me. "Lots of important people here. They're all very much impressed."

"Depressed, if you ask me," I come back.

"I am sorry you don't like it," he tells me. "But perhaps you will like my writing better."

"Writing?"

"Why, of course. I am writing the Great American Novel. I answer an ad just this week. *'Shake a Leg and Be Another Shakespeare! Just Clip This Coupon and Learn to Write!'* So I am only on my third lesson, but yesterday I start my novel. It is almost half through already."

I listen to this and start foaming at the mouth like a beer keg. And I am not the only one.

A little short fat personality stands right behind us. Now he taps Scrilch on the shoulder and stares at him. He is wearing a heavy pair of cheaters, with enough glass in them to cover a store window.

"Pardon me," he croaks. "But is it not Floyd Scrilch the artist whom I have the honor of addressing?"

"Right."

"And do you not just remark that in addition to your remarkable gifts as a painter, you are also a *literateur*?"

"Naw, I write stuff."

The little goggle-eyes smiles.

"Really?"

"That isn't the half of it," I butt in. "He is also a piano player, a social lion, and an all-around athlete."

"Wonderful!" breathes the goggle-eyes. "How I wish I might psychoanalyze such a genius!"

Then he introduces himself. He turns out to be none other than Doctor Sigmund, the psychiatrist—better known as Subconscious Sigmund.

Subconscious Sigmund grabs Scrilch by the collar.

"How do you manage to cope with such versatility?" he asks.

"I just take a little bicarbonate."

"I mean to say, how is it that you are so accomplished in so many different fields of endeavor?"

"Oh," blurts out Scrilch. "I just answer advertisements and they work out for me."

Subconscious Sigmund stares.

"You mean you just clip out advertising coupons that offer to teach you things and you learn them?"

"Sure."

"Then, Mr. Scrilch, I beg of you—permit me to psychoanalyze you at once."

"Does it hurt?"

"Certainly not. I merely take you to my office and ask you a few questions. I wish to probe your unconscious."

"You wish to what my what?"

"Look into your inner mind. You seem to be a most remarkable man."

Well, Scrilch is a sucker for flattery. The end of it is, he agrees, and we go off to the psychiatrist's office together.

"Come with me, Feep," Scrilch says. "I do not wish to get my brain drained without protection."

Subconscious Sigmund has a swell office downtown, and he takes us into a nice private room and we all sit down and have a drink.

"Now," he says, rubbing his hands together. "I am going to ask you to sit down here, Mr. Scrilch." And he puts Floyd Scrilch in a soft chair. Then he turns out all the lights except one lamp, which shines in Scrilch's face. "I will now ask you to answer a few questions," he purrs.

It is just like a high-class third degree.

So he begins to ask questions and Scrilch answers him. And now I see what Subconscious Sigmund is doing. He is pumping Scrilch for his whole life story. And the story comes out. About what a dull life Scrilch leads as a kid. About how nobody ever pays any attention to him, how he is just an average jerk.

And then Scrilch tells about the advertisements. How he answers the first one and gets muscles. About answering the piano-playing ad and getting lessons and being a wizard on the piano. About how he becomes irrestible to women like the hair ad tells him. About his hair growing with scalp restorer. About the painting ad and the writing ad and the life-of-the-party ad.

Subconscious Sigmund is amazed. I can see it. He walks around Scrilch, grunting and coughing and chuckling, and then he stops.

"I see it all," he whispers. "It is truly remarkable! Scrilch, you are that mythical cipher, that abstract integer, that legendary personification—the typical average man! The forces of heredity and environment conspire to blend perfectly the component elements of physique and mentality into the pure norm!"

Scrilch gives him the double take.

"What does this mean without pig Latin?" he inquires.

"It means you are the man all these ads are written for," Subconscious Sigmund tells him. "You are the average citizen these ads are slanted to appeal to. You are the normal man on which these preparations and lessons and exercises and products are designed to work. On a lesser personality or a greater one, they never succeed so fully. But by some kinetic miracle, you are the one person in the world who is perfectly attuned to advertising formulae. It is almost magical. The very words and phrases advertisers use come true in your case."

"You mean if an ad comes out saying you can live forever, I might live forever?"

"Who knows?" Sigmund comes back. "You are physiologically and psychically attuned to the vibrationary reflexes induced by advertising."

"It worries me," Scrilch confesses.

"How do you mean?"

"Well, lately, the ads work *too* good."

"*Too* good?"

"That's right. I mean, I learn piano playing, but I become a master. I take up drawing, and right away I'm a great artist. I tackle writing, and I write half a novel in one twelve-hour day. I send for a hair restorer and I get too much hair. I try to attract friends and women and I have too many friends and too many women. See what I mean? Something is working so that I just seem to get *too much*."

"So? That is most interesting, my friend."

"Sometimes I wonder if I answer the wrong ad, will it kick back on me? Will I get too wealthy or too strong or too talented?"

"I see," mumbles Subconscious Sigmund. "Overcompensation. A most illuminating development. We must probe further."

"What're you going to do, Doc?" asks Scrilch.

"Just look at me," Subconscious Sigmund says. He sits

down in front of Scrilch and begins to stare at him with those big cheaters wobbling.

I catch on right away. He is trying to put Scrilch to sleep. He talks to him and keeps the light shining in his face all the time, and he stares away and waves his arm around a little.

Scrilch just sits there.

Subconscious Sigmund stares harder and waves more. He begins to sweat.

Scrilch just sits there.

Subconscious Sigmund's eyes pop out under his goggles. His hands tremble. He sweats plenty.

Scrilch just sits there.

And all of a sudden, Subconscious Sigmund stops mumbling. His pop eyes go shut. His hands drop in his lap. He slumps down in his chair. Then he tumbles off on the floor and just lies there.

Scrilch gets up.

"Come on," he says. "Let's get going."

"But what about Subconscious Sigmund?"

"We'll leave him be," Scrilch tells me. "Can you imagine," he says, in a disgusted tone of voice. "This psychiatrist tries to *hypnotize* me! Me, when just the other day I answer that swell ad about *Hypnotism Made Easy!*"

That is the last I see of Floyd Scrilch for many a week. I do not hear anything more about his painting or his writing or his piano-playing. I do not see anything in the papers. I figure maybe he answers an ad on how to be a hermit or something, and let it go at that.

But one afternoon I am at the pool hall, minding my p's and cues, and a hand taps me on the shoulder.

I turn around and see Floyd Scrilch. His hand still taps me, because he is trembling. And because I do not recognize him there at first.

Floyd Scrilch is pretty pale. He looks thinner, and there are a couple rings under his eyes I would not like to see on bath tubs.

"Feep," he whispers. "You got to help me."

"Sure, what do you want me to do?"

"I want you to come out to my house," he mutters. "We're going to burn some ads."

"Burn some ads?"

"Sure. All of the ads. All the ones I answer and all the ones I plan to answer. Get rid of them. Before they get rid of me."

I give him a long stare and see he means it.

"There's a taxi waiting outside," he says. "Come on. There's not a minute to lose."

We hop in and drive away. It is a long ride.

"Make with the explanations," I request. "What happens to you? Why don't I see you around?"

"If I am around once more, I am dizzy," Scrilch tells me. "It is terrible. I have no peace. Friends calling me up. Women rushing in to visit me. Art galleries phoning. Agents after my book. And look!"

He is wearing a hat, and now he yanks it off. His hair falls to the floor. So help me, it is six feet long.

"You see?" he mutters. "It won't stop growing! Nothing stops any more. Just for fun I send in my picture to a movie talent bureau that advertises. I win a Hollywood contract. I win another contest. But I cannot go away. I am almost too musclebound to walk now!"

He waves his arm, and his sleeve rips. A bicep sticks out and he pushes it back.

"You see? Ads are good for everybody else, but not for me. They work too well. That is why I run away. I have to get away from people, from women, from advertising.

"That is another thing. A compulsion. That's what Subconscious Sigmund calls it. Every time I see an ad now, I must answer it.

"So I leave my studio and get myself a house in the country. I must. And that is where things go wrong. I hope we're not too late. We must destroy the ads and—something else."

He sits huddled up in the cab as we drive out into the sticks. At last the cabs pulls up in front of a rickety old frame house and we climb out. It is almost dark, and Scrilch runs up the steps so fast he nearly trips in the dim light.

I follow him in.

"No time to lose," he says. "Help me bundle this stuff up. I must get it down into the furnace while I'm still able to. At this rate of growth I may not even get into the cellar."

I see he is a little off the beam, but I do not comment. I merely look at the living room which is just filled with old paper. It looks like a government drive.

There is nothing but piles of clipped-out coupons. Thousands of them. And Scrilch begins to stuff them into boxes. So I help.

All the time he looks at the door.

"Smell anything?" he asks me. I shake my head. We pile some more. "Hear anything downstairs?" he asks. I shake my head.

I notice he is shaking again.

"What's the matter?" I ask. "What am I supposed to smell and hear?"

"It's the last ad I answer," he breathes, hoarsely. "I'll tell you about that later. We have to figure out a way to destroy it. Dynamite, or something. It's growing every hour. I'm almost afraid to go down there. I want to get this stuff in the furnace before it blocks the way."

"What?" I come back, while we bundle up the stuff and carry it out to the cellar door.

Then I hear a rippling noise. Scrilch wheels around. His eyes bulge.

"You don't smell anything, or hear anything," he yells. "But you must see something. Or am I nuts?"

I think I am. Because I *do* see something now.

It is the kitchen floor. It *bulges.*

Yes, the boards in the floor are bulging up. And the ripping noise comes from the wood.

"Growing!" Scrilch screams.

Then he grabs up a pile of coupons.

"I'll get these in the furnace anyway," he shrieks. "No matter how big it is! I'll do it—I'll show you no ad can frighten me!"

He opens the cellar door. It is black down there, but he does not turn on a light. Instead, he grabs his pile and runs down the steps.

I hear him yelling in the dark.

"Don't follow me!" he shouts. "It might be dangerous."

Then I just hear some thumping. All at once he yells again: "Oh—no—it can't be—growing—no—get away—oh—"

And I hear something else. An awful noise. A *rubbery* noise, like somebody is bouncing a zeppelin up and down like a ball. Then there is an awful grunt, and I do smell something, and I hear another sound.

The floor rips further. I hear Scrilch give just one last scream, and then I hear the other sound again.

But the other sound comes from far away, because I am already out the back door and running down the street.

I never go back. Because now I know what happens to Floyd Scrilch. He answers the wrong ads.

LEFTY FEEP took his elbows out of the butter plates and gave a long sigh. "Poor Floyd," he whispered, reminiscently.

I coughed discreetly.

"There's just one thing bothering me," I said.

"Name it and you can have it."

"Well—apparently, Floyd Scrilch was killed there in the cellar. But I don't see how it happened."

"He gets swallowed," Feep told me.

"Swallowed?"

"Sure, Bob. For answering the wrong ad."

"But what is this thing that grows down there and makes

the floor creak?" I asked. "What did you smell and hear at the last? In plain words—what was it that Floyd Scrilch kept in his cellar?"

"That I never know," Feep answered.

"I thought so!"

"Except for a lucky break of mine," Lefty Feep added, triumphant. "When I run out of there I happen to have an ad in my hand. I hang on to it unconscious. And later, when I look at it, I figure out what Floyd does. This is the last ad he tells me he answers. And it works too good again. So he gets killed."

"You mean this ad tells what he had down there in the cellar?"

"Look for yourself," said Lefty Feep.

He reached into his vest pocket and handed me the crumpled piece of paper.

The advertisement was quite small. I read only the top line, but that was enough.

*"Earn Big Money!"*the advertisement urged. *"Use Your Own Basement to Raise Giant Frogs!"*

AFTER WORDS

STANLEY: *Floyd Scrilch starts out as an underdog who gets no respect at all, and I couldn't help but think of Rodney Dangerfield when I re-read this story.*

BLOCH: Dangerfield was only twenty when this story was written. He couldn't even spell respect yet.

JS: *The Average Man is a compelling subject. There was a 1947 movie directed by William Wellman,* Magic Town, *that dealt with a community that symbolized the American national average. You seem to love writing stories about the Average Man. Besides the Floyd Scrilch story there's* "Nothing Happens to Lefty Feep," *which will be in a later Feep volume. You must have an affinity for the Average Man.*

BLOCH: I used to be one myself, before I had the brain transplant.

JS: *At the time you wrote this story, in early 1942, you were working for the Gustav Marx Advertising Agency in Milwaukee, and obviously were poking fun at your own profession, and the misguided power of advertising. The satirical underpinnings are quite amusing.*

BLOCH: We had ad libs long before Women's Lib.

JS: *And you were having fun spoofing the pulp magazine ads of those days.*

BLOCH: I remember I was inspired largely by the horrible little one- and two-inch ads that used to run in the back of the pulps. Ranging from *"Piles! Don't Be Cut!"* to *"How I Became a Father at the Age of 96."*

JS: The classic, of course, was Charles Atlas.

BLOCH: Yes, the dreadful "success" ads, and the full-page ads of Atlas . . . that 90-pound weakling guy getting sand kicked in his face was the most famous. I merely took those ads and decided to write a story around them. Around a character that would do what nobody would ever do; that is, profit and benefit from the ads.

JS: *The title is a take-off on the Lovecraft stories of the 1930s, the* "Weird Doom" *and all. Like something out of the Cthulhu Mythos. Similar to your* "The Strange Flight of Richard Clayton." *Or* "The Druidic Doom." *It has the ring of a story in* Weird Tales. *The only Lefty Feep story that slides into the genre of horror.*

BLOCH: Intentionally, that is.

JS: *And now we come to* "The Little Man Who Was Not All There."

BLOCH: "Not all there" was a slang phrase for mental deficiency . . .

In which Lefty Feep, slight of hand if not gland, pulls a disappearing act in an outlaw suit. Tragic Magic wracked and hacked with a fond wand and a glory storyline fine with doles and holes.

THE LITTLE MAN WHO WASN'T ALL THERE

I WALKED into Jack's Shack accompanied by a terrific appetite. It tugged me toward a table with a haste not to be denied. I didn't notice the thin and melancholy figure in the booth until a thin and melancholy arm grabbed my coattails.

"Hey!" said a voice, plaintively.

"Why, Lefty Feep! I didn't see you when I came in."

A grimace of positive horror crossed Mr. Feep's face, together with half of the sandwich he was eating.

"Don't say that," he pleaded.

"But I really didn't notice you."

Feep trembled violently.

"Please put a collar on that kind of holler," he begged. "It makes me queasy but uneasy when you say you do not see me."

"Oh, I see you now, all right."

"That's better." Feep pushed a relieved smile through the sandwich lettuce and waved me to a seat opposite him. "Now you're cooking with sterno."

I gave my order and sank back in my chair.

"Well, Lefty, what's new? Haven't seen hide nor hair of you for a few days."

"Don't say it that way!" Feep grated.

"What's biting you?"

"The finance company," Lefty Feep replied. "But that is neither here nor there. It is this stuff about not seeing me that disturbs and perturbs."

I began to feel a question coming on. I struggled to resist, but it was no use.

"What's the reason you're so upset when I mention not seeing you?"

Feep wiggled his ears impressively.

"Do you really want to know?" he asked.

"No. But you're going to tell me, anyway."

"Seeing you are so inquisitive," said Lefty Feep, "I suppose there is nothing else I can do but spill it. The whole thing starts out when I get tangled up with this Gorgonzola."

"The cheese?" I inquired.

"No—the magician," Feep replied.

Waving a stalk of celery in mysterious rhythm, Lefty Feep hunched forward and began his story.

I KNOW this Great Gorgonzola for many a year. In fact, I know him when he is just plain Eddie Klotz, doing a vaudeville act. Then he gets a magic show of his own, and pretty soon he calls himself the Great Gorgonzola and becomes tops in the sleight-of-hand racket.

I see his latest show just recently, and it is only a couple of days later that I run into him in front of a brass rail I happen to be standing on.

I give him the old once-over, because he is dressed very stylish, like a corpse, and he has a dance-floor mustache—full of wax. Then I recognize him.

"Well, if it isn't the Great Gorgonzola," I yap. "How are tricks in the magic game?"

"Fair," he tells me. "The legerdemain is all right, but the prestidigitation is lousy."

"I am sorry to hear that," I reply. "But by the way, as one

magician to another—who is that lady I saw you in half with last night?"

"That is no lady, that is my wife," he comes back, with a straight puss. "She is my assistant in the show we are doing. How do you like it?"

"Very nice," I tell him. "Strictly uptown. I figure I will go again this week."

He shakes his head.

"The show closes last night," he informs me. "I have a little business to attend to the rest of this week, so I close up and get ready to leave town. But I hate to do it."

"Why?"

"Do you ever hear of my rival?"

"Rival?"

"Yes," he sneers. "Gallstone the Magician."

"What's with him?"

"My wife, mostly," says Gorgonzola, looking very sad. "Gallstone is nothing but a bushy-haired wolf. He is making passes at my wife, and not just to practice his hypnotism, either."

"That is a tough break," I agree. "But why do you not give him a tough break too—say, his neck, for instance?"

"An excellent idea," Gorgonzola tells me. "But I simply must leave on this business trip. Meanwhile, this Gallstone will be hanging around my wife, trying to insinuate himself with her."

"That is a lousy thing to do," I pronounce. "There is nothing I hate worse than an insinuator. Isn't there a law?"

"You do not seem to understand me," says Gorgonzola. "He wants to worm something out of her."

"That is even worse."

"I mean, Gallstone is trying to get my wife to give away the secrets of my new magical effects for the next season's show. He wants her to tell him my new tricks."

"Aha! Then why don't you take your wife with you?"

"That's out. Private business, very important and just a

little dangerous. I'm leaving her out at the house. Futzi will have to take care of her."

"Futzi?"

"My houseboy," Gorgonzola explains. "He's a Filipino." Then he slaps his hand on the bar. "Say, there's an idea. Listen, Feep—why can't you come out to the house and stay there these next three days? It would solve everything if you'd keep your eyes open."

"I am sorry," I tell him. "But it is necessary for me to stay downtown and look after my interests."

"You mean those lousy two-dollar horse bets?"

"Well, if you choose to put it that way."

"But you can come down every day anyway. Just so you are on hand if this Gallstone shows up. It means a lot to me, Lefty—more than I can tell you now."

"All right," I agree. "When do I go, and where?"

"Today," Gorgonzola tells me. "Here's what I'll do—I'll go home, pack, and leave. Then I'll have Futzi come around and call for you with the car. You can carry your things easier that way."

"What things?" I reply, very bitterly. "One toothbrush and a pair of socks is not exactly a load."

"Nevertheless, Futzi will call for you. He'll bring the keys and everything. Expect him at your place around two. And thanks a million."

With that, Gorgonzola breezes out and I go home and dry out that pair of socks. I am shredding the bristles on my toothbrush when the doorbell rings.

I yank it open, careful, and look out into the hall. I do not see anybody. Then I glance down. Somewhere about a few feet from the floor is a little guy with a face like yellow jaundice.

This face is all plastered up in a big grin with the teeth sticking out like they want to use my toothbrush.

The little yellow guy bows up and down.

"Honorable Feep?" he asks.

I give him the nod.

"Honorable Feep, honorable Gorgonzola say for me to carry you to honorable house. Myself, humble Futzi, am yours truly to command."

This is Filipino double-talk meaning I am going to Gorgonzola's dump with him.

So I grab my handclasp—it is so small, you can hardly call it a grip—and close the door.

"O.K.," I tell this Futzi. "Lead the way, my Japanese sandman."

He turns and gives me an unlaundered look.

"Me Filipino boy, not Japanese," he hisses. "I do not enjoy it when you stick amusement at me."

"You mean poke fun at you?" I ask.

"Correctly. If I one of those Japanzees I go out commit hootchiekootchie."

"Hotsy-totsy?"

"No, hocus-pocus."

Then I get it. "You mean hari-kari."

"No. Hocus-pocus. I kill myself with magician's knife."

This kind of talk is hard to follow, and so is this guy's driving. We skid through traffic in Gorgonzola's car, and a dozen times I think we are morgue-meat, but little Futzi just sings away at the wheel. Then I decide to take advantage of the chance to find out a few things about the setup I am heading into.

"Does Mrs. Gorgonzola expect me?"

"Of coarsely. She expectorate you right away. Mr. Gorgonzola he tell her you coming down on weekend and then he take it on the sheep."

"On the lam, you mean."

"Honorable correction noted. And here we arrive."

We pull into the driveway of a two-story bungalow.

"What kind of woman is Mrs. Gorgonzola?" I ask, just to be on the safe side.

"She very female person," Futzi answers. "But so sorry.

Too skinny for suiting me. Not too skinny for honorable Gallstone though. He all the time dangle around like ants in the pants."

"You mean snake in the grass."

"Surely. Shrubbery serpent, that honorable skunk. Mr. Gorgonzola say if you catch Gallstone hanging around you cut his throat from ear to there."

We get out and head for the door. Futzi rings, grinning at me.

"Mrs. Gorgonzola arrive now," he says.

Sure enough, the door opens.

"Slide in," Futzi suggests.

"Not me!" I yelp. I do not like what is standing in the doorway. I dislike it so much my knees begin to knock.

"Listen, my fine Filipino friend," I whisper. "You tell me Mrs. Gorgonzola is thin, but you do not tell me she is *that* thin."

Because the thing that opens the door is nothing else than a white, grinning skeleton!

"Squeeze yourself together," Futzi giggles. "This is not Mrs. Gorgonzola. Is just a trick. Gorgonzola he very tricky honorable baby, you betcha! This just harmless bones."

Sure enough, I see the skeleton is attached to the doorpost. We edge inside.

"Now here are keys to honorable house," Futzi tells me in the hall. "Especially keys to Mr. Gorgonzola's bedroom. He does tricks up there so nobody steals. He say you take nice care of these, so Gallstone cannot stick honorable schnozzola into secret business."

I pocket the keys and then I hear somebody coming.

"So there you are," snaps a voice. Futzi turns around.

"Honorable Mrs., allow me to gift to you honorable Feep, Lefty, Esq. He is here to sit down on week end."

Mrs. Gorgonzola gives me the old eye, and a very pretty eye it is too, under all that mascara and pencil work. She is a tall, thin damsel with drugstore-blonde hair. I hold out my hand, but she must think I have a bad case of tattle-tale gray, because she does not take it. Instead, she hands me a stuffed-fish look.

"My husband tells me you're going to be here until he gets back," she freezes.

"I hope it does not put you out," I tell her.

"Oh, it's perfectly all right, I suppose. Futzi, show Mr. Feep to his room. Dinner's at seven. Now, if you'll pardon me, I must go lock myself in a trunk."

"What kind of talk is that?" I ask Futzi, when we walk upstairs.

"Straight from elbow talk," he says. "Mrs. Gorgonzola always lock herself in trunk or safe or something. She makes practice for magic act. What you call, escape artist?"

"I see."

When I get into Gorgonzola's room upstairs, I see a lot more. The place is filled with trunks and boxes and cases, and when I hang my coat in the closet I find still more. There are decks of cards under the bed, and artificial flowers and flags and wands. I head for the bath to wash my hands and Futzi leaps for the door ahead of me.

"Wait!" he hollers. "You wish to release rabbits?"

"Rabbits?"

"Honorable Gorgonzola keeps rabbits in bath. Bathtub full of lettuce, you notice."

Sure enough, the place is full of bunnies. I start to wash, and the lop-ears flop around and jump up on me, while Futzi tries to shoo them off.

"Oww!" I mention, with my eyes full of soap, because a rabbit jumps onto the washbowl and starts tickling my stomach. But it is too late for me to do anything, and I get my coat splashed up plenty.

"Do not spend any attention to that," Futzi grins. "I send honorable coat to honorable cleaners."

"Fie upon that noise," I bark. "If I do not get back downtown this afternoon I am going to the cleaners myself.

(TURN PAGE FOR DETAILS)

THE LEFTY FEEP READER'S SCRATCH SHEET SCROLL

Identifying you as a dedicated Lefty Feep reader . . . Just send your name and address to: CREATURES AT LARGE, P.O. Box 687, Pacifica CA 94044.

You will also receive information about future Lefty Feep publications

I have to place a bet on a pet, and I cannot run down there in my shirtsleeves. The snappy dressers at the pool hall will laugh at me."

"Why not wear coat of Mr. Gorgonzola?" Futzi suggests. "He got plenty clothes in closet. Enough for whole nudist colony, I gamble you."

This seems to be an idea. After Futzi takes my wet coat away and tells me I can use the car to drive down, I go to the big bedroom closet and start looking around.

The place is full of magic paraphrenalia like I say, but there do not seem to be any clothes hanging there at all, except costumes. I do not wish to wear a turban or a Chinese kimono, and I am about ready to give up when I see this trunk.

It is a great big iron chest locked away at the bottom of the closet, and I pull it out and see that it is closed very tight indeed. For a minute I give up, because I do not carry any nitroglycerine on my person for many years. Then I remember the keys Futzi gives me.

Sure enough, the first key I try unlocks the trunk. It is filled with mirrors and folding stuff and glass balls—and I realize this must be the trunk full of new tricks that Gorgonzola is so anxious for me to watch over.

But there at one side is just what I am looking for—a nice tuxedo. There is a coat, a vest, a pair of pants, and a top hat to match.

I merely remove the coat and slip it on for size. It fits pretty well and I am just going to yank on the trousers when I look at the clock and see I must beat it downtown in a hurry if I wish to catch the fifth race.

So I keep my old trousers and wear Gorgonzola's coat. I run down the hall and out into the yard, climb into the car, and make like crazy.

Ten minutes later I am entering Gorilla Gabface's pool palace. It is here that I make my modest investments on the races from time to time.

There are quite a bunch of bananas standing around phoning in their wagers, and big fat Gorilla Gabface is making book. When I rush in, they turn around and stare.

Now I admit it is unusual for me to wear a tuxedo coat and checkered trousers. Such a spectacle is worth a stare any day of the week. But the kind of look I get from the personalities around the phone is quite queer indeed. And there is a very quaint silence along with it.

I rush up to Gorilla Gabface and hold up my hand. He is standing there with his mouth open and his tongue hanging out a mile, and when I come close he sort of shudders and puts his hands over his eyes.

"No!" he gasps. "No—no!"

"What's the matter, you big ape?" I ask, kindly. "You look like you never see me before in your life."

"I don't!" he gasps. "And if I never see you again I am very satisfied."

"But you know me. I'm Lefty Feep!"

Gorilla moans a little.

"The face is familiar," he groans. "And so are the trousers. But what happens to the rest of you?"

"Nothing at all," I tell him. "I merely borrow this tuxedo coat to wear here."

"What tuxedo coat?" Gabface asks. "I don't see any."

"Then what do you think I'm wearing?"

"I don't know." Gorilla is sweating. He backs further away. "From the looks of you, you should be wearing a shroud. I don't know what holds your neck up."

"Are you giving me the rib?" I ask.

"No—you're giving me the shivers," he says. "Coming in here like that; just a face and a pair of pants underneath. What happens to the rest of you?"

He pulls me along the wall by the seat of my trousers, very careful, until I am facing a mirror.

"Tell me what you see," he whispers.

I look, and then it is my turn to gasp.

K.D.
8

Because in the mirror I see a pair of pants, a neck, and a head. There is nothing in between. I am cut off at the hips, and my head and neck are floating around about three feet above in the empty air!

"You must do a lot of betting in the first races today," Gorilla whispers. "I hear of guys losing their shirts on the horses before, but you go ahead and lose your whole torso!"

I just stand there. Looking down, I can see my tuxedo coat very plain. But it does not show in the mirror and it is not visible to anybody else.

"You say you borrow that coat?" one of the specimens at the phone inquires.

"Yes, I find it in a closet."

"Maybe the thing is full of moths," he suggests.

"Very hungry moths," Gorilla chimes in. "So hungry they not only eat up the coat but your chest and arms, too."

I just stare at the mirror. Because now I find I know what happens. I look around for clothes in a trunk where Gorgonzola keeps his magic tricks and I get a trick coat. One that makes me invisible.

Just to prove it, I take the coat off. And sure enough, I am all right again. I stand there in my shirtsleeves looking foolish, but not so foolish as the rest of these mugs.

"How do you do it?" Gabface asks me.

"It is a magician's coat," I admit.

"Well, do not put it back on," he begs. "You give us all quite a shock with that trick. For a minute I think you must be suffering from an overdose of vanishing cream."

"Never mind that," I snap. "I want to place a wager in the fifth race at Santa Anita. On Bing Crosby's horse."

"You are too late," Gorilla tells me. "It just finishes."

I let out an unkind remark. "Curse this coat business," I suggest. "It spoils a sure 15-to-1 shot for me."

"Cheer up," says Gabface. "You are lucky you do not make the bet, because you lose anyway."

"How come?"

"Well, Bing Crosby's horse is disqualified at the post, so Crosby runs the race himself instead. And loses."

This cheers me up a little, and so I take my leave and go back to Gorgonzola's house for supper. I am very careful not to wear this coat in the car, because if I do it will look like the jalopy has no driver in it.

Besides, I cannot get used to the idea of what I see when I look in the mirror. Being invisible is a very funny feeling, and every time I remember it I have to close my eyes and shudder.

The last time I do so I am just ready to park. And I run smack into the back of a big Packard.

"Aha!" yells a voice from inside. "Watch where you're going, you hoodlum!"

I look around to see what kind of uncouth person he is talking to, and then I realize the remark is made to me. More and over, the owner of the voice jumps out of the Packard and climbs up to the running board. He is waving one hand in front of my face and he does not have any flag in it, either. Just a big fist.

"I am sorry," I say. "I must be driving with my eyes closed."

"That is the way you will drive for a long time, you oaf," he says. "Because I am going to black both eyes for you."

I notice he is a big, beefy fellow with a red face and a shock of bushy hair that stands out from his head like a dust mop.

"Can't we talk this over?" I suggest.

One big arm reaches in and grabs me. He lifts me out of the car and holds me up by the neck.

"The only thing I will talk over is your dead body," he snarls. "You smash both my rear fenders and that is what I am going to do to you."

Just then the front door opens and Mrs. Gorgonzola runs out. She smiles at the big bushy-haired specimen.

"Why, Mr. Gallstone, you've arrived for dinner," she simpers. "I see you and Mr. Feep already know each other."

"Yes," I gasp. "I bump into him just now coming in."

"Mr. Feep is a house-guest," says Mrs. Gorgonzola.

"So?" Gallstone drops me down to my feet and takes his paw off my collar. "I am pleased to meet you," he snarls, and holds out his hand. I take it, and he nearly breaks my fingers off at the joints.

"So you are Gallstone the Magician," I manage to get out. "Gorgonzola tells me a lot about you."

"He does, huh? Well—he can't prove it." Gallstone sneers. Then he turns to Mrs. Gorgonzola and gives her a look at his big teeth.

"I hear your husband is away," he says.

"That's right."

"Too bad. Ha-ha!"

"Yes, isn't it, tee-hee!" cracks Mrs. Gorgonzola.

So right away I figure it is one of *those* things. I get out of the way to avoid being hit by any flying mush they are slinging at each other.

Then Futzi sticks his head around the door.

"Dinner is swerved!" he yells. "Rush to put on honorable food-sack."

Mrs. Gorgonzola turns to me. "When you leave, I think you're not coming back for dinner," she says. "So—"

I catch on to this, also.

"I eat downtown," I lie. "I will just go up to my room, if you don't mind. You two go right ahead and entertain each other. If you don't mind, of course."

Gallstone smiles and now I know what he reminds me of with his bushy hair. A wolf. It is like Gorgonzola says. And now he is sneaking around Gorgonzola's wife.

I just go upstairs but already I have an idea in the old noggin. When I get into the room I make for the trunk and pull out the rest of the tuxedo, also the top hat. I put these on, and then go for the mirror.

For a minute I am afraid to look. I stare down at my coat and pants. They are very ordinary-looking to me, and I can see them very plainly. So naturally I know I must be able to see them in the mirror.

But when I do look in the mirror, there is nothing. Nothing at all. The coatsleeves come down over my hands and the pants cuffs cover my shoes, and the top hat pulls down over my face—all this I know, but I do not see it in the mirror. The mirror is blank. Absolutely blank.

Maybe there is some new chemical in the cloth, or some fiber that does not reflect light. Whatever it is, Gorgonzola has an invisible suit, and I am wearing it. This is enough for me.

Because I have this plan. I do not like Gallstone the Magician and I promise to watch Gorgonzola's wife. So I decide to go ahead.

I wait awhile and then I sneak downstairs wearing the invisible suit. Sure enough, Gallstone and Mrs. Gorgonzola are at the supper table, flirting with each other.

When I slide in, he is showing off by juggling three water glasses in the air at once. She giggles and watches him and he smirks all over the place. Pretty soon he puts down the glasses and pulls out his napkin. A big rubber plant grows from underneath it.

"Oh, Mr. Gallstone, you are so clever," she says.

"Just call me Oscar," he says. And pulls a live snake out from the potatoes. "I'll bet your husband can't do this," he remarks.

"Oh—*him*," sniffs Mrs. Gorgonzola. "He doesn't do anything. Before we marry he is so cute—always grabbing rabbits out of my neck and surprising me by turning coffee into champagne. Now he doesn't even juggle the dinner plates any more."

"Such neglect! Shameful!" says Gallstone. He reaches over and tweaks her ear. A gopher jumps out.

"You're wonderful, Oscar," she tells him.

"That's nothing at all to what I can do," boasts Gallstone. "Come into the living room."

"Why?"

"I want to show you some of my parlor tricks."

They go into the living room. Mrs. Gorgonzolla grabs his arm. I follow right behind, but of course they cannot see me at all.

"You ought to leave that clumsy oaf of a husband," Gallstone suggests. "A woman like you deserves only the best kind of thaumatugry, to say nothing of a little goety now and then."

"Oh—I couldn't," she says.

"Why not? What has your husband got that I haven't got? What if he does saw you in half? I've got a trick where I can saw you into four parts. Six, even. And if you'll join my act instead, I'll promise not to stop until I can cut you into sixteen pieces."

"That would be thrilling," she blushes.

"Why, your husband doesn't even know how to stick knives into you in the basket trick," Gallstone sneers. "Me, I can use axes on you."

"You make it all sound so fascinating," she simpers, snuggling up against him.

"Tricks? Why, I've got tricks Gorgonzola never even dreams of," whispers Gallstone, grabbing her in a half nelson and giving her the kind of look a rat gets when he grabs a piece of cheese.

"I know what kind of tricks you have," I burst out. "And you can stick them back up your sleeve, Gallstone."

"What's that?" Mrs. Gorgonzola shrieks, jumping up.

"Huh?" Gallstone looks around. "That voice—it spoke to me out of empty air."

They stare but they do not see me, of course, even though I am standing right in front of them.

"You must be imagining things," says Gallstone, with a puzzled look.

"*Ouch!* I didn't imagine *that*," snaps Mrs. Gorgonzola.

Because I decide to pinch her in a likely spot at this moment, and do so, hard.

"What?" asks Gallstone.

"*That!*" shrieks the lady. "There—you did it again. You naughty boy. You pinched me."

"Where?"

"On the davenport there."

"How can I pinch you when you're holding both my hands?"

"Well, somebody pinched me."

I stick my face down close.

"You'll get pinched again if you don't stop holding hands with that bushy-haired baboon," I mutter.

"Eeek—that voice again!" Mrs. Gorgonzola wails. "Don't tell me you don't hear it this time, Oscar."

Gallstone is on the spot now. All at once he smiles.

"Oh, *that* voice," he says. "Just another little trick of mine your husband can't duplicate. That's a spirit. A ghost. I'm psychic, you know. I can call ghosts out of the empty air."

She gives him a sick-calf look.

"Oh, how wonderful you are!" she says. They go into another clinch. I break this up by stepping on Gallstone's toes, hard. Then I let out a long groan. They jump apart fast.

"Cut out that romantic stuff, Goldilocks," I grate. "Or you'll be a ghost yourself in a couple of minutes."

"I don't think I'd like to live with such spirits," Mrs. Gorgonzola wails. "Oscar, make that voice go away."

Gallstone is plenty confused. But he stands up, and tries to smile.

"Listen, darling—once and for all, let's forget all these things. I want you to go away with me and join my act. That's what I've come to tell you. You and I can take your husband's new tricks with us and—"

Aha, that was it! He was after those tricks, just the way Gorgonzola warns me. I watch the two of them close.

"I'm not sure," Mrs. Gorgonzola flutters. "You must let me decide."

"No time for that. I'll prove to you that I'm a better magician than Gorgonzola any day. And then you must come with me."

"Well—"

"Come on. Name a trick your husband can't do and I'll do it for you right now."

"Let me see. Oh yes, that safe trick. You know that big iron safe he has. He tries to get out of it after it's locked and he just can't seem to master the combination."

"Let me at it," Gallstone boasts. "Lead me to it. I'll show you."

"It's in the cellar," she says.

"Show me."

They go downstairs and I follow. I try to trip Gallstone on the stairs, but miss. And there we are in the cellar; the two standing in front of a big iron safe and me invisible next to them.

The safe is really a terrific box, big and heavy, with a large lock on it. Gallstone looks at it and laughs.

"Why, breaking that is like breaking a baby bank," he sneers. "I'll climb in and let you lock me up. In three minutes I'll be out again and we'll be off together. Is it a deal?"

Mrs. Gorgonzola blushes.

"Very well, Oscar," she says. "You have my consent. If you can break out of this safe I'll run away with you."

"Kiss me, darling," moos Gallstone. They clinch, but I stick my face in between and Gallstone kisses my neck. He blinks a little but breaks away. Then he wraps his coat around himself and opens the safe.

"Here I go," he says, crawling inside and bending himself double to squeeze in. "Lock the door, darling. I'll be out in no time."

I stoop down and notice, when he pulls his feet in, that there is a little steel pick attached to the sole of one shoe. But

Mrs. Gorgonzola does not see this. She closes the door and blows him a kiss and then steps back to wait.

In about a minute I can hear this Gallstone fumbling around inside with his pick, working on the combination. I just wait. The tumblers start to click.

Another minute goes by and another. Still no Gallstone. Mrs. Gorgonzola stoops down.

"Are you all right, Oscar?" she calls.

"Sure—be with you in a jiffy," he gasps.

But a jiffy passes and so do five minutes. And no Gallstone.

Mrs. Gorgonzola is getting impatient.

"Can I help you?" she asks.

"No—I'm—getting on fine—just a second," he groans.

Fifteen more minutes go by. Gallstone is thumping around and rattling the combination and panting for breath.

Mrs. Gorgonzola is getting redder and redder. All at once she looks at her wristwatch.

"You get in there twenty-five minutes ago," she calls. "I'll give you five minutes more."

There is a grunt from inside and a lot of rattling. But five minutes pass, and Gallstone is still in the safe. The noise stops. Gallstone gives up trying to get out. Mrs. Gorgonzola gives a sigh and looks stern.

"Very well, Oscar, you show your true colors. You are nothing but an impostor. You are not a good magician. You cannot find your way out of a telephone booth, let alone a safe. I will never run away with you. Good night!"

She turns around and marches upstairs. I follow her, because there is nothing more I have to do. I do my job when I keep turning the dial of the safe after Gallstone lines up the tumblers.

So I go to bed very happy. Gallstone will sneak away like the pup he is. Now I know Mrs. Gorgonzola is all through with him, and there is nothing to worry about. Gorgonzola will be back in a day or so and his tricks are safe after all.

I take off my coat and hat and am just going to remove the tuxedo trousers, when the door opens. Futzi walks in.

"Honorable Feep, I expect you are—oh mercy, what in name is honorable that?" he yells.

He is staring at my trousers, or rather at the place where my trousers should be. But because of the pants I wear, he does not see anything below my waist at all.

"Oh what unhappy accident!" he wails. "You get cut in twice by auto car?"

"No, of course not," I say.

"Then perhaps you lose on races?"

"There are some things," I answer with dignity, "which I will never bet. No, I do not lose anything."

"But you have no limbs downstairs," Futzi wails. "Just head and torso."

"I have more so than torso," I assure him, stepping out of the trousers. "There, you see? All that happens, Futzi, is I wear this suit of Gorgonzola's. It is some kind of trick suit, because when I wear it I am invisible."

"So?" whispers Futzi. "That is remarkable, also strange."

"Sure," I say. "This must be one of the new tricks that Gorgonzola wishes me to protect. I prefer you do not mention this around. Now I lock the suit up again and that is that."

So I haul out the trunk and lock up the tuxedo and hat. Futzi hangs around staring at me.

"Where is honorable Gallstone?" he asks.

"Downstairs on ice," I tell him. "He locks himself up in a safe like a war bond."

"Then he does not rush away with Mrs. Gorgonzola?" Futzi asks. "I expect they lope off together." His face falls.

"No elopement," I tell him. "You better go down and unlock the safe now and let Gallstone go home."

Futzi still hangs around.

"Maybe you like me to press honorable suit?" he asks. "Make it nice and fresh for Mr. Gorgonzola to be invisible in? Gorgonzola always proud to look his best even if invisible, I gamble you."

"No, get out of here," I snap.

"I press and iron plenty fast," he begs. "Please, let me press nice invisible coat and trousers."

"I'll press your trousers for you with my foot if you don't scram," I suggest.

So Futzi scrams.

I go to bed. I tuck the keys right under my pillow, too, because I do not wish to lose them. An invisible suit is plenty valuable and I am taking no chances. I figure on keeping awake.

But I am not awake a couple of hours later. In fact, I am very much asleep, and dreaming about rabbits with big teeth and bushy hair that are locking me into a safe. The dream is so real I can even hear the tumblers clicking.

The clicking gets louder and I wake up. Then I know what is making the sound. The keys under my pillow.

They are sliding out, in a hand.

It is a yellow hand. Futzi's hand.

He is standing over my bed in the dark, grabbing for those keys.

"Hey!" I yell, jumping up.

"Hey!" I yell, going down again.

Because Futzi's hand drops the keys and grabs my wrist. He jerks it and I go back on my head. Then his other hand gets hold of my waist. I turn over on my stomach. Then he uses both hands in a very busy fashion and we have quite a scramble.

In a minute I am sitting on the bed looking straight into a pair of legs wrapped around my neck.

Something about them looks quite familiar to me. And I suddenly realize that these are my legs. Around my neck. I am tied up like a Christmas package.

Futzi stands in front of me, grinning.

"Very sorry to disturb," he says.

"What is this?" I gasp, trying to get loose.

"Jiu-jitsu," he tells me.

"Jiu-jitsu? But that's a Japanese trick, isn't it? Then you're not a Filipino, you're a—"

Futzi bows.

"That is most correct," he tells me. "I am not a Filipino, Mr. Feep. Nor do I need to continue the disguise with that ridiculous accent, either. All I require now are those keys of yours. I shall take the suit and leave."

"But I don't understand—" I say.

"Of course not." Futzi laughs, very low. "Why should I disguise myself as a Filipino house boy, get a job in a magician's house, and act as a servant?

"The answer is obvious. Gorgonzola is a clever man, but I know his secret. He does not leave town—he's here now, down at local headquarters of Army Ordnance. He'll tell them he has a new chemical treatment which renders clothing invisible and offer it to the army as a military weapon. Like Dunninger's work in camouflage that makes battleships invisible. The invisible suit is just a sample of the material. Quite a valuable secret.

"Now I have that suit. I shall wear it, slip downtown and put Gorgonzola out of the way once and for all. Information comes to me that his conference with ordnance officials is scheduled for late tonight.

"Naturally I would not be admitted to such a gathering under normal circumstances." Here Futzi gives a little smirk and bow. "But with this suit on as a passport I think I can slip in quite freely. With your curiosity thus satisfied, I leave you."

I still sit there with my legs tied into Boy Scout knots while Futzi goes over to the closet, hauls out the trunk, and opens it. He gets the dress suit and hat and slips them on very fast. He is so small the clothes hang over him and in a few seconds he is gone. Disappears into thin air. I see the door open. His voice chuckles.

"Goodnight, honorable Feep," he says, sarcastic. "We must discuss hari-kari again some time. Perhaps you will prefer committing it yourself when you think of what's going to happen to your friend Gorgonzola."

Then the door closes and I am left tied to be fit. I grunt and groan and wrestle with myself, but I cannot get my legs loose. Finally I roll off the bed onto the floor. That does it. It cracks my skull, but it loosens my legs.

I stagger downstairs to the phone and look up the ordnance headquarters number. I ring and there is no answer. Then I decide to call the cops—until I remember this invisible suit stuff is a military secret. Also, it will not sound so good to ask the cops to chase an invisible man at midnight.

So there is only one thing to do. I spot Gallstone's Packard still standing outside. Futzi has the other car, of course.

I have some trouble sitting down inside, with my sore legs, but no trouble at all in getting that car up to ninety. When I think of that invisible little Jap sneaking around and trying to knock off Gorgonzola and steal his plans, I know there is no time to lose.

In exactly seven minutes I pull up in front of the old destination. The joint is dark, but open, and I make the stairs very fast to the second floor. There is a light burning in an office room and the door is open. They are inside—and I am sure from the open door that Futzi is with them. Invisible.

I tiptoe in and look through the inside door. There are four characters sitting around a desk, and sure enough, Gorgonzola is with them. He has a briefcase open in front of him and he is talking very fast.

I am the only one who sees what is behind him, though. It hangs in the air very still, but it is ready for action. A big black revolver, in the hands of that invisible Jap.

I throw myself through the doorway and grab the revolver. There is a lot of yelling, but I get it in my hands. Then there is a real yell.

Naturally, all these birds can see is me, waving a gun. They do not see any invisible Futzi, and I cannot yell out to them to look for him, either. He can be hiding anywhere in the room and nobody can spot him.

So I just turn my gun around, point it at a perfect bull's-eye, and shoot Futzi.

And that is how I save a military secret.

LEFTY FEEP stopped waving the celery and put it in his mouth.

"I can understand now why it upset you when I spoke of not seeing you," I said. "You must have had quite an experience."

"Sure. But it is O.K. now. Gorgonzola gives the ordnance department his new chemical invisibility formula, his wife gives Gallstone the air, and I give that little Jap spy some lead poisoning where it does him the least good."

I coughed.

"About that business of shooting the Jap," I said. "There's just one question that bothers me."

"Yes?"

"Well, you say he was wearing this invisible suit and nobody could see him. Yet you managed to shoot him at once. Just what were you aiming at?"

Feep blushed.

"I do not like to say exactly," he confessed. "But I will mention that I get suspicious that night when Futzi hangs around wanting to get his hands on the suit. I decide to figure out a way to make the suit a little less invisible, in case it is worn by anybody else. So I do, and as a result when Futzi wears it he gives me a target he does not notice himself in his hurry putting it on."

"What target?" I persisted.

"I refuse to say," Feep grinned. "All I can tell you is that before I lock honorable suit up for the night, I take a scissors and cut a big hole in seat of honorable pants."

AFTER WORDS

STANLEY: *You have a reference to Bing Crosby's horse, of all things.*

BLOCH: If something was current when I was writing, I'd find a way to stick it into a story. Racing was a big thing in Hollywood in the 1940s. And Bing was quite a habitue of the track. Louis B. Mayer of MGM had his own stables, and many major stars owned or bred horses. Crosby was publicized for this and often talked about it on his radio series, *The Kraft Music Hall,* and other shows written for him.

JS: *Here's an amazing thing: You have a reference to Dunninger, who was then a popular stage entertainer specializing in hypnotism and so-called mind reading. You refer to his tests of invisibility for the U.S. Navy's war effort. This is astounding because there are legendary stories that in 1943, a whole year after your story was written, the U.S. Navy conducted invisibility experiments with* the U.S.S. Eldridge, *a destroyer escort sailing out of Norfolk, Virginia. Allegedly the warship vanished and reappeared a short while later in Philadelphia. It was written up in an alleged nonfiction work,* The Philadelphia Experiment: Project Invisibility, *and New World Pictures made a fictional film version of this story in 1984. Did you have some psychic foresight?*

BLOCH: (Arching eyebrows) You must be joking. As far as my story is concerned, I made it up. Nothing more. Those things happen once in a while. After all, any real invention starts as the product of someone's imagination, just like a piece of fiction. There's nothing strange about the idea that reality can emerge from the mind as well as fantasy.

JS: *You were dealing with H. G. Wells'* Invisible Man *in this story. Is that a favorite novel of yours?*

BLOCH: Not particularly. I liked the book, of course, but I was hurt by the 1933 film version with Claude Rains. I was irritated by the final scene when The Invisible Man walks naked into the snow, and footprints appear, wearing *shoes!* I thought that was very sloppy. Amazing how a thing like that can irritate me. In the context of a production, someone spends a fortune to do a film, and then a little inconsequential detail is overlooked or ignored, or someone says, "Nobody will notice; who cares," so there is an inconsistency which is unnecessary.

JS: *We now come to your Flying Carpet yarn.*

BLOCH: Let's hope it doesn't get unraveled . . .

LEFTY FEEP

In which our checkered hero is called on the carpet when his willing shilling backfires . . . and finds himself cutting a snug rug with a Wizard of Odds in the fly-sky over Buffalo.

SON OF A WITCH

WHEN LEFTY FEEP approached my table at Jack's Shack, I rose to my feet with a gasp of indignation.

"Here, let me brush you off," I said. "The nerve of those careless waiters—spilling a tray full of chop suey on your suit."

Feep's eyebrows rose and circled above his thin, morose face. His hand motioned me back into my seat.

"Nobody spills chop suey on me," he corrected. "This is not Chinese hash on my coat—it is the weave of my suit." I took another look. What I saw on Feep's suit was more of a writhe than a weave. The threads cascaded snakily through a baggy tweed in a riot of clashing colors.

As Feep sat down I shook my head.

"I don't understand you, Lefty," I murmured. "These loud clothes you sport—your taste in color! Don't you ever wear anything quiet?"

"Sure," snapped Feep. "Earmuffs."

"I mean, why these awful patterns and color combinations? Have you no love of beauty?"

"Certainly. Me, I like blondes."

"No," I amended, hastily. "I speak of aesthetics."

"Aesthetics? I have aesthetics last year when they yank my tonsils out."

"That's anaesthetic," I told him. "But don't you like soft, pastel shadings in paintings and tapestries? Don't you like the quiet richness, say, of a fine oriental rug?"

"Rugs!" snapped Lefty Feep.

"But you haven't—"

"Rugs!" howled Feep. "Bugs to rugs!"

"What's the matter, man? I only asked you if you liked rugs."

Feep's eyebrows bristled like twin toothbrushes. He leaned even closer and spoke from between tight lips. "Rugs are for mugs, thugs and slugs," he grated. "On my floor at home you find only tile, linoleum or empty gin bottles. Rugs, never!"

"Why? What have you got against rugs?"

"You ask me that? Can it be that I do not tell you about the time I go to Out-of-Business Oscar's auction?"

"Can be," I answered. "I never knew you attended an auction in your life."

"It is very nearly the last thing I do attend," murmured Lefty Feep, closing his eyes. "When I think what could happen to me because of it, the cold chills still use my spine for a racetrack."

Something about Feep's voice made me want to hear the story. Or perhaps it was just the fact that he now grabbed me by the lapels and held me so I couldn't escape.

"I will tell you about the experience I have with a rug," he muttered. "Then we will take you out to be defrosted."

"Why?"

"Because," whispered Lefty Feep, "it will turn your blood to ice."

I sat there, refrigerating slowly, as Feep began to unwind his tongue . . .

I AM ALWAYS a very active personality, as you know. I am hep to pep. Making lazy drives me crazy. Well, I get up bright and early one afternoon, all ready for a big day.

I am just pulling the cork out of my breakfast when I realize there is nothing to do.

This is a terrible feeling for an ambitious guy like me, but it is true. Today there is nothing for me to do at all. No races are running. No football pools are going. All the pinball machines are shut down. There isn't even a crap game going on over at Gorilla Gabface's pool hall. In other words, I am unemployed.

Naturally, any sensible citizen will realize the only way out is to crawl right back into bed until at least the burlesque shows open. But I am all energy today, so I decide to go out and stroll around.

I am toddling down the old stem about an hour later when I find myself passing Out-of-Business Oscar's.

This Out-of-Business Oscar is a personality who runs a second-hand joint down the street. He derives his nickname from the big signs he plasters up all over the front of his rubbish palace.

GOING OUT OF BUSINESS says the big banner across the front.

MUST VACATE IN THIRTY DAYS. FORCED SALE—LEASE EXPIRES.

It is hard to read the words on these signs. They are pretty faded, because the signs must be about twenty years old by now.

But Oscar has some new ones up today.

PRICES CUT says the first one.

PRICES SLASHED says the second one.

PRICES BLEEDING TO DEATH says the third.

Then there is one just under these that reads *FIRE SALE.* But I do not pay any attention to that. Out-of-Business Oscar is the kind of guy who starts a fire sale every time he lights a cigar.

Which is pretty often, because Oscar finds a lot of cigars in front of the curb.

The sign that does interest me is hanging over the door.

Sure enough. I peek in and see a lot of specimens around a big counter; and Oscar is standing up on top looking like a judge with a gavel in his hand.

So I figure I got time to kill and maybe I can murder it by taking a look at this auction. I walk inside and listen while Oscar begins to deal out the spiel.

"Gentlemen," he yaps, just as though there are some in the crowd. "As you know, today we auction off the estate of the late Mrs. Bobo Grope. We are privileged to dispose of the household effects of this millionaire-ess—her valuable collection of old masters, her antiques and art treasures, and her priceless oriental curiosities."

Then he starts the sale. Well, to make a long story tedious, he is not doing so hot. The stuff he auctions off is very high class, but the customers aren't. They bid only a half buck or a dollar on all the lovely pictures and pottery. This is a shame—I am not a corner sewer of art, but from the way he describes it, I see that this is all the real McCoy, if oriental furnishings are ever made by any McCoy.

Poor Oscar warms up and sweats. He hauls out the bric and the brac and gives with the tongue. He grabs a couple pots and waves his arms.

"I have here two gorgeous specimens of the Sung Dynasty," he hollers. "Two exquisite Chinese cuspidors."

They go for a mere six bits.

"And here is a rare Ming mustache cup," he says—and knocks it down to an old goat for a dime.

So it goes. He sells an Egyptian mummy case to a musician who wants it to carry his bass viol in. He disposes of Hindu idols and Siamese carvings for a buck or two. It is breaking his heart.

On top of it, some smart alecks in the crowd keep making wise remarks, and it is very embarrassing to poor Oscar.

He hauls out a big rack and says, "We will now proceed

to dispose of this remarkable collection of Persian and Oriental rugs."

A jerk in the rear hollers out to him. "Get rid of that junk and start auctioning off the harem!"

This is too much for Oscar. He announces that there will be a five-minute pause in the sale, and slides back of the counters.

I know he is going for a drink, so I quick scoot along after him and nab him in the act.

"Why, it's Lefty Feep," he says, recognizing my lips on the bottle. "You are a sight for sore eyes. And my eyes are plenty sore today from looking at that crummy mob."

"Too bad," I sympathize.

"Well, it is my fault," he shrugs. "This collection of Mrs. Bobo Grope's is famous all over the world. A dozen big experts and orientalists wire and phone that they will show up today. I expect they will pay thousands for some of these rare and curious pieces. So I send out regular engraved announcements, very high class.

"Only I make a mistake. I print that the sale begins at three in the afternoon. And when I file notice legally, I set the time for two. According to law I must start the auction at two, and so here I am, an hour early. None of the big shots arrive yet, and this stuff goes for next to nothing."

I pat him on the back with one hand and reach for the bottle with the other. Then Oscar looks at me.

"Feep, I must get prices up. Maybe you will shill for me?"

"You mean, bid against some of those customers and make them bid higher?"

"I appreciate it if you do it," Oscar tells me. "Have another drink and let's get to work."

So we go back to the auction room and that is what I do. Whenever Oscar holds up a rug and somebody offers two dollars, I offer three. And so forth. Prices rise. We auction off a dozen Arab blankets in a row.

Then Oscar gets to the bottom of the pile. He hauls out

a dusty old roll, all tied together with wires at the ends. And he makes a little speech.

He says, "Friends, I have here a very unusual item, just brought in from abroad."

"What broad?" hollers the heckler in back. But Oscar gives him a nasty look and he shuts up.

"This is one of the rugs Mrs. Bobo Grope buys on her last trip to the East. It does not arrive until after her death, so I cannot tell you its history. It is not unwrapped but will be sold sight unseen in its original condition. I can assure you it is a very fine piece, because of the elaborate way in which it has been wrapped and crated. Yet I am willing to let it go to the highest bidder to expedite this sale."

Oscar holds up the roll of carpet, tied together at the ends by wire, and waves it around.

"What am I offered?"

"Two bits," yells a guy at my right.

Oscar glares. "Two bits? I am insulted. Who knows what this precious bundle contains? Remember—Cleopatra herself comes rolled up in a rug when she visits Anthony. Perhaps she is hiding inside."

"In that case, fifty cents," says the heckler. "Though I prefer Gene Tierney."

"Fifty cents!" snorts Oscar. "Why, this rug maybe is worth thousands for all we know. Mrs. Bobo Grope pays plenty of money for her rugs. She has plenty of filthy lucre."

"I don't care if she is a filthy looker. I don't care how she looks. I bid fifty cents!" snaps the heckler.

So I see I must do some shilling here. I bid a dollar. The heckler bids two. I come right back with three. He bids five. I have him going, so I bid seven. He bids eight. I shrug and bid ten.

"Ten dollars!" yells Oscar. "Do I hear more?"

I wait for the heckler. He is going to raise now. But—he doesn't.

All at once Oscar bangs his gavel.

"Sold for ten dollars," he shouts.

I just stand there with my mouth open. I never expect such a situation, at all. All at once I find out I just buy a lousy piece of carpet for ten dollars. It is awful.

But there is nothing else to do but go up to Oscar and take the rug. I give him ten dollars. Then I put my shoe back on.

"Double-crosser!" I whisper under my breath.

"Sorry," Oscar tells me. "But who knows? Maybe you really got something there."

"Sure. I get a backache carrying home this hunk of burlap," I answer. And I pick up the heavy rug and march out, burning up.

I am still smouldering when I hit the sidewalk. So much so that I do not notice a guy coming in and he runs smack into me at the doorway. I stumble and almost drop my rug.

He turns around.

"Please pardon," he says.

I am all set to give him a few hot remarks when I take another look. I see he just climbs out of a big limousine, about half a block long. So I modify my remarks before I open my mouth. I look again and realize he is a pretty old pickle. Quite a pappy guy, with a long white beard hanging down to his waist. So I modify my remarks still further and finally come out with, "Don't give me the bump, chump."

He gives me the old eye and I suddenly get a shivering spell. Because he has a pair of very dark peepers with a glare in them like the neon lights on a funeral home. Those eyes are now boring a hole right through what I am carrying.

"You attend the auction inside?" he asks, very fast.

I admit it.

"Is it very far along?" he questions, excited.

I tell him yes, nearly everything is sold by now.

Pappy jumps up and down on the sidewalk when he hears this. He almost falls on his face or vice-versa, only his beard is tangled up in my coat and it holds him up.

"Tell me I'm not too late," he gasps. I realize he must be one of the big collectors Oscar tells me about, who get the wrong announcements.

"What about the rugs?" he yells to me.

"I am afraid the rugs are going now," I answer. "In fact, I purchase a couple yards of oriental cheese-cloth myself."

Pappy's face turns a rich purple, which looks very nice with his white beard. He hops up and down, almost pulling off my coat.

"Ten thousand dancing demons," he yells. "I may be too late to find it! Out of my way, by the high-hung, hammered, heated, hissing hot hinges of hell!"

And he tears through the door into the auction, almost knocking my rug out of my arms.

I shrug, and then I start to lug and tug. Carrying that rug home is a mean job. I walk along trying to remember that swell curse the old boy gives out with, because right now I am in a cursing mood. To make it worse, I cannot even seem to hang on to the rug properly. It is all the time slipping down under my arm, hanging down in front or wriggling out behind. With the result that I am tripping over the curb and walking sideways, and making very slow progress.

That is how Out-of-Business Oscar manages to catch up with me before I get home.

I hear feet clicking behind me; somebody running very fast. And along comes Oscar, his face purple just like the old pappy who bumps into me.

"Oscar," I say, surprised. "I figure you are auctioning. What brings you here?"

"My conscience," Oscar gets out, puffing for breath. "Feep, I realize I play you a dirty trick when I make you take that rug. After all, you are working for me, and can you help it if the bidding goes wrong? It bothers me so much I have to drop everything and come after you. The thought of my misdeed stabs me to the quick. To the quick."

Now I do not know what Oscar's quick is, which he is being stabbed to, but I get interested right away. Oscar has me by the collar and his left hand grabs for the rug.

"I am going to give you your ten dollars back, Feep," he says. "Is that square?"

Well, it sounds square to me, and that is just what is wrong with it. Coming from a personality like Oscar, it should be crooked.

So I stall a little.

"Maybe I don't want to sell," I say.

Oscar's face gets almost black.

"You must," he begs. "This is on my conscience. It touches my heart."

Then I know he is lying. Because Oscar has no conscience, and his heart is so hard nothing can touch it except a pneumatic drill.

"I will keep the rug for my room," I say. "It will cover up the cigarette butts."

Oscar splutters. "I know how you feel and I don't blame you at all. Just to make it up for all your trouble, I'll give you fifteen dollars for it."

"No," I answer.

"Twenty."

Right then and there I get the score. Somebody else wants to buy this rug at a higher price, and Oscar thinks he can get it away from me. So I just shake my head and keep on going.

"This rug is not for sale," I yell. "And that's that!"

Oscar wails, but I ignore him and walk away. Now I can hardly wait to get home. I wonder just what kind of a rag this rug is. I remember Oscar telling about how Cleopatra comes rolled up in a rug, and I can just imagine unrolling it and seeing Lana Turner bounce out. Or anyway, something valuable and rare.

When I climb the stairs to my room I get another idea. Perhaps somebody hides gold or jewels in the rug roll. Maybe some Arabs smuggle diamonds out of the country in it. Who can tell? The carpet is heavy enough, and it is tied up very tight indeed. I am very eager to open it up.

But just as I open the door, there is a rush on the stairs and who comes running up but the old pappy guy.

"Wait just another moment," he hollers. "You are Mr. Lefty Feep?"

"That's the name of same," I admit.

"Oscar directs me here," he wheezes. "It is quite important."

"Who are you?" I ask.

"You read English? Here's my card—don't bend it," says the old fuddy. I take the card and read the name:

BLACK ART
Thaumaturgist

"What is this, a gag?" I ask. "In the first place, you are not black, and in the second place what is a thaumaturgist—some kind of chiropractor?"

He gives me a little bow and a smile.

"I admit it is all a little unusual," he tells me. "But you see, a thaumaturgist is a magician. And Black Art is really a very appropriate name."

"Well, I got no time to see any card tricks," I answer. "So if you will excuse me, I must go inside and milk a goat."

He holds up his hand, and I see those deep red eyes of his burning at me again.

"Don't be a fool," he says, in a real soft voice, like a dentist's drill. "I am not a conjuror. I am a sorcerer. An evocator. An enchanter. A goetist. A geomancer."

"Calling yourself names won't help any, buddy," I tell him. But I am really impressed. It is dark in the hallway and here is this old man with his red eyes shining at me and his long skinny claws scrabbling at my coat.

"I want to buy your rug," he whispers.

"What, another?"

"Believe me, it is most important to me that I obtain it. I need it and I am prepared to pay well. I offer five hundred dollars."

"Five hundred—"

"A thousand, then. Money is no object. A thousand dollars for that rug!"

"Sears should see me," I whisper. "I can be a star salesman."

But I am doing some quick figuring. First, Oscar wants to buy it back, and then this Black Art. Maybe they are both crazy. And then again—Oscar tells the crowd that this rug is wrapped up and shipped in and nobody sees it. He says Mrs. Bobo Grope pays big money for her stuff. Maybe the rug is worth the money. Maybe it is worth a lot more.

I think of the gold and jewels that might be hid away in it. I think about Cleopatra. And then I turn to Black Art and shake my head.

"No, I do not sell this rug," I tell him.

"Two thousand," he hisses.

"No."

It is very hard for me to say no this time. Two thousand is a very convincing argument, and his two eyes are also quite convincing. They glare at me, and when they look at the rug they are *hungry*.

"Come back some other time," I manage to say. "I must think it over."

"Very well, Mr. Feep. But Black Art is not to be foiled, I warn you! I shall get that rug, sooner or later."

And he beats it down the stairs.

I beat it indoors. Now I'm almost crazy to open this carpet up. I throw it on the floor and run into the closet to hang up my hat and coat. It is very dusty in the closet and I am coughing and clearing my eyes when I come out.

I look at the rug on the floor and then I rub my eyes some more.

Because the wires at the end of the rug are snapped.

I can swear they are tied a minute ago when I throw it down, but now they are untied. Thick wires, too. And the rug lies there.

I rush over and unroll it. Very careful, inch by inch, so if there are any jewels or coins wrapped inside I will not miss them.

But there is nothing there. I unroll the rug completely and it stretches across the floor. I stare at it.

What do I see?

A platinum border with jewels in the pattern? A gold fringe on a silver carpet? A solid weave made out of ten-dollar bills and war bonds?

No.

I see a dirty, dingy old hunk of burlap I wouldn't use to cover the floor of a hen-coop. It is torn and ragged on the edges. The fringes are raveled and there is a pattern running through it that looks like a map of Hitler's retreat in Russia, and twice as messy.

And I refuse two thousand dollars for the thing!

I let out a whoop and hit myself on the forehead in rage. In fact, I hit myself quite a solid smack, and it knocks me so groggy I reel over to the washstand to put cold water on my noggin.

This I do, cursing under my breath and under the faucet. Then I wipe my head off and turn around again, feeling better.

But one look tells me I am still groggy. Worse.

I stare down at the rug I unroll on the floor. Only I do not have to stare *very far* down.

Because the rug is floating.

Floating in midair!

That dirty old hunk of carpet, that hotel for Persian fleas, is floating around in the air, about a foot off the floor.

I just stand there with my mouth open, showing my

adenoids and tonsils. Then I sneeze, because a cloud of dust rises from the rug while it swoops across the floor.

The damned thing is alive!

All at once I remember how it slips out from under my arm all the time I carry it, and how the wires break open of their own accord, and now I understand. The rug is alive. It moves by itself!

I am so upset I watch it without doing anything for a minute. And it floats up, moves over toward the open window. It is going out the window!

"No you don't," I remark, hurling myself across the floor and giving it the flying tackle. No rug worth two thousand dollars is going to run off and leave me, even if it floats like Ivory Soap. I bring the rug down and hold it against the floor.

I pant for a minute, because it is a long time since I do a flying tackle, not running around with jitterbug girls any more. The rug sort of wriggles under me, like a big snake.

I reach over and grab a floor lamp and put it down on the carpet, anchoring it to the floor. Then I haul a chair over to hold it, and stick the fringes under the bedpost legs.

The rug thumps to the floor and lies still. I get off and stoop over to take another look. But it doesn't seem any different. It is still a dingy rag, all dirty and torn. I watch it, see it is quiet, and slip the lamp and chair off it. Then I squat down on it and try to scrape away the dirt to see if I can find some kind of pattern underneath which tells me what it is supposed to be.

All I get is a mouthful of dust. I sneeze again, and my temper blows out right through my nose.

"Blast the whole business," I yell. "I wish I do not get mixed up in such messes—why can't I be enjoying myself at a nice crap game at Gorilla Gabface's joint instead?"

All of a sudden there is a terrible wind blowing. I look around to see if I am still sneezing, but no. I am not making this wind. The rug is.

K.
D.

Because the rug is moving. And I am sitting on top of it!

This time we sail right for the open window, and through it. In another second, I am whizzing along through the air over the street, riding on the rug!

"Put me down!" I yell. But the wind chokes the voice right out of me. And before I can holler again, there is something caught in my throat. My heart.

Because we are zooming across the sky, over the streets and houses, and when I figure the speed I just lie down on my face and close my eyes. A second later I feel an awful thump and I know we are crashing. So I open my eyes and sit up.

The first thing I look for is broken bones. But there are no broken bones. In fact, there are no bones at all—except two. These two bones are rolling right on the floor next to me. A four and a three.

Because when I open my eyes, I am sitting in the back room of Gorilla Gabface's pool hall, watching a crap game!

Here is an item for Ripley. I sit on the rug, wish I was at a crap game at Gorilla's joint, and the rug flies me there!

I look up, still confused, and see we come in through the open skylight. We come in very quiet, too, because nobody notices us, the rug and I.

They are all kneeling in a knot around the game on the floor—four of them, including Gorilla Gabface himself. And in front of them is a pile of lettuce big enough to choke Rockefeller. So it is no wonder they are too interested in the game to see me make my three-point landing.

I am very shaky, but I am beginning to understand a few things about the rug now. Why this Black Art the magician wants to buy it, and why it is such an unusual item. So I roll it up very tight under my arm before I move over to the game and introduce myself.

"Well, if it isn't Lefty Feep!" yells Gabface. "Another dog come to rattle these bones, I presume?"

Which means I am in the game.

Now I am very fond of African polo myself, in fact it is a

sort of a passion with me. And I am indeed eager to rattle the ivories. But I do not wish to lose this rug of mine, either, and it is such a tricky gadget I cannot figure out where to park it, without a horse-anchor. Then I get an idea.

"I would dearly love to play marbles with you gentlemen," I say to these rats. "But I wish you to humor me a bit. I have here a piece I call my lucky carpet. I desire we should all shoot craps on its surface. Besides," I add, courteously, "I do not like to see you all kneeling on the bare floor this way. It is undignified, and it wrecks the knees of your trousers."

So they let me unroll the carpet and we all kneel down and I get the dice in my hands and begin to make like castanets with them.

In a very short while I have enough lettuce in front of me to make a full-size Victory Garden, and I am very happy.

Every time I place the dice down I get either a seven or an eleven, and every point I roll I make.

I suppose this is all very technical talk to you, if you do not understand the intricate technique of shooting craps, but the idea is, I win a lot of money.

This does not please the others a small bit. Finally, when Gorilla Gabface gets the dice, he is very irate, having lost about two hundred berries. He grabs up the cubes in the oversize catcher's mitt he calls a hand and shakes them until the spots come loose.

"Now roll, curse you," he remarks, in a voice like thunder. But the storm breaks when he lets go of the dice and gets snake eyes—which means he loses. He picks up the dice again, very displeased, and they make a noise in his hand like a couple of skeletons doing calisthenics on a tin roof during a hailstorm.

"Come on," he chants. "Get going. *Off to Buffalo.*"

That does it.

I make a mistake when I do not warn him in time. But it is too late now.

Because when he says "Off to Buffalo," the rug rises up with a bounce and we are through the skylight. But quickly.

There is yelling and screaming and howling. All five of us get pitched forward into the center of the carpet, and we tangle up our arms and legs. Maybe it takes a minute, maybe it takes ten. Meanwhile, we are howling through the night. And when I finally manage to get my head out from under that pile of jerking bodies, I look down at the ground and what do I see?

Niagara Falls!

We are off to Buffalo, all right!

We land about a minute later, right on the edge of town, in a vacant parking lot.

It is a moonless night, and I am glad, because if anybody sees us coming down the anti-aircraft will get busy in very short order. As it is, I have enough trouble explaining things to Gorilla Gabface and his pals. They are naturally flabber from gasted.

So I tell them the story.

"Jeez!" remarks a character name of Dime-Mouth McCarthy, who is a scholarly type. "What youse got is probably that there Magic Carpet like in them Arabian Nights."

"Magic Carpet?" I say, while the idea suddenly clicks in the old brain.

"Sure," says Dime-Mouth. "A flying carpet, see? What them there oriental rug-cutters use to cruise around for a quick getaway. Just the thing to keep in the parlor for a powder, see? I always figure it is one of these here missological things, but youse can see I am wrong. On accounta here it is. And there we are."

The other lugs listen to Dime-Mouth's explanation and shake their heads, trying to calm down.

"Now what do we do?" asks Gorilla Gabface.

"Maybe we can get it to take us back to town," Dime-Mouth suggests. "It don't cost nothing to try. There ain't no meter on it. If I was youse, Feep, I'd beat it back to the house in a hurry and wait for the customer to show up. He will pay big money for a rug like this."

"Yes, but why?" I ask. "What use has he got for it?"

"Very simple," Dime-Mouth tells me. "He shows up in a big limousine, doesn't he? That's it. He wants to put the car away and use the flying rug during the tire shortage."

This sounds logical to me, so we all hop back on the carpet.

"I wish to be back at Gorilla Gabface's," I say, very loud. And the rug swirls around, takes off, and we are on our way.

This time nobody is quite so frightened. Me, I am even getting used to traveling by air, so I look down on all the scenery as we pass, and in no time at all we are coming down into the street. Gorilla Gabface nearly gets his head knocked off when we skim under the telephone wires, but outside of that there is no trouble. The rug steers itself perfectly, and we sail through the skylight and land without even a bump.

The minute we are all landed, they crowd around me and begin to make with the brains. The whole gang is loaded with schemes.

"Why don't youse open a travel bureau?" suggests Dime-Mouth.

"Nuts to that. Use the rug for a taxi," says Gorilla Gabface.

Somebody else suggests sight-seeing tours over the town. And naturally, there is a shifty-faced little rat in the crowd who comes out with a proposition to smuggle liquor.

This I turn down, of course, pointing out that it is not only dishonest, but also that there isn't enough room on the rug to carry much alky on a trip.

Besides, I do not wish to get myself all involved with these oafs on any deals, until I figure out this situation for myself. I have a Flying Carpet. It is such a matter as requires thought. I do not wish to go for a fly-by-night scheme.

So in the end I pop back onto the rug and say, "Home,

James." The rug lifts me back out of the skylight and I fly through the air with the greatest of ease.

All the way home I wreck my brains trying to figure out what to do about all this. But when I finally glide in through the open window and land, a new problem arises.

It arises from the chair in my room, where it is sitting. And its name is Black Art, the thaumaturgist.

He stands there giving me the glare and stare when I come down. I flash him a weak smile and anchor the rug under the bedposts again, trying to act like nothing happens.

But it is no use. He can see what the score is.

"So," he greets me. "You know the secret."

I nod.

He shrugs, lifting his beard up and twisting the end. "Too bad. For years I search for the magic carpet in vain. I haunt the *souks* of Ispahan, Teheran, Damascus, Alepo. I comb the bazaars from here to Hyderabad. Agents of mine are on the trail of the fabulous Flying Carpet.

"And in the end, a silly woman, this Mrs. Bobo Grope, stumbles on the prize by accident. She buys it as part of a lot consignment, never dreaming that she is acquiring the legendary rug of oriental fable. She dies. And a stupid auctioneer raffles it off to a witless lout."

"You are wrong about that, pal," I correct. "I buy this rug myself."

He smiles. "Well, let it pass. The important thing is that you now know the true value of this carpet. And I am again prepared to offer you a good price. Shall we say—ten thousand dollars?"

Now, there is nothing I rather hear somebody say than "ten thousand dollars." It is a very cute phrase and tickles my ears. But I am still playing my hunch, so I stall.

"Why is this rug worth ten grand to you?" I ask. "If you are one of these wizards like you claim, what do you need with a flying rug? The way I hear it, you guys can do almost anything you want."

Black Art sits down again and sighs. The wind ruffles his white beard. Then he sighs again and tears come into his eyes. He pulls up the end of his beard and wipes them away. Then he blows his nose.

"Being a wizard isn't so easy," he moans. "It is a terrible life. If you know how hard it is for me to get along, you would have pity on me and give me the rug."

"Don't sluff me that guff," I answer. "Wizards can do anything."

"You are wrong," says Black Art. "Maybe I can make you understand if I tell you my secret."

"Your secret?"

"Yes," Black Art whispers. "You see, I am the son of a witch."

"Don't tell me."

"It is true," he sighs. "And I wonder if you know what it means? To be born in a horrible little cottage way off in the woods. Without the comforts of a city home, without a furnace, without plumbing. Never to have a father. Never to have any other kids to play with. Just sit in this awful cottage all day long, with the horrid smell of sulphur and brimstone in the house.

"Your mother is always brewing up stuff on the fire—big cauldrons of herbs and awful messes that stink up the place. She brews so many philtres she doesn't have time to cook for you."

"I never have such an experience," I admit. "Though the way I remember it, Ma sometimes whips up some bathtub gin."

"That is different," Art sighs. "You don't have any toys to play with if you are the son of a witch. Just poppets—not dolls, but poppets. The little wax figures witches stick pins in. She gives them to you to play with and that's all. And that awful black cat—her familiar! If you pet it, it scratches you up in a jiffy.

"And then you are alone so much. She is always going out

to Black Sabbaths and stuff, and her broomstick is never in the corner. On May Eve and Halloween, and all times during the year you are left alone in that hideous cottage. One time I remember drinking some love-philtres as a boy, when left home alone. They only upset my stomach."

Black Art sighs again.

"That's my life," he goes on. "No school. I have to study books on sorcery and black magic every day. Cast spells and study horoscopes, learn awful subjects like anthropomancy and lithiomancy and divination. I work for years all alone. It is a dog's life. And when she dies, I am left to myself. Before I know it I am all mixed up with second mortgages to the Devil and a lot of legal stuff. I inherit nothing but a bunch of debts to demons. And I am already an old man before my time.

"Look at me—look at my wrinkles and beard! Do I look like a young and happy man? Do I look as though I enjoy practicing magic powers?"

He starts crying, and my own eyes are a little misty. It does sound terrible. Imagine this poor enchanter—probably never even gets to see a floor show or play a juke box or do anything with culture!

"Then to make it worse, I find out I cannot even attend the Black Sabbath. On account of Ma falling down and busting her broomstick when she dies.

"You know what this means to a wizard? It means disgrace! It is like not attending union meetings or paying lodge dues. If I do not show up at least once a year at Sabbath meetings, I am all washed up."

Then he explains to me about these Black Sabbaths, which are stag parties for witches and wizards. Sort of a picnic, like, only just a little wilder. They all get together on a hilltop or mountain over in Europe someplace and dance around for a while and talk shop. Then the Big Boss shows up and pitchforks around and gives them their orders for the coming year.

And this is what upsets Black Art so much.

Without the broomstick to ride on, he cannot get to his Sabbath. And there is one coming up pretty soon, on Halloween.

"What about a plane?" I ask.

"Don't be foolish! In the past, I travel by plane or boat. But with this war going on—how can I get to Europe? Or the Hartz Mountains? Priorities fix it so I cannot even buy a private plane for myself, let alone get booked as a passenger. And that is why I need your Flying Carpet. That is why I search for it. It is the one means of transportation left to me—and unless I get to this Sabbath, it will be all up with me. All down, rather. Because the Big Boss has a nasty habit of disposing of we wizards when he is not obeyed."

Well, this song and dance he hands me has me all softened up. I figure I might as well take ten grand and let the carpet go. What good is it, anyway? And if he has to get to this Black Sabbath of his—

"But just what arrangement have you got with the Big Boss?" I ask.

Black Art smiles. "I see you are clever," he mumbles. "So I will not conceal it from you. I am anxious to attend this Sabbath in particular, because it is my only chance to see the Big Boss. And if I can see him I am going to make a deal that will give me tremendous power. If you wish, you and I can share it together.

"Because you *are* right, Feep. A wizard *can* have anything he desires—if he will pay the price. You know what that price is. Your soul. You have a soul, haven't you, Feep?"

"I guess so."

"Good. I still have mine, too." Black Art chuckles. He is not so sad now, and the chuckle is something to hear. "Yes, even though I owe the Big Boss a number of debts, I still have my soul to bargain for. And I shall make a bargain."

It is pretty dark in my room, but Black Art's eyes are shining very bright. His teeth gleam, too. Somehow I would feel better if I don't see them so well. They bother me. So does his chuckling voice.

"Yes, and what a bargain it will be! Because I want power, Feep. Great power. Now, in a time of war, there will be new chances to rise, to rule. Imagine a wizard, with a knowledge of spells and enchantments, capturing control of entire nations! Ruling armies! Directing destinies!

"I, who haunt in darkness, who must study and pore over musty tomes, waste my life as I do, am sick of sitting in the shadows. I want to rule. And the time is now.

"There is a man in Europe, Feep. A sick, neurotic, half-crazed man, who believes in magic. In astrology, and the stars. He is always willing to listen, to be guided by those who profess to be sorcerers. Fakes. But I am no charlatan. I want to get to that man—make him believe in me. Make myself his master. Give him orders and see that he obeys.

"That is the kind of bargain I am going to make at the Sabbath, Feep! Now do you understand why I must get there? Now do you see why I want your carpet?"

I see all right, and I do not like it a little bit.

"It is no dice, buddy," I tell him. "I still am not selling the rug."

Black Art stands up. I never notice how tall he is before—how nasty he looks in his long black coat. He points a skinny finger at me.

"You dare to refuse, you miserable lout? Why, it means riches for you! You have nothing here—sitting in this dirty, dingy little room. I wouldn't keep a pig in this filthy sty."

"Get out, then!" I holler. And push him over to the door.

"I'll be back!" he yells. But I slam the door on his beard, and it is all he can do to tug it out and bounce down the stairs.

I am really burned up now. I do not mind him suggesting a foul deal like he does, but when he tells me I live in a crummy dump, I get very angry.

Because I know only too well I *do* live in a crummy dump,

and something inside me tells me I am a fool not to take his ten thousand. Only I'd rather be a fool than a rat.

Still and all, my temper is ruined. It is late, and I must get some shut-eye, so I undress for bed. Just before I climb in, I remember the rug. I do not wish it to fly away on me, so I grab it off the floor and stick it in the closet and lock the door on it. The closet is so dusty I start to cough again and this makes me madder still.

I lie in bed and burn up. What a day! I get hooked into buying a rug, I get a reputation for being some kind of a screwball with all my friends, and a crazy magician comes around and threatens me.

Maybe he will show up again with some phony trick or other. But I do not think so. Anyhow, that is a problem for tomorrow.

So at last I fall asleep.

And I have a nightmare.

In the nightmare it is the next morning. I am waking up when I hear a knocking at the door. I sit up and ask, "Who's there?"

And a voice says, "Black Art," and I say, "Shut up and go away, you bewhiskered baboon!"

Then I turn over and all at once I hear a rustling sound. I sit up again.

I stare at the door.

Something is oozing in through the keyhole. Something white, like fog. A little cloud of smoke. It trickles in very slow and swirls around. All at once it gets thicker. There is a burning red center to the fog. Deep red. And then I recognize it.

It is the color of Black Art's eyes. Deep red eyes. And all at once a face forms around the eyes. And the fog turns into a long white beard. Then a body.

Black Art is standing in my room!

"I will teach you not to thwart a wizard's desires!" he whispers.

Before I know it, he is over at the closet door. He opens it. I see him stooping over on the floor, scrabbling around. He picks up the rug. He comes out—

And then I do sit up in bed.

Because I am not dreaming. I am wide awake, and Black Art is stealing the rug before my eyes!

"Hey, you carpet-goniff!" I holler.

He just turns and looks at me.

His red eyes stare. I stare back. And all at once I find out I can't look away. I am what you called hypnotized. I gawk at him like he was a chorus cutie instead of an old geezer with a long white beard.

"So," he whispers. "A wizard has powers. And you are not going to move. I am taking your rug, Feep. I have a flying trip to make to the Hartz Mountains. There is just time enough to make it."

He steps on the carpet and stands in front of the open window. I try to jerk my eyes away. All at once I do it. I jump out of bed.

Black Art smiles. One hand goes to his waist. I think he is pulling a rod on me, but no. He just lifts up his beard. I see underneath it. Hanging from his neck, hidden by the beard, is a very long, very sharp knife. He takes it out and waves it. I can see he is used to waving it.

"Do you like mince-meat?" he asks. "Well, that is what you will be if you come one step closer to me."

So I just stand there while he gets on the rug. He pulls his beard to one side like it was a handkerchief and waves goodbye.

"Well, I am off," he tells me. And then he stares at the rug and mumbles, "Hartz Mountains, please."

The rug gives a flap, and floats out the window.

I shiver myself out of it. There he goes. It is all over. My rug is gone, he is gone, and that deal is going through. There will be hell to pay—and I know who will pay it. All of us, if Black Art has his way.

And then, while I am standing there, I hear a thump.

It comes from just outside my window.

I rush over and look out.

There is a terrible crash from down below, and I stare at the back alley. Lying on the stones is Black Art. On top of him, like a shroud, is the Flying Carpet.

I am downstairs in three leaps. I pick Art up and phone for an ambulance. First I hide the rug. When the medicos get there I tell them he falls out of the window—and after one look at the body, they believe me.

And when they go away I take a look at the rug again.

Then I understand what happens. I take another look at my closet and get the whole story straight.

For the first time in my life, I thank my lucky stars that Black Art is right when he says I live in a dirty old dump.

Because that is the one thing that saves us all from the bargain Black Art wants to make.

Of course, the rug is no good any more since it does not fly, and I throw it in the ash heap. But maybe it is just as well the way things work out. I get a bicycle to travel by, anyway.

I SAT BACK in my seat with a frown. "Sounds like you have a pretty close call there, Lefty," I admitted. "But—"

Feep gave me a sour look.

"You and your 'Buts.' Always something bothering you, friend! Well—what is it this time?"

"Nothing," I said. "Nothing at all. Only, you see, I can't figure out what it was that made the Flying Carpet fall down and kill the wizard. It always flew before, didn't it?"

"Yes."

"So why did it fall?"

"That is my lucky break, Bob," Feep said. "Like I said, if I take the ten thousand dollars, I never get rid of this Black Art and he goes out and does his dirty work. It is pure luck that I refuse and he gets bumped off."

"How do you figure that?"

"Well—if I take the ten thousand, I move out of my room, into a better apartment. And you know what a dump I live in. All dirty and dusty. And if I am not in my dirty and dusty apartment, then I do not put my rug overnight into the dirty and dusty closet, and it does not get fixed there so that it will not fly any more."

"You mean keeping that rug in the closet overnight killed Black Art when he used it?"

"Sure. That is the lucky break. Because of what happens in the closet to the rug—what gets into it to make it fall down."

"All right, Feep. Just what did get into the Flying Carpet?"

"Moths!" said Lefty Feep.

AFTER WORDS

STANLEY: *This Black Art character . . . He's bazaar. There's a tragic touch about him as he describes the trials and travails of being a witch's offspring. And he introduces the line "I'll be back," which of course was borrowed by Arnold Schwarzenegger for* "The Terminator."

BLOCH: I recall that Black Art is a character who comes from *In the Land of the Sky Blue Ointments*. He's a character I used extensively. In fact, I put him in a little section about a traveling salesman and later excerpted that section to be printed in a fan magazine under the title, "The Traveling Salesman." And twenty years later that story was in *Playboy* under the same title. So Black Art has been around. And undoubtedly I'll make use of him again in the future.

JS: *There are references to "a sick, neurotic, half-crazed man who believes in magic." Obviously, Black Art is hoping* to meet Adolf Hitler. Wouldn't it have been extraordinary if he had, and Lefty Feep had been there?

BLOCH: Three of a kind . . .

JS: *We now come to the Lefty Feep story in which you have your head in the clouds . . .*

In which Lefty Feep hears and fears a tall seedy tale about a spry guy who uses his bean to stalk a growing mystery. A story that lays an egg more than once and harps repeatedly at the reader.

JERK THE GIANT KILLER

I WAS SITTING at my usual place in the usual booth of the usual restaurant the other night, when Lefty Feep made his unusual entrance.

At first I didn't notice anything out of the way about him. His face still looked like a fugitive from a pair of moosehorns. His suit was as gaudy as ever, and his necktie spilled over the front of his shirt like a raspberry sundae.

Then, as Mr. Feep slid into a seat across from me, I noticed the difference. "No cuff on your trousers," I remarked.

Lefty Feep nodded.

"From now on the only cuffs I get will be about the head," he grinned. "And at that, I do not think she will catch me. In fact, I am sure of it."

"Who?" I asked.

Feep shrugged. I let it go at that. Some aspects of his private life won't stand close scrutiny. If he chooses to live as a one-man matrimonial bureau, it's his business.

"No," Feep continued. "No cuffs for me—on trousers or hands. This is the new Victory Suit."

"Looks like it's been through some pretty gory battles," I said. "Such a color scheme! It certainly isn't camouflaged."

Feep pouted.

"Do not criticize," he said. "I merely do my part for the war effort. I give up my cups, I bust my record of *The Japanese Sandman*, and I spend my dough for bonds instead of blondes."

"Very patriotic."

"Oh, it is nothing," Feep sighed. "I only wish I can do something really fine, like my friend Jack does."

"Jack? Jack who?"

"I do not know his last name," said Lefty Feep. "We just call him Jack because he never has any."

"Poverty-stricken, eh?" I observed. "But what can a poor man do that's really going to aid the war effort?"

A gleam kindled in Feep's eye. I shuddered, because I knew what was coming.

"It is quite a story," he murmured. "I know you will be happy to hear all about it."

"Sorry," I gasped. "I have a heavy date."

"Never mind your fat girl friend," snarled Feep. "This is such a tale as does not come your way every day in the week."

"Thank God!"

"What's that? Well, never mind. I will tell you the story just as I hear it from Jack when I run into him the other day."

Lefty Feep's tongue shot out of his mouth, and we were off. Way, way off.

THIS GUY JACK (began Lefty Feep) is what you might call a very down-and-out personality. He is down because he is only five feet tall and he is generally out about two hundred dollars to the bookies.

About a year ago he gets so far out that he is living in the suburbs—Pennsylvania, in fact. Maybe he goes there for the cool climate, because it is pretty hot for him around town.

The next time I see him Jack tells me he gets married. This does not surprise me, because Jack always has a soft spot for women—in his head.

The dame he hitches up with is in the neighborhood of six feet tall, which is quite a neighborhood to be in for a guy of Jack's stature. In addition, she is built along the lines that Longfellow thinks of when he writes *The Village Blacksmith.*

But it turns out she owns a little farm in the Pennsylvania hills, and so that is where Jack now lives.

Just about this time the war breaks out and everybody is talking about the defense effort. Jack is very patriotic, like I say. He is willing to do his part. In no time at all, he drives into one of the towns around there, steps up to the employment office and gets his wife a job in the mills.

The war comes closer, and even this is not enough for Jack. He goes to another mill and gets his wife a night-shift job as well.

"We must work night and day," he tells her. And then a star-spangled gleam comes into his eye, and he says, "My only regret is that I have but one wife to give to my country."

So you see how it is with Jack. His wife goes to work and he stays home and tends to the farm. Not a day passes but he is doing something—like carving his initials in a tree, very fancy, or decorating the porch with some beautiful fishing flies. A great fellow to brighten up the place is Jack—in fact, he is almost always lit up.

For some reason or other, dames being funny like they are, this does not altogether please his partner in matrimoaning.

One morning she comes home from the night shift in order to cook the meals before she goes back to work on the day shift, and she is feeling very cranky. It seems that Jack cooks up some overtime for her at another plant.

"Listen, you lazy bum," she says—it pains me to use such vulgar language, but that is the way this coarse woman phrases it—"I want you to do some work around this place. Here I am, day and night, working my fingers to the bone over a hot blast-furnace, and you sit around the house and loaf. You do not even sew the buttons on my overalls. What kind of a husband are you, anyway?"

In order that Jack does not miss any of this lecture, she picks him up and holds his ear next to her mouth. Now she drops him down on the floor again in such a rude fashion that Jack cannot even answer her last $64 question.

But this does not matter.

"Go upstairs and clean out the attic today," she says. "It is time for spring planting, and you will find all the seeds up there that Papa saves when he comes here from the old country."

"I should go out in the dirty fields and plant seeds?"

"By tomorrow morning one thing or the other will be planted—the seeds or you," says his wife.

And she grabs up her lunch pail and storms out.

So, poor Jack picks himself up off the floor and hauls his hips way up to the attic. Of course, after such a walk, he has to sit down and rest a while. Which he does, stretching out on the sacks of seeds up there.

He lies there looking at all the big bags, and the more he looks the more discouraged he gets. Some of them weigh fifty or a hundred pounds. And he cannot imagine himself carrying a hundred-pound sack a mile out into the fields and then dumping it.

You see, Jack is not a farmer, he just bets like one. And he does not understand the first thing about crops like the local yokels do. He is strictly an uptown boy, and the only way he knows how to raise corn is in a bottle.

So he is very discouraged, but when he thinks about his wife he is even more discouraged. Finally he gets up and starts to haul the bags around. He is looking for the smallest sack he can find.

He stirs up a lot of dust—because these things are up in the attic now for many a year, ever since papa kicks off after coming from the old country. But in the middle of his wheezes and sneezes, Jack finds a very tiny leather pouch, way at the bottom of the piles.

He figures at first maybe it is only tobacco, but when he shakes it he knows it is seeds, all right.

"That's the sack for me," he decides. He puts it in his pocket and goes downstairs.

On the way down he accidentally finds some very nice fishing tackle in the closet next to the stairs, and he figures he might as well stop by the creek on the way to plant the seeds.

Well, one thing leads to another, and one road leads to the creek, and then one fish leads to a string. So when Jack sits up and takes notice, it is after dark.

His wife will be coming home from the day shift and making supper before going back on the night shift. So Jack realizes he must get back to the house in order to grab some grub.

He gallops across the fields and then he remembers the seeds. It is too dark to see, and too late to waste time. He stops, scuffs a little hole in the ground with his fishing rod, and pours a handful of seeds into it.

At least this gives him the old alibi that he actually does some planting today. So he puts the rest of the seeds back in the pouch and trots home.

When his wife asks him if he engages in any agriculture, he answers yes. So she goes to work that night very happy because Jack reforms this way. And Jack goes to bed very happy for the same reason.

The next morning, when the Former Farmer gets up, he forgets all about it. Today he figures on going back to the creek, because the fish are biting faster than a crowd of relatives at Thanksgiving dinner.

Right after breakfast he tackles his tackle and does a sneak to the creek.

On the way he crosses over the fields again. At least, he crosses part way.

But he does not get any farther. Because right smack in

the middle of the last field, down away in the valley, hidden from the house and road, is this plant.

When Jack sees it, his lower jaw drops so far he can rest his shoes on it.

The plant just sticks right up out of the ground. How far is hard to tell, because Jack cannot see the top. It is all made of green stalks, but it is not a tree. Jack looks up to the branches, but all he sees is clouds.

It is a sort of a horticultural Empire State Building, if you know what I mean, and if you do please tell me.

Anyhow, such a sight in a bare field is very unusual. Jack pats his hip, feels that the flask is still full, and pinches himself to find that he is awake. He takes another look.

"What kind of seeds do I plant, anyhow?" he wonders. "Possibly they come from some mail-order catalogue. That is the only place where things grow so big."

The more he looks at the big tall stalks on the plant, the hotter he gets to find out what it is.

"Maybe if I shinny up a ways I can see the top and find out if this is a plant for peas, or potatoes, or rhubarb," he decides.

So Jack drops his fishing tackle and grabs hold of a big tough stalk and boosts himself up. He climbs very easily, because there is plenty to hang on to. Before he notices it, he is way up out of this world, and the air is getting thin. But still he is not at the top.

He climbs a little higher, stopping now and then to rest. The further he goes, the more anxious he gets to figure out what kind of a vegetable he raises.

Pretty soon he is so high he is afraid to look down at the ground. But he is now very far away from the good earth.

This is certain, because he is getting quite damp from tangling with a cloud.

A minute later he is damp inside as well as outside, from tangling with his flask. But he needs strength, where he is.

Soon there are clouds all around him. He has to take

another nip. He wants very much to get down now, but he cannot see his feet any more. There is nothing to do but keep climbing up.

Which he does, hauling away with his hands until he gets them blistered, and hauling away at the flask until his lips are blistered, too.

"I am thankful for one thing," he mutters. "Imagine how big this thing grows if I put fertilizer on it last night."

All at once the clouds start to thin away. He goes about the distance of the Washington Monument and he is in the open. In fact, he is reaching the top of the plant.

Only the top is not exactly what he expects to see. There is no raw vegetable dinner waiting up there. No beets, no succotash, no cauliflowers, no tomatoes, no spinach.

Instead, the top of the plant goes right through a hole in the clouds, and when Jack crawls through this hole he is on solid ground!

"So this is China," says Jack, getting a little mixed up in his geography—to say nothing of the flask. But there he is, and very glad to be standing on some firmer terra, too.

He looks around. The scenery is nothing much—just country, with a lot of hills. And there is a path running along a ways off.

When he gets his breath back in his lungs and his cork back in the bottle, he is about as high as the scenery. He decides he might as well amble down this path and see what the score is.

So he walks along. Not exactly in a straight line, but he gets places.

Before you know it, or he knows it, he is going up the path to a big stone apartment house on a hill. At least it looks like an apartment house to Jack, but when he gets a closer glimmer at the turrets and all, he knows it is nothing but a castle. A genuine castle, stuck right out here in the hills!

Jack knows that there is only one explanation for a castle standing out on a country road—it must be a filling station.

So he footsies up to the door, wondering where the gasoline pumps are.

The door is open, and all at once he notices somebody is standing there in the entrance.

This turns out to be nothing less than a very pretty filet of femininity—a little red-headed ginch, with enough curves to strike out DiMaggio.

"Greetings," says the ginch, just as if Jack is expected. "Who art thou and from whence dost thou hail?"

Jack figures he is getting the old double-talk, see? But he is a very hep number, and always ready with a line.

"Why, I am a traveling salesman," he says. "And might you be the farmer's daughter?"

"I know no villiens, churls, nor peasantry," the ginch comes back. "I am the Lady Imogene, and this is the fief of my husband. And what," she coos, "might a traveling salesman be?"

"You don't know?" says Jack. "Well, well—"

He gives this Imogene ginch the old eye. And she smiles right back in a way which tells Jack that her husband isn't home. Probably out tending to his fiefs, or something.

Which suits Jack perfectly. In no time at all, he is inside this joint. It turns out to be a real castle, with sure-enough stone walls.

The whole place is terrifically big, like a downtown movie lobby, but what impresses Jack most is the size of all the furniture. The chairs are almost twenty feet high, and the tables even higher.

"Who is your husband—King Kong?" he asks.

"No. He is King Glimorgus," answers Imogene.

"Sounds like a dandruff remover," says Jack. And the ginch giggles.

She is throwing off plenty of smiles and such, and shows Jack around the joint very sweetly.

"I am glad you are here," she confesses. "I am so lonely."

"What does old Glimorgus do for a living?" asks Jack.

"Verily, he is a cattle tender."

"You mean he is out all day taking care of his herds?"

"Not exactly," simpers the ginch Imogene. "It is other people's cattle that he takes care of. Also he is a renowned sheep-raiser. He raises them from other people's land and carries them here."

"In other words, this husband of yours is no better than a thief," says Jack.

Imogene turns pale.

"Prithee, I implore you not to speak thusly in his presence. Such gibes make him exceedingly furious. And when he is furious, he is apt to become very angry. And being angry makes him mad."

"What you are trying to tell me is that he has a bad temper. I get it," says Jack. "Well, I do not wish to tangle with this cowboy husband of yours anyway. I would just as soon stay a stranger to this Lone Ranger."

"I grieve to hear you speak thusly, for King Glimorgus would like you."

"You don't say."

"Verily. He likes men."

"He does, eh?"

"Yes—with a little salt and pepper. Some he likes roasted and basted. Others he likes raw. Lean as you are, methinks he wouldst relish you in a fricassee."

Jack gulps.

"Pardon me, I got to catch the Chattanooga choo-choo," he gasps, diving for the door.

But Imogene grabs his arm.

"Tarry a while," she suggests. "I do not expect him for many an hour. And I promise, I shall not permit him to eat you." Here she gives out with another dreamy smile, and Jack wavers a little.

"Speaking of food," Imogene goes on, "methinks that after your travels you might be hungry. Wouldst do with a roast duck or two?"

"Wouldst do plenty," says Jack. "Lead me to it." Because he is really strictly from hunger.

So he follows the redhead into the kitchen, which is a huge place like all the other rooms. There is a terrific stone oven in the middle, and next to it stands an oversized table and some big chairs.

The ginch Imogene helps Jack climb up into one of these seats, and he sits there looking like a brat in a high-chair while she fusses around the oven with a couple quackers she is going to roast for him.

Jack is plenty curious to find out more about this setup, which strikes him as more fun than usual.

"Isn't it a little trying to live with this nee and derthal?" he asks.

"I fail to comprehend."

"I mean, aren't you afraid of Hannibal the Cannibal?"

"You mean King Glimorgus, my husband?" laughs the ginch. "But pray what must I fear?"

"Well, you tell me his diet is a riot. So I figure maybe he will gobble you up between meals."

Imogene smiles and shakes her head.

"He needs me to cook for him," she explains. "Truly, were I gone, the servant problem here wouldst be most vexing."

"I can understand that all right," Jack agrees. "But still, if he is a brutal type like you say, it is a wonder he does not beat up on you all the time."

Imogene looks a little frightened.

"Let us not speak of that," she says. "Often do I wish to be free of him, but there is no way." Her smile turns on again. "Verily, it is my hope that perhaps you might be the champion who could rescue me."

She comes over to Jack and waves her ducks under his nose, very temptingly, and how can he resist?

He gets up on his chair and pounds himself on the chest.

"You got the right idea there, baby," he says. "I'm going

to do just that. When I set my peepers on you I say there is a little number that is too classy to be cooped up with an oversized cattle-thief like this Glimorgus. And when that big tramp shows up I'm going to—"

What Jack intends to do is never settled. Because all at once the big tramp shows up.

Merely the big tramp of feet, but that is enough. Jack can hear the feet just outside, and they are pounding along like a couple of twenty-ton tanks. Standing on the chair as he is, he can just see outside the window when a head passes. One look at the size of that head and Jack changes his mind.

"Here he comes!" he yells. "Hide me somewhere, quick!"

Imogene looks around wildly.

"Here—do you climb into the oven," she suggests.

"Do I? And how!" Jack dives off the chair and runs to the big stone oven. He can hardly reach up to the door and it takes a lot of effort to get it open, but the sound of those huge feet echoing through the house is all the encouragement he needs.

"Boost me up," he whispers.

"I cannot."

Just then the problem is settled. Because a big hand sticks itself around the kitchen door. Jack takes one look and then gives a flying jump up into the oven. He slams the door just in time as the giant walks into the room.

Jack lies there in the dark, squinting through the air-holes in the oven door. And there is certainly plenty for him to see.

Plenty of the giant, anyway. Because this King Glimorgus turns out to be thirty feet tall. He is so big he could black Jack's eyes for him with his knees. Jack does not wish to give him such an opportunity, so he watches very quietly from behind the oven door.

The giant comes in and stands there for a minute. He does not shake hands with his wife, either—because he is carrying a calf under each arm. He swings the calves around like they were chickens and then tosses them down on the table.

"Here is a little snack for lunch," he announces. Then he grabs Imogene up and kisses her.

This makes Jack shudder. The idea of anyone having to come close to that great big face is very unpleasant. He has a tremendous black beard, and kissing him is the same as falling into a pile of bushes face-first.

But Imogene smiles, being used to it, and the giant smiles back. His smile is like grim death, because he has teeth as big as tombstones.

He sets Imogene down very carefully, and then he yawns. This isn't so bad, even if he does make all the dishes rattle and the clock on the wall stops dead.

"Anything happen?" he asks, in a voice like a sick foghorn.

"Naught, my lord," says Imogene.

"Guess I'll eat then," the giant decides.

"Very well."

"Roast these calves for me," says the giant.

Jack gulps. Imogene turns pale.

"Just shove them in the oven under a hot fire," the giant orders.

"But—but my lord—"

"Eh?"

"You know it is not wise for you to indulge in roast meat during the midday. Remember the advice of the leech—cooked meat is bad for the pressure of the blood."

"Is that so?"

"Of course." Imogene begins to coax. She climbs up on the giant's lap and strokes his forehead.

"You are so delicate, my lord. So anemic. You must guard your health. You are not strong."

This is fine talk to hand somebody who looks like the big brother of Gargantua the Gorilla, but it works with the giant.

"Perhaps you are right, my little pet," he says. "I do not feel my best. In fact, I am not even very hungry. So I will just eat those two calves raw."

Jack breathes a sigh of relief as the giant begins to pick at his food. He merely toys with it, dabbles around—in fact, it takes him nearly ten minutes to eat the two calves. Just an invalid's diet.

Imogene bustles around, bringing him salt and pepper, and rolling out a pony of ale for an appetizer. She is doing her best to keep King Glimorgus from noticing anything wrong.

But all at once he holds up the leg of a calf and turns his head.

"I smell something," he says. This time his voice is so loud that the clock on the wall falls off completely.

"What do you mean?" quavers the little ginch.

"Aha!" yells the giant. "I thought so."

"Thought what?"

"Fee, Fi, Fo, Fum
I smell the blood
Of an Englishman."

This is bad poetry, but the thought behind it is worse. At least to Jack. Because he is not an Englishman, but Irish, and this is quite an insult, to say the least.

To say the most, if the giant finds Jack it is curtains. So he trembles inside the oven. The giant gets up.

"Are you hiding a man in this castle?" he booms.

"Verily, you jest," trembles Imogene.

"But I smell one."

"Perchance you suffer from a cold in the head."

"I know a man when I smell him," insists the giant. "And when I smell him I find him. And when I find him—I eat him!"

Jack begins to feel like a hunk of sandwich meat already. The giant is striding back and forth across the room.

"Where is he?" he yells. "Show him to me and I'll tear him limb to limb! I'll clean his wishbone and use it for a toothpick."

"The use of toothpicks is vulgar," Imogene says. "And you are mistaken, my lord. That is no man you smell—merely the hen."

"Hen? What hen?"

"Why, the marvelous hen I purchase from the itinerant wizard who chanced by this morning."

"Honestly, you women are all alike," grumbles the giant. "Every damned peddler that comes along, you have to buy something—"

"Wait until you see it," says the ginch. "Truly, it can perform a miraculous feat."

She runs out into the other room and brings back a live chicken. It is an ordinary-looking white bird and the giant scowls at it.

"I see nothing remarkable in this fowl," he sneers.

"Ah, but there is something remarkable in it. And wait until it comes out."

She sets the hen down on the table and strokes it. It clucks a little.

"Lay!" she says to the chicken. "Lay!"

The chicken squawks. All at once it sits up. Imogene lifts it off the table. Underneath the chicken is an egg. An egg of solid gold!

"Is not this a remarkable thing to find in a chicken?" she asks.

"It lays golden eggs, does it? And all you do is tell it that you want one?"

"Merely stroke its back and command it to lay."

So King Glimorgus the giant sits down and begins to stroke the chicken and yell, "Lay!" And the eggs pour out.

"Eighteen karats!" chuckles the giant. "Nice, grade-A size, too. My dear, all is forgiven."

He scoops up a pile of golden golfballs and gets up.

"I shall take these down to have them assayed," he says. "Mind you, guard the hen well until I return."

And he tramps off.

A couple of minutes later, Jack crawls out of the oven.

"Nice work," he tells Imogene. "You saved my life. Now I must beat it before my wife beats me."

"You are wed?" says Imogene. Her face falls. "I am sorry. For I was of a mind that you should stay here with me and console me."

"A very noble idea," Jack answers. "In fact, nothing suits me better. But pretty soon your husband comes back and starts poking his big nose around again, so I figure I will keep out of his way. And my wife is not quite so big, but she is just as tough."

So Jack heads for the door with Imogene after him.

"Perchance you will return?" she asks.

"Who can tell?"

"If not," sighs the ginch, "I will bestow a parting gift. Take this hen."

And she gives him the hen that lays the golden eggs.

"A very sweet gesture," Jack says. "And thank you for giving me the bird."

He leaves Imogene then and puts the castle behind him. Jack makes time on the path now with the hen under his arm. He looks around to see that the coast is clear, and when he comes to the plant sticking through the ground, he slips down through the hole.

Going down doesn't take so much time. He manages to slide quite a bit of the way, and he is very willing to hurry.

He figures on getting home and doing some planting before his wife arrives. He wants to plant seeds, and he also wants to plant this remarkable chicken where she won't find it.

Sliding down, he does his best to figure out this adventure he has.

The whole thing reminds him of a yarn he reads in a book when he is a tiny tot—a little epic entitled *Jack and the Beanstalk*. In fact, this seems to be almost a duplicate.

His name is Jack, and he finds some seeds and plants

them, and they grow. He plants them in the dark, but now he is almost sure they are beans. The stalk comes up, he climbs it, and there he is with this giant. The giant even talks like the book, with his hi-de-ho about sniffing the corpuscles of a British subject.

And now Jack gets a hen that lays nuggets. It all adds up, somehow.

So Jack hits the earth feeling pretty pleased with himself. He hops back to the farmhouse and sticks the chicken away in the back of the hencoop.

Then he grabs up a sack of corn and goes out to plant it. He is so happy he even feels like doing a little work, and by supper time he has the satisfaction of spreading more corn than a politician does at election time.

He heads for the house, very happy. His wife is all smiles when she sees he is working.

"I am glad you reform, you bum," she greets him. "I fix an extra nice supper for you."

Which it is.

But right in the middle of the meal, Jack stares down at his plate.

"Where do you get this lovely fried chicken, darling?" he asks.

She smiles at him.

"Why do you ask, you naughty boy? From the hencoop, of course."

"The hencoop—"

"Certainly." She wags her finger at him. "You are so thoughtful to go and steal one of the neighbor's chickens for me."

"Neighbor's—"

"But of course, just like a man, you do not realize they will recognize it if it is running around in our yard. So I kill it and fry it."

"You fry the chicken I put in the hencoop?"

"Of course."

And all at once Jack does not like his fried chicken any more. In fact, he loses his appetite. So his wife has to take the rest of the chicken in her lunch pail when she goes off to work on the night shift.

Jack lies in bed thinking about what a rotten deal he gets. Here he has a chicken that can lay golden eggs—he has Fort Knox right in his own backyard—and he loses it. It is enough to get anybody up in the air.

And that, finally, is where he decides to go.

There is nothing else to do, after such a disappointment, but to climb the beanstalk again tomorrow and see if he can lay his hands on another hunk of this precious poultry.

He can hardly wait. For the first time in years he is up at dawn and running out into the field in the valley where the beanstalk stands.

Sure enough, it is still there, and when Jack gets there it is far from still. He boosts himself up hand over hand and makes like a monkey.

Pretty soon he is high and dry, not bringing a flask with him this trip. The going is tough, and for a minute Jack gets a bad attack of qualms.

After all, why should he risk his neck again by playing around with a thirty-foot bozo whose idea of a complete hamburger dinner would be Jack with a bottle of ketchup poured over him?

So Jack stops to think things over. And he looks down at the ground. It is so far away that he gets the shakes about falling and there is nothing to do but look up again—and climb some more.

In a little while he is up in the clouds again, looking for silver linings. But all he gets is water on the knee trying to wade through the dampness, so Jack climbs as fast as he can and shortly he is crawling through the hole at the top of the beanstalk.

He is on the path in the hills again and this time he knows his way. He walks very slowly, looking to see if he can notice the giant's footprints in the dust. But there is no mark of any size 44 brogans treading this way, so he skips along until he comes to the big stone castle.

The door is still open, and Imogene is standing there. When she sees Jack she smiles and tucks up her pretty red hair.

"I am so glad you are back," she says. "I wight you wish to console me?"

"Wight you are," says Jack, who is catching on fast to her brand of conversation.

"Shall we step inside?" asks Imogene.

"Is Shorty home?" Jack comes back.

"King Glimorgus?" she giggles. "Nay, he is out hunting."

"Deer?"

"Nay—you."

"Me?"

"Verily. He suspects the presence of a stranger about. It is his belief that you are responsible for the disappearance of his chicken, and he will not rest until he finds you."

"If he finds me, I will not rest," says Jack. "Maybe I better jam on the scram."

Imogene's pretty blue eyes cloud up and look like rain. She sighs.

"You wouldst desert me?" she wails. "And here it is my hope that you are a gallant champion come to rescue me from that miserable ogre! Could I be free again to live as other women, instead of being cooped up here with that monstrous tyrant—oh, I should do anything to reward the noble rescuer who saves me!"

"Anything?" says Jack.

"Anything," sighs Imogene.

Well, this is a pretty big proposition, and Jack knows it. So he takes his time thinking it over. Then he makes up his mind.

"Would you get me a drink?" he asks.

"Surely—we have mead and ale in plenty! Come with me into the castle."

So Jack wanders into the castle again. He keeps his eyes open this time, because he is really on the lookout for another hen to grab. If he can only find an 18-karat chicken or a platinum-producing pullet, he is satisfied to run a few risks.

But the castle rooms are empty, and when they come to the kitchen he gets his drink and sits down on the floor—not having a stepladder handy to climb up to the table.

Then he decides to pump Imogene for information.

"Do I hear you mention raising that chicken from a gizzard?" he asks her.

"No. I purchase it from a wizard," she answers.

"Do you suppose he has any more fowl like that?" asks Jack. "I am in the market for another chicken, or maybe a duck that lays bucks."

"That is the only chicken of its kind, he tells me."

"What?" moans Jack, disappointed. "No turkeys? No ostriches?"

She shakes her head. Then she smiles.

"But wait until your eyes rest on the purchase of today," she tells him. "This is indeed a wondrous bargain. 'Twill interest you greatly."

"Let's have a squint," Jack suggests.

But he does not get a squint. He gets a scrunch. The scrunch of the giant's feet outside the castle.

"Here he comes," yells Jack. "Open the oven and start in shovin'!"

"But you are to rescue me—"

"How can I rescue you unless I rescue myself first?" Jack argues, running across the big kitchen tiles. "I go to hide safe to save my hide."

But when they get to the oven and Jack reaches up, the door is stuck. And so is he, because he can hear the giant coming into the front hall.

"Now where?" Jack yells.

"Here—lift yourself into the bread box." Imogene points

out the big canister on the floor. So Jack pops off the cover and pops inside.

Meanwhile, the giant is coming up like thunder through the house. Jack tips the lid a little to see what's going on.

King Glimorgus stamps into the room, with a very nasty look spread all over his face.

"Don't tell me," he yells, before Imogene can open her mouth. "I can sniff him a mile off—the paltry poultry pilferer."

He gives her the old leer and sneer from ear to ear.

"It is in my mind to wring your pretty neck," he growls.

"But my lord—there is no one here. Seeing you approach, I have come to pour your tankard of ale."

And she offers him the drink she fixes for Jack.

"Ale—bah!" hollers the man higher up. "There is but one drink for me—the blood of that thieving rogue!"

"I do not see him."

"Use your nose," grunts the ogre. And he goes off into his poetry hour again, in a voice that would melt rocks.

"Fee Fi Fo fum
I smell the blood
Of an Englishman!
Be he alive
Or be he dead,
I'll grind his bones
To make my bread."

Jack lies in the breadbox and almost shakes the lid off.

"Why doesn't he try some of that new enriched bread?" he grumbles to himself. "A little vitamin B_1 is all right. Why does he need my bones in the stuff?"

But this is not a question to ask any thirty-foot giant, so Jack keeps strictly from silence.

"He's hiding here," the giant yells. "Maybe in that

oven!" And he strides over to the oven door, yanking it open. The door is still stuck, but this does not stop the ogre. He wrenches the door off and looks in.

Of course the oven is empty.

"I'll search everywhere," yells King Glimorgus. But Imogene pouts and tugs at his knees.

"You'll spoil my surprise," she says. "You will find its hiding place."

"Surprise? What surprise?"

"The surprise I bought from the wizard today."

"He here again?" But the giant looks interested.

"This item is truly rare," says Imogene. "Do you be seated, whilst I bring it to you."

She scampers off and comes back in a minute carrying a lot of wires under her arm.

"What manner of trash is this?"

"A harp, my lord. A wonderful harp."

"Harp? I don't play a harp!"

"No need to play it. It plays itself."

"Plays itself?"

"That is the marvel of its minstrelsy. Merely command it to play, my lord."

So Imogene sets the harp down on the table and the giant sits down and gawks at it for a minute. Then he says, "Play!"

And the harp plays.

Jack cannot believe his peeping eyes. The strings on the harp move and a tune comes out. Of course, it is not anything that is leading the hit parade, but the stuff makes music.

And the giant begins to smile.

When the chorus is over he says "Play" again, and the harp swings out. Pretty soon there is quite a jam session going on, in a corny sort of way. The giant taps the table with his fingers—very gentle, so as not to splinter it to bits—and the harp goes through its repertoire. It is better than a juke box, because you don't have to put nickels in it.

After a while it starts playing some real soft stuff—

regular slumber music. And in no time at all, the giant is snoring. In fact, he snores so loud it drowns out the music, and the harp shuts up.

So there is the giant, slumped over the table fast asleep. As soon as she sees it is safe, Imogene gives Jack the old high-sign and he climbs out of the breadbox.

"Glad to get out," he whispers. "Too crowded. Loaves of bread jamming my knees and rolls all over my waist. I do not mind getting a bun on, but not on my head."

"Quickly," pants Imogene. "He sleeps now. You must go."

"Mind if I take a souvenir?" asks Jack, pointing at the harp.

"Very well."

So Jack tiptoes over to the table, reaches up, and grabs hold of the harp.

The result is very startling. Because the harp sort of tugs back on him and then it plunks out some sounds that resemble words:

"Help—Master—Help—"

Jack grabs it under his coat to stifle the noise, but too late. The giant opens his eyes and sits up.

"So!" howls the ogre. "There you are—you chicken-hearted chicken thief!"

Jack is on the spot. In fact, he will *be* a spot if the giant's foot ever smashes down him.

He thinks fast.

"Yes, I am the yegg who snatches your eggs," he admits. "And now I am taking your harp. So what are you going to do about it, Gus?"

King Glimorgus makes a lunge for him. This is just what Jack wants, because he runs right between the giant's legs. Glimorgus turns around, but Jack is scampering down the hall, with the harp tucked inside his coat.

"Stop thief!" yells the harp.

"Fee, Fi, Fo, Fum," yells the giant.

"Same to you, brother," remarks Jack, running very sincerely.

But the giant is right behind him.

Jack races out of the castle and down the trail, but Glimorgus stomps along right after him. He has to run stooped over with his hands out, because if he takes too much of a stride his legs pass right over Jack and he cannot see to grab him.

Jack weaves and ducks but keeps to the trail. And the giant's hands come scooping down behind him in the dust, trying to grab hold.

Jack spies the hole and the top of the beanstalk and dives for it. He starts climbing down.

Then he starts *sliding* down.

Because the giant comes right after him!

He tears away an acre or so of ground around the hole and jumps down on the stalk. The beanstalk shakes and sways, but Jack does not stop. He slides for dear life—his own.

Right down through the cloud layers he goes, skinning his hands and knees. Beans pop all around his head, but he does not hesitate. The giant bellows behind him, and then he seems to get stuck in the fog from the clouds. Jack can hear *Fee*-ing and *Fi*-ing, and when he comes down closer to the ground Jack hears the thunder of his *Fo*-ing and *Fum*-ing.

At last Jack hits solid earth. He is panting and gasping, but he is also planning and grasping.

"If this is really such a beanstalk like in the story," he wheezes, "then there is only one thing I need to do. I must chop down the beanstalk with my little hatchet."

This is a very cheerful idea. But Jack is not George Washington.

I cannot tell a lie. He has no hatchet!

So there is Jack, staring up the shaking beanstalk, waiting while the giant's feet start sticking out from the clouds. He is coming down fast. The stalk is wobbly, but it is not falling. And there is not a hatchet in sight!

Jack grabs at himself and beats his chest. Then he hits it.

The harp!

He yanks it out.

"Hey—leggo of me!" yells the harp, in a very impolite manner.

But Jack has no time to be polite. He rips the wood away from the harp and grabs a handful of loose wires. He twists them together at the ends.

Then he kneels down and saws away at the base of the beanstalk. The wire is sharp. It cuts.

Now the giant's knees are showing. And Jack hears his voice out of the clouds.

"Fee, Fi, Fo, Fum
Ready or not—
Here I come!"

Jack saws away. And the beanstalk gives. He looks up and yells.

"Fee, Fi, Fo, Fum
Here you go,
You oversized bum!"

And that is just what happens. The beanstalk suddenly snaps with a twang and a bang. The whole stalk swings free and a gust of wind lifts it straight up in the air.

From above, Jack hears the giant giving what the poets call one hell of a yell. But it is too late. The beanstalk shoots up into the clouds and disappears. The field is empty. There is nothing left.

So Jack goes back home to his wife.

"After all," he figures, "maybe it is best things happen like this.

"The giant is gone, and that means I really rescue Imogene from him, and make good my promise.

"It is nice to have a lot of golden eggs, but the government war tax won't leave you anything but the shells.

"A harp that plays itself is also fine—but what has it got that a portable radio hasn't got?"

Such is the story Jack tells me when he comes to town a couple days later. His wife thinks he is a jerk for not doing the planting like he promises, but Jack has plans. He tells me the plans, too, and he is very happy about the whole thing. Remarkable, is it not?

LEFTY FEEP sat back and balanced an olive on his tongue.

I leaned forward and exploded.

"It's not remarkable—it's downright screwy! I have never heard such exaggerations in all my life."

Feep looked hurt.

"Do not say such a thing, Bob," he snapped. "It may be that I lie a little from time to time, but I never exaggerate!"

"But Lefty—do you actually expect me to believe that the Jack and the Beanstalk fable happened here in real life?"

Feep shrugged.

"Who can tell? Jack's wife says the beans are very old when her Papa brings them over to this country."

"Nuts to beans," I sighed. "But there's one thing that really puzzles me."

"Name it and you can have it."

"In the fable, the stalk falls down, and the giant gets killed. In your story, it flies up in the air. That isn't much to believe, it is too much."

Lefty looked injured, even a trifle hurt.

"It only shows you don't understand science," he snapped. "The giant is closer to China than he is to me, so he falls up."

"Up?"

"Sure. That's gravity."

I nodded slowly, because I could see he was right there. But another thing bothered me.

"When you started out, you told me Jack was making such a wonderful contribution to the war effort. And nothing in your story even hints at such a thing."

"Oh, that." Feep smiled. "What Jack does for the war effort is something he tells me the other day. Remember, I mention he has plans."

"So?"

"The night Jack plants the beanstalk he uses only a couple of beans. He still has a lot left over in the pouch he finds."

"Well?"

Feep shrugged again. His smile broadened.

"Very simple. Jack is going back to the farm right now. He is going to plant the rest of those beans in a Victory Garden."

AFTER WORDS

BLOCH: I enjoy all of the early Lefty Feep stories except "Jerk the Giant Killer." Today I would write it as a Feep adventure—and find a better payoff. Must have been turned out fast because I needed the money. Story of my life, or all too much of it.

STANLEY: *It does seem strange that Lefty is not an active participant.*

BLOCH: At the time it didn't seem in character for Lefty. He didn't fit the storyline, the plot. The motivations . . . weren't characteristic of Lefty, so I told it once removed.

JS: *And now we come to a story where Feep meets a crazy inventor,* "The Golden Opportunity of Lefty Feep."

BLOCH: Midas well get right to it.

The Golden Fleece is a beholdin' piece of this inventive darn yarn in which a goldbricking scientist turns dingy Phyrgian Kingy, forcing Lefty to feel gilt. Definitely a lot of bullion.

THE GOLDEN OPPORTUNITY OF LEFTY FEEP

LEFTY FEEP slumped into his seat across my table and beckoned to a waiter.

"Bring me a glass of water and a toothpick," he ordered. "And kindly knock the point off the toothpick first, so I am not tempted to cut my throat."

I stared at Feep in astonishment.

"What's the matter, Lefty—aren't you eating any more?"

"Not any more than I can get," he muttered.

I searched his long morose face for a possible explanation. All I saw were eyebrows and a frown.

"You certainly look down in the mouth," I told him.

Lefty Feep sighed. "Everything is down in the mouth with me, except food."

"Broke?"

He nodded.

"Yesterday I am the richest man in the world. Today I am a bum."

"Why should today be an exception?" I asked, but under my breath. He didn't hear me.

"Yes, yesterday I sits at the Ritz. Today I mutter in the

gutter. I am all set to go over the hill to the poorhouse, only I am too weak to climb hills."

I patted him on the shoulder to cheer him up. Then I patted him in the face with a roll. This did the trick. His mouth opened gratefully, and the roll disappeared. Also his frown.

"Don't take it so hard," I consoled him. "After all, money isn't everything. All that glitters is not gold."

The frown came back.

"Gold!" rasped Lefty Feep. "Please do not exclaim the name of same. Do not meddle with that metal."

"Why, what's wrong with that?"

"Everything. It is gold which causes all my troubles. In fact, I go from a gold rush to a bum's rush all in one day."

The waiter returned with the water and toothpick. Feep gargled noisily, then balanced the toothpick on the end of his nose in a wistful fashion.

"I still don't understand," I mused. "Why this dislike for gold?"

"It is very hard for me to talk about it," Feep sighed.

"All right, then. I'll change the subject."

A gleam entered Feep's eye. He began to breathe heavily as he rose and grasped my shoulders.

"But if you insist," he said, "I will spill the story to you."

"Oh, I don't insist at all—"

"You are forcing it out of me," Lefty Feep accused. "So you ask for it, so you'll get it."

Pushing me back in my seat with a half nelson, Feep arranged my right ear for a target, aimed his mouth, opened, and fired.

And I got it.

AS YOU KNOW (began Lefty Feep), I am the kind of personality who likes to go places and do people. It is very difficult to get me embarrassed.

But the other day I wake up and find myself embarrassed

in the worst way—financially. I am caught with my pants-pockets down. I am not only broke, but fractured.

You see, a couple weeks ago a medico looks me over and advises me to go off to a summer resort hotel for change and rest.

Well, the bellboys get the change, and the hotel gets the rest.

So there I am, flatter than last night's beer.

To make it worse, I am all tangled up with a very neat little number name of Sweetheart Singer. I do not know how she gets such an unusual name, but that is what the Navy calls her.

Do not get the wrong idea, now. Sweetheart is really a very intellectual type of ginch. She is very fond of etchings—particularly the kind the Government puts out on $20 bills. So you see, I am now mixed up in what you call a love triangle—I love Sweetheart, and Sweetheart loves money.

And here I am, dead broke. In order not to be heart-broke also, it is necessary for me to lay my pinkies on some coin, but swiftly. In fact, I have a weighty date this very evening. But the way it stands, I do not possess enough cash to rent a telephone booth.

So to make a long story wrong, there is only one thing for me to do. I hop back to town and pay a visit to Out-of-Business Oscar.

This Out-of-Business Oscar, you may recall, is a loveable old cutthroat who runs a combination auction mart and hock shop where I once purchase a rug. He is called Out-of-Business Oscar because he is always advertising a close-out sale. Although the only thing Oscar ever closes is his fist—over money.

Even so, Oscar and I are friends of many years' standing—principally me standing in front of him trying to get two or three bucks when I pawn my watch. Getting dough out of Oscar is like trying to squeeze tears out of a landlord.

Still, today I know this is the only chance I have of raising a few chips to take Sweetheart out on, so I amble down to Oscar's store and unbuckle my watch chain before I go in. I also take off my rings, my cuff links, and tie pin. This ought to get me at least a fiver, I figure. But just to make sure, I bring along a small hammer—in case he makes me knock the fillings out of my teeth.

When I get up to the doorway of the hock shop I see a big sign outside:

OUR LEASE EXPIRES!
GET YOUR BARGAINS—IT'S OUR FUNERAL!
ATTEND THE BIG PRICE MASSACRE!

So I know business is still going on as usual. And I walk inside.

The place looks empty. It is very dark, and there does not seem to be anybody around. I stand there for a minute, and all at once I hear a voice gasping behind my back.

"Turn around and let me look at you—at last, at last, somebody to talk to. Speak to me!"

It is Oscar, of course. He rushes up to me and grabs my hand, pumping it like he was running a meat-grinder and expected hamburgers to drop out from under my arm.

"You don't know what a pleasure this is," he wails. "Nobody comes into this joint for an entire week. It is a week since I see a human face."

Then he recognizes me and frowns. "Of course, I do not exactly feel that I see a human face yet when I look at yours."

I choose to ignore this remark.

"Speak up," he says. "What brings you here?"

"A bicycle," I tell him.

"I mean, what's on your mind?"

"Hair-restorer, mostly," I confess. "What I am mainly interested in is raising a couple guilders on these family jewels of mine."

"You wish to hock this junk, in other words?" he says.

"I do not care for your other words, but that is the idea."

"It is a good idea," says Oscar. "But it will not work. Because I have not more and not less than no money. Here," he says, "I will prove it to you." And he steps over to the cash register and rings it open. Something flutters out of it and then falls back.

"See?" Oscar shrugs. "A moth. And it is so starved, it is too weak to even fly. Around here is strictly from hunger."

"What's the matter?" I ask, very mystified.

Oscar sighs and shrugs some more.

"I don't know, Lefty, I can't understand it. This week is the most baffling one I ever live through.

"On Monday I start out as usual with a big sign. *PRICES SLASHED TO RIBBONS.* Nobody comes in. So on Tuesday I put up my bigger sign. *PRICES CUT TO BITS.* Still nobody enters. On Wednesday I hang out the sign that reads, *PRICES TORN TO PIECES—COME IN BEFORE THE BARGAINS BLEED TO DEATH!* And nothing doing.

"On Thursday I am so burned up I put out the sign *FIRE SALE.* Nobody shows up—not even the Fire Department.

"Today I got all the signs up, but they are staying away from me in droves. I am about as popular as leprosy. Nobody wants to buy anything. Too much prosperity. If it keeps up, I am ruined."

Oscar rubs his bald noggin until it begins to shine like a street lamp.

"Maybe you got a few suggestions to help me with?" he asks. "I will appreciate same, Lefty."

I hesitate. It is a terrible thing to even think of, but I can see no way out of it in such a case. So I let my voice sink very low and try to keep it from trembling.

"Well, Oscar—there is only one thing left to do. You'll have to get out the hook."

"The hook?"

"Yes. That's all you got left."

"You really think so?"

"I'm afraid that's all."

"All right."

Oscar sighs and creeps behind the counter. He stoops down very carefully and pulls out a long iron pole with a scythe on the end of it. It looks very mean indeed.

He tries not to look at me while he creeps over to the door. He is ashamed, but he is still an old master when he goes to work, so I watch him carefully.

Oscar half-opens the door. He sticks his bald noggin out and squints up and down the street. His mustache bristles with anticipation, and dried noodle soup.

Then he hears it. Footsteps from the left, coming down the street.

Oscar sticks his head out further and frowns when a pair of socks hanging in the doorway hits him a mildewed blow in the face. He draws the hook up and begins to slide one end of the pole out of the door.

"Shh! I think I hear a fink approaching now," he whispers.

Now Oscar is not a sports lover, and he does not care for fishing—even though the river runs right in back of his shop. But I can learn more about fishing by watching him land a customer than old Izaak Walton could ever teach me.

So I watch this fink coming down the street. He is a little old guy with a face like a prune that wears glasses. He walks along very swift, and Oscar waits from behind the doorway, playing his hook over the sidewalk down low.

All at once the old bird is just ready to pass the door. Oscar jerks the hook up very sharp and trips the guy. Then he digs the hook into his belt, very careful, and plays him from left to right across the sidewalk. Oscar now braces his feet against the threshold and pulls his victim in. The old guy flies across the floor of the shop, and Oscar jumps right behind him and locks the door.

Then he turns to face the old buzzard with a smile—because he is now a legitimate customer.

"What can I do for you, sir?" he asks.

"Where am I?—hey—what's the idea—ouch!" wails the little old bird, trying to get up off the floor.

Oscar promptly taps him over the temple with a rare old New Jersey Ming vase. And the customer promptly falls down again.

Oscar turns to me.

"I am sorry, but I learn from experience this is the best way to make such a customer forget exactly how he happens to come in here."

Then he very carefully gets a glass of water and revives the little old guy. He opens his eyes and sits up.

"Nasty fall you just have, buddy," he remarks.

"Fall?" squeaks the customer.

"Sure—remember? You pass out just in front of my store. And say, that's lucky for you—because of the way you rip and ruin your clothes when you fall."

Then Oscar whips into his old routine. He runs behind the counters and begins to grab at his stock of flour sacks, mumbling to himself.

"New coat—the old one is torn—let's see, I got something handy and dandy here, just imported from the Bronx. And a new hat now—the old one is busted, and anyway you must just come from walking near a pigeon loft—here's a beautiful homburg from Hamburg—only $1.88, costs me $2.00, but it's yours for $1.00, I make it up by saving on string—a new tie instead of that greasy hunk of rope you're choking yourself with—aha—"

He races back to where the guy stands, bewildered, and begins to tear off his vest and coat. Then he rips his shirt, and replaces all the old clothes with stuff from the shop. The little old fink stands there in a cloud of dust while Oscar pats the new clothing into shape.

"Pity you ain't taller," says Oscar, throwing on a size 42 vest. "But you're young—you'll grow yet."

Then he grabs the trousers.

"You must tear these when you fall," he comments, showing the guy the place where the hook rips his pants. "Well, don't worry, here is a new pair that will give you legs like a chorus queen."

He jams a pair of pants over the scrawny legs, thrusts a cane into the guy's hand, and plunges a tie-pin into his neck. Then he steps back and registers ecstasy.

"Marvelous!" he croons. "You look just like a page out of *Esquire*."

What he looks like certainly would be tore out of any magazine, quick, by whoever would see it. But this is all part of Oscar's song and dance.

"Now let's see," he mumbles. "That's $1.49 and $2.76 and $7.63 and $9.27 and $3.04 and $.18 for Social Security, and $.05 for the glass of water I revive you with. Comes to a grand total of not more and not less than $43.77 you owe me."

The little old customer looks bewildered.

"But I have no money," he says. "I'm sure I'm grateful to you for taking care of me, and getting me all fixed up with these splendid new clothes. But I'm not in a position to reimburse you. Ouch!"

He makes the last remark because of Oscar the Tiger, who is already snarling at him and clawing off his clothes in one furious leap.

"Wait," pleads the customer. "I can pay later—soon."

"Later!"

Oscar rips off his tie.

"Soon!"

He tears the shirt open.

"Pay me later, eh?"

He reefs the trousers.

"A wise guy! Huh!"

Off goes belt and socks.

"But," pants the old bird, trying to resist while he is whirling around in the air like a pinwheel, "I am an inventor.

Ouch! And I am just on my way to the Patent Office today to get my model registered and I am sure it will make me a lot of money."

"Money?" Oscar pauses, clutching the trousers. "What kind of invention, Buddy?"

The little old guy strikes a pose in his underwear.

"Well, sir, I'm glad you ask me that. Most people just laugh at me when I mention it. They think I'm crazy. But just yesterday I terminate my experiments and complete the invention of what I call the Midascope."

"Midascope?"

"Simple. Named after Midas, the king of the well-known legend."

"The bozo with the golden touch?"

"Exactly."

"I don't get it."

"My invention is a super-reagent which has the property of turning all inanimate matter into gold."

"You mean you could turn wood into gold, for example? Like that King Midas did in the story by touching it?"

"Definitely. Hence the name. However, there is nothing supernatural about my discovery. Supernormal, perhaps, yes. But this does not operate by touch—it consists of a ray. A simple ray, which, if directed properly at an object, will transmute its atomic components into the structural equivalency of gold."

"Cut the double-talk," Oscar tells him. Then he turns to me. "What do you say, Lefty? I think you better call the zoo and tell them one of their squirrels is out of his cage."

"You mean to infer I am demented?" hollers the old bird.

"Not at all. I think you're nuts," Oscar replies.

"Then you'd better take a look."

He stoops down and fumbles in his old discarded coat and pulls out a small metal tube that looks like a flashlight. There is a cap over the end.

"By removing this cap the ray is released," he says, smirking.

"Oh, yeah?" I put in my two cents worth. "Then how come the cap does not turn to gold?"

"Because it is made out of a metal specially treated to resist the action of transmutation," says the guy, going back into his scientific double-talk. "But take the cap off and you get gold right away wherever you point the ray."

Oscar steps up and yanks the cylinder out of the old bird's mitts.

"Looks like a fake to me," he yaps. "I bet if I open it up and look in, I get a black eye—like those ones with the hula dancers' pictures inside."

The small article sniffs and looks very haughty.

"There is no trickery involved, gentlemen," he says. "This represents my life-work. I guarantee its genuineness. To prove it, I will allow you to point the ray at whatever article you may choose in this shop."

"Nothing doing, buddy," says Oscar. "How do I know it ain't one of these disintegrator-rays like you read about? Blow my furniture or clothes to bits."

I personally do not see where this will be such a great loss, considering the quality of Oscar's furniture and clothing stock, but I keep still.

"Wait a minute," Oscar says. "I will step outside. There is a fruit store right across the street, and I will get hold of something to experiment on."

So he ducks off and comes back in about a minute with something in his hand. A banana.

"Here we are," he says. "Now, buddy, you turn on this thing and let's see you coin some gold."

The little stranger takes the cylinder and holds it in his hand. He sets the banana down on the counter, then looks at it. He smiles. All at once he pulls the cap off his cylinder and points it at the monkey-cigar.

Nothing happens.

No light shines out. Nothing explodes. The little fink just waves the cylinder at the banana, that's all.

"Fake!" sneers Oscar.

The banana lies there on the counter, and Oscar snatches it up in disgust. All at once he stands frozen with the banana in his hand.

"It feels different," he mutters. "Heavier."

I take a good look. The banana is still yellow, but it is *shining*. Shining like gold!

"It is gold!" yells Oscar. "Solid gold!"

He begins to dance up and down, waving the jungle pig-knuckle in the air.

"It works, you see? It really works!" he shouts.

I grab at the banana. Sure enough, it is heavy metal now. I can't peel it. The whole thing is a golden lump.

"Now what do we do?" I ask.

"What do we do?" echoes Oscar, staring at the banana. "What do we do? Why—we just run right over to that fruit store again and bring back a watermelon!"

I do not wish to go into details about the next hour we spend. Oscar does bring back a watermelon, and the stranger does turn it to gold with his cylinder. Then we sort of go goldbugs, I guess.

Because we start to turn the junk in the store to gold. We wave the cyliner at the stuff on the counter and on the shelves. We get golden golf-clubs and tennis rackets, gold fountain pens, vases, pictures, microscopes, candid cameras. We even get gold leaf pages in the books when we point the cylinder at them. It is like one grand and glorious bingo game where we always hold the winning corn. Nothing is impossible. An hour ago we are lower than a worm's toenails and now we are kicking around the pot at the end of the rainbow. No wonder we do not have much of the old self-control.

Finally Oscar climbs up on a golden stepladder and points the cylinder at the stuffed moose-head hanging over

219 THE GOLDEN OPPORTUNITY OF LEFTY FEEP

the door. He looks at the golden moose for a minute and then he stops and frowns. He climbs down slowly.

"Why are you rubbing your forehead?" I ask.

"Because a thought hits me."

"You should have concussion of the brain," I remark, but he ignores this. He points at me and the little inventor.

"We are wasting our time," he says.

"Meaning what?"

"Meaning just this—why should we hang around here trying to turn this petty stuff into karats? We can go out and really coin money with this thing.

"Why not turn it on the sidewalks, on the trees, on the buildings? Imagine owning a whole skyscraper of gold! A 22-carat Empire State Building? Or a golden Subway? I can picture Radio City—"

"Stop!" says the little old fink, striking another pose in his longer underwear. "You talk like a fool."

"I do, eh?"

"Certainly. Allow me to remind you of a few elementary truths. Don't you realize that if you run around indiscriminately transforming everything into gold, that gold will lose its value? Don't you understand that if you create too much gold it will become common and therefore worthless?"

"I am willing to risk it," Oscar sneers.

"Well, I'm not," the stranger snaps. "As I say, I am on my way to the Patent Office with this working model. I intend to register it and present the formulae involved to our government; to keep, not to use. In times of need, the cylinder can be employed. But it must be worked with discretion.

"I can see that common men cannot be entrusted with such great power. You, my friend, have already bruised your knees bowing down to the Golden Calf. It is an object lesson to prove mankind is not yet ready for easy riches."

I get the little fink's point all right, but Oscar grunts.

"Get off your soapbox and come down to earth," he says.

"Here we get a fortune in our grasp and you want to give it away."

"We?" says the inventor. "It's *my* cylinder. I demand that you return it to me at once so that I may proceed on my errand to the Patent Office."

"Cylinders you want?" Oscar sneers. "Nuts you get!"

This is a very discourteous statement, and it seems to make the little guy quite angry, because he suddenly makes a dive for Oscar and tries to grab the cylinder out of his hand.

There is quite a lusty scuffle, and all in a moment the two of them are rolling on the floor.

I look on, very shocked. Because I would not roll on a floor as dirty as Oscar's for all the gold in the world. Not even dice would I roll.

But in a minute I am even more shocked. Oscar jumps up on his feet and grabs the cylinder. The little old guy starts to dive for him, with his underwear flapping in the breeze. And all at once Oscar whips the cap off the cylinder and points it—right at the inventor's legs and feet.

There is a hideous scream. Then, an awful thump.

The little guy stops short and stares down at his waist. He is still screaming, but every time he tries to take a step the thumps drown him out.

Because Oscar turns the bottom half of the shrimp's underwear to solid gold!

"I can't move," wails the inventor fink. "It's too heavy!"

"Good," Oscar grunts, putting the cylinder back on the counter.

"Get me out of here," yells the little stranger. "The underwear is frozen tight. Even the buttons are solid, and the buttonholes. Get a can-opener or a pick-axe and chip me loose!"

"You mean I should go to work on you like a miner?" asks Oscar. "Not on your life. Seeing how you cannot move, I am going to carry you into the back room and let you cool off for a while. Do not make any noise, or I will turn the rest of your longerie to gold and you will be a statue from the neck down."

"What are you going to do with me?" quivers the little old guy.

"Nothing, if you are a good boy. I will let you stay in the back room and see that you are fed and that nobody melts you down into wedding rings. Meanwhile, I will make use of your little invention—very good use."

While he is talking, Oscar is shoving the half-man, half-statue back of the counter to the back room overlooking the river.

It all happens so fast I scarcely make up my mind. And just as I do make it up, Oscar comes back and raps me on the knuckles. So I drop the cylinder back on the counter again.

"I can't trust you either, can I, Feep?" he says. "Maybe I better tie you up, too. In a little burlap bag. Then I can turn the bag into gold and toss you into the river. You always say you want a luxurious funeral."

"Honest, I'm not going to steal the cylinder."

"I'll say you're not," Oscar tells me. "And you're not going to say anything about our inventor friend, either. You are going to be very quiet while I figure out what I want to do with this little money-maker."

So while Oscar sits there trying to figure out what to do with his little money-maker, I am sitting there trying to figure out what to do with my little money-spender.

Because I do not forget that I have a date with Sweetheart Singer this evening, and I still do not raise any money to raise whoopee on.

I do not see which way to turn, but it it is any consolation, neither does Oscar. He sits there grumbling to himself under his breath, thinking up scheme after scheme. But always something is wrong.

"What if I do turn sidewalks into gold," he says. "I don't own the sidewalks. Also, the Empire State Building is out—why should I make money for King Kong? Of course, I already got a fortune right here in the store, but I must figure out a way to get more. I need a lot of stuff I can turn into gold."

Every time he makes a remark, Oscar rubs his bald spot. And he makes so many remarks I figure he will wear himself down until he has nothing above the forehead in a little while. But he is so greedy that no scheme he thinks of will satisfy him.

All at once he sighs and gets up.

"Well, maybe I better figure some more," he yawns. "After all, there is plenty of time. The cylinder will not run away."

"That is right," I say.

"Oh, I forget!" he shouts. "Quick, I must lock up the store! With all this gold lying around I don't want any customers wandering in."

He races to the door, pausing only to turn the hook into gold and then going on his merry way.

"Better close the awnings, too," he decides. "Don't want anybody looking in through the windows tonight."

"I'll do it," I volunteer.

"Good."

So I step outside while Oscar waits.

When I skid past the door I do not hoist any awnings. I merely hoist my coattails and race away down the street.

Because Oscar is right when he says the cylinder will not run away. He just does not figure that I will run away, and that I will take the cylinder with me.

Which I do, lifting the thing off the counter just before I go out, when his back is turned.

So now I make very fleet with the feet, and behind me I hear Oscar yelling, "Stop, thief, stop, thief!" at the top of his voice.

Only this does not do any good. Because on such a street as the one where his store is, this command can apply to almost anyone passing by.

I just keep running, holding the cylinder under my coat, and I do not pause until I dash into the lobby of Sweetheart's apartment building.

It is already dark, and I do not wish to be late for my date. Because I am really gooey for this ginch. I got no more chance when I get near here than a hot marshmallow has around a Girl Scout.

I hold the cylinder very tight under my coat when I step up and ring the bell.

Already I am making plans. I will tell her about this cylinder and it will make her very happy and then perhaps we will get ourselves wedlocked. And this suits me fine. Some people do not approve of such an idea, because they say this Sweetheart is too mercenary. Me, I know different. She is not mercenary at all—only greedy.

And I figure the cylinder will take care of that. I mean to return it to the inventor, naturally, but I merely need to use it tonight.

So I have my little act all prepared. When the door opens I strike a pose with my arms stretched out and I whisper, "Sweetheart!"

"Ain't youse a little bold, stranger?" says a deep voice.

To make a long story embarrassing, it is not Sweetheart at all in the doorway, but a big lug.

I look up into a bristly red beard. Then I look further up into a big red mouth and a bigger red nose, and then I look way up into little red eyes.

This is quite a squint, because the lug in the doorway is over six feet tall in his stocking feet. Which is probably the way they measure him, because he does not look like the kind of personality who ever wears shoes.

"Is youse looking for somebody?" the lugs suggests. "Or maybe just a sock in the jaw?"

I stand there figuring out what to do. The way I see it, the only chance I have of punching him in the nose is to jump up and hit it with the top of my head.

Just then Sweetheart sticks her attractive puss around the doorway.

"Oh, hello, Lefty," she says. Then she turns to the lug. "Will you excuse me a minute?" she coos, very sweet. And steps out in the hall with me, shutting the door behind her.

"I'm sorry, Lefty," she tells me. "I forget all about our little date for this evening. I am going out with this gentleman friend of mine from Alaska."

"You mean that polar bear with the henna fur?" I snap.

"Don't talk that way," she pouts. "He is none other than the famous Klondike Ike. He is a very wealthy prospector."

"Prospector, eh?" I mention, in a sarcastic manner. "What does he own—a halitosis mine in Breath Valley?"

"He is rich," sniffs Sweetheart. "Why, he always carries a bag of raw gold dust around in his pocket."

"That's nothing," I tell her. "If it's gold you want, I am plenty dusty with it myself. I am so rich I am filthy."

She gives me a fishy stare.

"What are you trying to hand me, Lefty Feep? The only way you make money is by playing a slot machine—with a hammer."

"Give me five minutes," I yell. "Just five minutes. I'll be back here with more gold dust than this Eskimo Elmer of yours ever has."

"His name is Klondike Ike," Sweetheart says. "And yours is mud."

She slams the door on me.

Well, I am far from discouraged. I run downstairs and into the backyard of the apartment building. I find the janitor's shovel and a couple paper bags from the garbage incinerator. I fill the bags with dirt and get out the cylinder. I uncap it and point it at the dirt.

"Midascope, do your stuff," I whisper.

In thirty seconds I am puffing up the stairs again, lugging two sacks filled with gold dust. I take out a couple nuggets and pound on the door.

Klondike Ike sticks his beard out.

"Oh, it's you, is it?" he sneers. "What do you want—darling?" he says, in a very effeminate manner.

"I am a traveling dentist," I tell him, politely. "When you snarl at me, I see your teeth are decaying. I think they need some gold fillings."

Then I smash him one in the teeth with the nuggets. He looks very dented at my dentistry and slumps down on the floor. I march over him and into the apartment.

Sweetheart just stares at me when I pour the bags out over the carpet.

"See what I mean?" I tell her.

"Oh Lefty, darling, you're so rich—I mean, wonderful," she sighs, falling into my arms.

"What about our date?" I ask her, coming up for air a few minutes later.

"Let's go," she murmurs. "Oh honey, I never could resist a wealthy—a masterful man."

So she puts on her hat and face over at the mirror and steps out the door.

"Wait a minute," I call to her. "I want to wash up."

Saying which, I close the door and get to work. I figure on one grand gesture. I will turn on the cylinder all over her apartment. I will transform the floor, the walls, the furniture, everything into solid gold. Then when we come back later in the evening she will really see what I can do. This will certainly put my number up on her hit parade.

So I let fly with the Midascope, flashing it around like I am spraying with a Flit gun. In a minute I am standing dazzled. My eyes hurt. Everything sparkles and glitters. Yellow, tawny, shining gold surrounds me on all sides. The place looks like Rockefeller's delight.

Then I tiptoe out and lock the door. Sweetheart is waiting for me in the hall and we go downstairs. On the way down I pick up another bag of gold dust I leave stashed in the hallway. We are all set.

Well, I am just the kind of a personality to entertain a gold-digger this evening.

"Where shall we go?" Sweetheart asks.

"Why, the Ritz, of course," I tell her. And we do, in a taxi. When we get out I do not pay the driver, but hand him the bag of gold instead.

"Jeez," the cabby whispers. "There must be a fortune here, mister."

"Sure," I remark. "Almost enough to buy yourself a new tire."

And we swoop into the Ritz. On the way I duck off at the cloakroom until I find one of those big urns with the sand in it they use for throwing cigarette butts in. I scoop out sand, turn on the Midascope, and come back with pockets bulging from still more gold dust.

We go in and order the best—meaning plenty of champagne. Because I have just the appetite to drink a hearty meal.

All of this makes Sweetheart almost hysterical.

"I don't understand it at all, Lefty," she keeps saying. "Where does all this money come from?"

I just look mysterious. But after two quarts of the champagne, maybe I only look confused.

Anyway, she will not rest until she gets the story out of me. She keeps coaxing me all the time we are dancing, and she is some coaxer.

"You must tell me, darling," she sighs. All at once her eyes get very soft and tender. "I know—my great big wonderful man holds up a bank."

"Guess again. Gold is where you find it," I quote.

Her eyes get still more tender. She is wild about me.

"Maybe you kill a tax collector?" she breathes, sweetly.

"No. You're still cold."

This is a lie. Sweetheart is a lot of things, but she is not cold.

"Do you hijack a Brink's truck?"

"Uh-uh."

I lead her back to the table.

"I hate to disappoint you, Sweetheart," I say. "But I do not do anything dishonest to get this stack of chips. I just discover I am one of the long-lost Gold Dust Twins."

"They're black," she pouts. "And you are kidding me."

But she cannot pump the secret out of me. All she can do is pump champagne into me.

After we leave the Ritz—where I leave a cupful of dust to tip the waiter with—we go on to a couple of other hot spots. In fact, by midnight we see more joints than a chiropractor.

And all the while Sweetheart is itching to discover my secret. I keep stepping out for a minute on her to find some more sand or dirt to make dust out of with the Midascope—looking for rubber plants or cuspidors or sawdust—and every time I come back with a fresh batch she stares again. The Midascope cylinder is hot from being used so much. And Sweetheart isn't much cooler.

Finally, in our fifth joint and our sixth quart of champagne, I pop another bottle and the question.

"Sweetheart," I say, romantically, "let's you and me try a little wedded blitz."

"Are you proposing matrimony?"

"Matrimony hell—let's get married!" I snap.

She turns her big baby blue eyes up at me.

"Lefty," she says, "I think you are the one I am always waiting for. You are kind, and generous, and brave, and generous, and strong, and generous, and cultured, and—well, generous."

"I am glad you see it this way," I tell her. "Personally, I always look for a girl who agrees with me. And if you think I'm wonderful, I agree with you. So what are we waiting for?"

"Just one thing, darling," she tells me. "We must have no secrets between us. You must explain where it is you get all this gold from."

"All right," I say. The champagne is bubbling around in my head, and I figure it will not hurt to tell her.

So we leave this last dump and taxi home, and in the cab I explain the whole picture to her. Or at least part of it. I tell her I have this magic gimmick that turns anything I want into gold. And I also tell her that I have a little surprise waiting for her when she gets home.

"How wonderful you are," she says, softly. "To think that I am marrying a man with the Golden Touch! I hope we spend money—I mean, many—years together."

Right then and there I begin to feel maybe I am making a mistake.

I also begin to feel her fingers digging into my pocket and trying to snatch the cylinder.

I slap her very gently on the nose, but I am really just a wee bit burned up. She may not make such a perfect wife after all, I figure—like the other three I marry at one time or another.

In fact, from the way she speaks, she does not want a man at all. She would be happier with a cash register.

But it is too late now. I ask her, and a gentleman cannot back down. Without being sued for breach of promise, that is.

So I decide to make the best of it. We get up to the apartment door and she can't wait to get inside and see the surprise I promise her.

She runs up the stairs ahead of me, and I lurch behind. I hear her open the door and scurry in. Then I hear her give a screech.

"She must be plenty surprised," I figure.

But she is not as surprised as I am a minute later.

That is when she comes out just as I get to the head of the stairs. On her face is a very nasty look, and in her hand is a lead bookend.

The bookend does not stay in her hand long. It comes right down on my skull.

"Take that!" she shrieks. "You four-flushing phony! You and your fake gold bricks!"

I keep staring at the bookend. Only a couple of hours ago I turn it into gold. Now it is lead—

"My whole apartment," she screams. "Turned to lead—everything turned to lead! You—you counterfeiter!"

She catches me one across the side of the old noggin that spins me backward down the stairs.

When I get to the bottom I do not stop. I just keep right on running.

All the way to Out-of-Business Oscar's I am trying to puzzle it out in my aching orange. First gold and then lead—is something wrong?

Oscar and the little inventor fink are the only ones who can tell me. That is why I streak for the store.

When I get there the joint is still lighted behind the drawn awnings and shades. I bang on the door.

Oscar opens it.

"Something terrible happens," I yell. "I got to tell you—"

He glares and drags me inside by the scruff of the neck. I have a very tender scruff, too.

"You want to tell me?" he hollers. "Something terible happens to *you*? Look at what happens to me!"

I look. I stare straight up into a stuffed moose-head of solid lead. I look around at the lead clothing, the lead microscopes, the lead counters. Everything that the Midascope turns to gold is lead now. Dirty grey lead.

"It happens an hour ago," Oscar groans. "The gold just seems to fade away and there is nothing but lead all over."

He picks up the lead banana from the counter and throws it on the floor in a rage. He kicks out at the lead watermelon and then yells.

For the next minute all he can say is *ouch*.

"What about the inventor fink?" I ask.

"He is locked up in the back room," Oscar reminds me.

"Well, let's tell him—he ought to know what's wrong."

"So quiet back there I figure he goes to sleep," says Oscar. "But you're right. He might know what the trouble is."

We go up to the door and knock.

There is no sound.

"Come on in there," Oscar hollers. "Wake up."

"What is it?" asks the little stranger from behind the door.

"Something terrible happens to your Midascope. The stuff it turns to gold is all changing to lead now."

"Not really?"

"Absolutely."

All at once we hear a funny sound.

It is the little inventor fink, laughing.

"I am glad," he chuckles. "Something must be wrong with my discovery after all. And I am glad! Because your greedy behavior proves that the world isn't ready for such a miracle yet at all. I'm happy I make this failure.

"But now I must be leaving you—"

The voice stops.

"What does he mean?" Oscar yells. "How can he leave us?"

"The window in the room," I pant. "It opens on the river."

"But his heavy underwear is too heavy—" Oscar begins. I shake my head.

"Listen to that."

There is an awful bumping sound.

Oscar unlocks the door, throws it open.

There is the little inventor guy, balanced across the window-sill. He is ready to dive out. We stare at the heavy bottoms of his underwear.

"Hey—wait—don't jump—you can't!" we scream.

But the little inventor fink jumps. He tips forward, topples over, and disappears.

There is a terrific splash from below.

Oscar grabs the Midascope from my hand and runs to the window. "Come back here!" he shouts, hurling the cylinder out into the river.

"Missed him," he says. "Oh well—he's done for."

"It's suicide, swimming with that gold on him from the waist down," I admit.

"Gold? What gold? It changes, remember?" Oscar reminds me. "He probably drowns because of all the lead in his pants."

LEFTY FEEP cleared his throat in order to push another one of my rolls down it.

"So that's what you mean by being rich yesterday and poor today," I mused.

"Tragic, isn't it?"

"Very. I suppose Oscar is pretty mad at you for all this?"

"Why should he be?" Feep asked. "The cylinder turns out to be no good, so he doesn't need that. The junk in his store he can't sell, and now that it's turned to lead he can maybe get rid of it to the army for bullets. So he is all right.

"As for me, I get out of this mess with Sweetheart, so I am not behind on the deal."

"Then everything works out all right."

"Well, yes and no. Oscar *is* sore about just one thing. You see, this inventor fink is screwy when he says his Midascope turns stuff to gold. And he is also wrong about one other point—when he claims the cylinder does not work on flesh."

"Meaning what?"

"It's this way. Oscar is pretty blue last night when it's all over. He asks me what he's going to eat the next day without any money.

"So I tell him to hang a line out of his window and catch some perch from the river. He does, and that is why he is mad."

"How so?"

"Because he hangs his line in the spot where he throws the cylinder after the inventor. And instead of perch, he gets a string of nice, cute little goldfish."

I smiled.

"Too bad. But after all, he could still eat them, I suppose."

Feep frowned.

"That's what I tell him. And he does eat them. So now, you see, he's in the hospital."

"What's the matter?"

"Lead poisoning," said Lefty Feep.

AFTER WORDS

STANLEY: *This is a wonderful variation on that old joke about having lead (or ants) in your pants.*

BLOCH: If you try to shoot the ants you may end up with both.

JS: *The character of Klondike Ike looks and behaves like Bluto, Popeye's antagonist. Was that image in your mind?*

BLOCH: The only images I have in my mind would offend the Moral Majority.

JS: *You must have really had a great time writing these stories—dreaming up the funny names and situations. Almost like writing sketch material for a comedian.*

BLOCH: Writing for comedians is a special form of masochism which is best avoided—I did a little at one time and learned my lesson. I prefer the freedom which comes of writing for my own amusement.

JS: *We've seen the theme of avarice personified in our media by Auric Goldfinger, by Humphrey Bogart as Fred C. Dobbs in* The Treasure of Sierra Madre, *and by characters in the Batman comic book series. What or who did you specifically have in mind when writing* "The Golden Opportunity of Lefty Feep"?

BLOCH: Initially, I was prompted to do something about gold by my disgust for the government decree which made it a federal offense to own more than one hundred dollars in gold bullion or raw gold—i.e., about three ounces at the pegged price back then. To me it smacked of the very dictatorial policies we were supposedly fighting against in World War II. I determined to say a few things Erich von Stroheim hadn't managed to convey in what MGM preserved from his original cut of *Greed*. Then, just in time, I realized that it would not be appropriate to come on too strong in the type of story I was telling; I'd have to show the ridiculous lengths people resort to when wealth is the goal, but eliminate any overt comment on it. That was when I hit upon my ending—the ultimate example of "all that glitters is not gold"—which expressed my sentiments exactly, yet did not violate the Feep canon.

JS: *This last story in the book,* "A Snitch in Time," was written especially for this edition.

BLOCH: It was a challenge to see if I could still recapture the style. Actually, I found I'd really never learned to change it very much. As the old saying goes, "You can't teach an old dog new trees."

A brand-new grand-brew 1987 Lefty Feep story, in which Lefty traverses thirty-seven years of history. A timely story with cultural overtones.

A SNITCH IN TIME

I SELDOM get to New York nowadays, and when I do, New York gets to me.

Too much traffic, too much confusion, too many people—it's a combination I try to avoid whenever possible. But this trip was necessary, and I had no choice. Knowing in advance that my actual business errand would take a good half-day of my time, I planned my schedule accordingly, and arranged for a three-day stay. It turned out well—after making the necessary allowances for a delayed flight, the wait and search for my luggage, the efforts to hail a taxi, the hassle at the hotel where they'd fouled-up my room reservation, and the usual complications of trying to make a direct-dial long-distance call home, I found I'd used up the first day just as expected.

Next morning all I had to do was phone and confirm my business appointment, and again my time-estimate proved to be correct. After six wrong numbers and eleven calls, during which I sat and listened to recorded music before being cut off, I finally got through to my party and was told by his secretary that he'd left for the day. But I managed to set up a meeting for tomorrow afternoon, so progress was being made.

And sure enough, on the third day, just as I'd hoped, I did take a meeting. Granted, I only got to spend ten minutes with the man I'd come to see—make that two minutes, if you allow the time he spent on the telephone during the conference—but that was all to the good. It meant I could still get to the hotel, check out, commandeer a cab to the airport, and board another delayed flight which would land me back home by midnight. My three-day journeying had not been in vain after all, and the man I'd come to see for a decision had given me a definite maybe.

As a result I was feeling pretty good when I left his office and took an elevator down to the lobby. Once there, I took a deep breath, put one hand on my wallet, clenched the other hand into a fist, and prepared to fight my way through the crowd until I reached the street.

Fortunately, there was help at hand. All I had to do was walk behind two lawyers and a union official who were apparently late for a meeting with the Mafia. As they swung their attache cases, knocking down an assortment of obstacles ranging from school children to little old ladies, I merely followed in their footsteps on my way to the streets of Fun City.

I had almost reached the door when I saw him.

For a moment I blinked. Everyone knows about *deja vu* but this was ridiculous.

Or, rather, he was ridiculous—this tall, thin man standing against the far wall, and waving frantically. He was distressingly dressed in chalk-striped trousers and a checked jacket which should have been chucked long ago. He wore a felt hat of a type which had not been felt on a human head for years, and his alligator shoes were not the kind any self-respecting alligator would wear.

I blinked again, but when I opened my eyes he was waving and weaving his way through the crowd. Towards *me*.

"Oh no!" I muttered. "It can't be!"

It couldn't be, but it was—

"Lefty Feep!"

I gasped his name and he nodded. "I know who you are

the minute I recognize you." He eyed my stomach, then my head. "More there, and less hair. You do not change as much as I expect."

"But you haven't changed at all," I murmured. "How long has it been since the last time I saw you?"

"Who's counting?" Feep grinned.

"That's not the question," I told him. "What I want to know is what you're doing here."

"Looking for you," he said. "And here you are, just as nifty as in nineteen-fifty."

"You really thought I'd be in the same place after all these years?"

Feep shrugged. "Don't I always find you somewhere around Jack's Shack?"

I sighed. "If you're talking about the restaurant that used to be here, forget it. They tore the place down and put up this high-rise instead."

"What happened to Jack?" Feep asked.

"He died some years ago."

"That figures." Feep shook his head. "I always warn him not to keep eating the stuff he serves his customers."

As we spoke the lobby crowd kept brushing past, nudging us closer to the front exit. "Look," I said. "There's another restaurant around the corner. And I've got a million questions to ask you."

"Copesetic," Feep said. "I get a meal and you get a deal."

Taking his arm, I escorted him outside and down the street to an East Indian place—the Delhi Deli. And it was there, after working our way through two bowls of the house specialty, rhinoceros curry, that I finally asked the inevitable question.

"Nineteen-fifty was a long time ago. Where have you been since then?"

"Nowhere. Up until today I am still in nineteen-fifty."

"But that's impossible!" I stared at my long-lost new-found friend and frowned. "On the other hand, you certainly look exactly the same as you did the last time I saw you. Even your clothes haven't changed—"

"Only my underwear. I change it every week, rain or shine."

"Never mind the weather report. If you were still in nineteen-fifty until today, then how did you get here?"

"Time travel," said Lefty Feep.

The echo of his words jarred my memory. "That's right, I remember now. Didn't you tell me something about using a time machine way back when?"

The waiter brought us some cookies for dessert and Feep removed his hat, probably out of respect for their age. Then he nodded.

"The fact is exact," he said. "I make several time-machine trips in the past, to say nothing of the future."

"So you claimed." I shook my head. "But frankly, I never quite believed you. Time travel is a scientific impossibility. Any man-made vehicle capable of reaching the speed necessary to advance or reverse itself in time would be destroyed the moment it started to move. The effort to overcome the forces of entropy is enough to make such a machine fall apart if only because of the friction."

Feep shrugged. "Truth is stranger than friction," he said. "So here I am."

I had no answer for that—only another question. "But why?" I asked.

"You remember what I tell you about Sylvester Skeetch and Mordecai Meech. These are the characters who send me through time before. And they know how to do it, on account of they are scientists."

"That's right." I nodded. "As I recall, their methods are highly unorthodox."

"Leave religion out of this," Feep said. "Both Skeetch and Meetch happen to be born-again atheists. But they run this Horsecracker Institute which has plenty of money to spend on experiments for learning how to find out about things. It is funded by the same charity that operates the Society for the Contribution of Delinquency to Minors. Also they sponsor this big campaign to donate sex transplants to the poor in other countries. It is called Glands Across the Sea."

I frowned. "What has all this to do with you?"

"Plenty," Feep told me. "I do not live in another country and I do not need a sex transplant, but I am poor. So when Skeetch and Meetch tell me they have invented a new, improved time machine, my ears perk up. And when they say they need somebody to take the machine into the future, my spirits perk up too. And when they offer me ten cents for every day I travel through time, coming and going, I am tempted."

"Just how much money does that amount to, in actual cash?" I asked.

"I am not sure, because I count with my hands. But I know it runs well into five fingers."

"So you agreed? You were willing to risk your life just for a deal like this?"

"Of course not." Feep grinned. "I tell them it is very dangerous, and I will not go unless they come up with a better offer. But then they throw in a ten-dollar tip, so how can I refuse?"

"I still don't understand," I said. "Why did those two dingalings need to invent another time machine if they had one already?"

"Because this new model is bigger."

"What difference does that make?"

"It means the machine has more room to carry stuff."

"Like what?"

"Like the things they send me here to get. That is why I am here—to bring back things from the future which they can study. Like from the year 2000."

"But it isn't 2000 yet."

"This I find out when I arrive." Feep sighed. "Maybe I run into a detour. But I am sure Skeetch and Meetch will be happy just as long as I bring them what they ask for."

"Such as?"

Feep produced a notebook from his jacket. "They give me a list. Also the money to buy stuff with." Our check arrived and he grabbed it before I could, shaking his head. "You always buy our meals twenty-three times before, so I figure it is my turn to grab the tab."

He stared at the bill. If the waiter had been clearing the table he might have picked up Feep's eyes by mistake, for they were as big as saucers.

"Holy Toledo!" he said. "Fifteen bucks apiece for curry? A dollar-fifty for a cup of coffee?"

I shrugged. "Times change. Haven't you heard of inflation?"

"Sure. That's how you blow up balloons." He shook his head. "But Skeetch and Meetch do not."

"They don't blow up balloons?"

"They don't hear about inflation." Feep pulled out a wallet and emptied its contents on the table-top. "Look what they hand me to buy things with! Three hundred dollars will cover my expenses the way a band-aid covers Jane Russell's cleavage."

"Don't tell me you're supposed to bring her back too?"

"No such luck." Feep sighed. "But prices are a crisis."

"What *do* they want?"

Feep scanned his list. "A half-dozen books, for starters. At three bucks a throw, that's eighteen dollars for six."

"Eighteen dollars for one, if you're lucky," I told him. "Three bucks is just enough for one magazine."

Feep's eyes expanded from saucers to dinner plates. "That's only the beginning. They also request clothes, a radio, and one of those big TV sets with the twelve-inch screens and—"

"Twenty-six inches," I corrected him. "You can pick one

up for around six hundred or so. Also you should get a VCR."

"A what?"

I described a videocassette to him. "Lots of other new things around they'd be interested in. Perhaps they'd like a nice Apple."

"Now you are batting in my league." Feep looked relieved. "Apples they like. And even with this inflation you tell me about, I figure I can pick up an apple for maybe ten cents."

"Make that ten thousand dollars, if you get all the extras and the software."

"Ten thousand in loot just for fruit?" Feep's eyes were now the size of platters. "What kind of apple is that?"

"It's a computer."

"You mean they now have apples that are adding machines? Since when does an apple know how to add?"

I gave him a brief explanation of computer technology and he nodded.

"You are right. Skeetch and Meetch would love a computer, seeing as how they are the forgetful type and are always overdrawn at the memory-bank. But how can I purchase such items?" He riffled the bills. "All I hold is three C's—maybe two-fifty after I deal with this meal. And the way you say, two hundred and fifty smackers do not smack very loud."

I glanced at my watch. "I wish I could help you, but in two hours I've got to catch a plane for home."

"You no longer reside in Manhattan?"

"For the past twenty-five years or so I've been writing television and screenplays out on the West Coast."

"Like Hollywood?"

"Exactly."

"I like Hollywood too." Feep nodded. "I am very big on Judy Garland and John Wayne, all those Andy Hardy movies—"

"Sorry," I murmured. "Garland has wilted, John has waned, and Andy isn't very Hardy either. Hollywood changed."

"Take me with you," Feep said.

"Why on earth—?"

"Because I *am* on earth. One of the things Skeetch and Meetch want most is for me to bring back a movie. It is on the list—see for yourself."

"I see, but I don't understand. What could you do in Hollywood?"

"Maybe I can find employment there."

"But I thought you didn't like working."

"Do not tell me Hollywood is changed that much," Feep said. "If you get the right job you don't have to work." He leaned forward, gripping my lapels. "Besides, if I earn enough money I can buy the stuff I am sent here to get."

I considered his request for a moment. It did make sense in a way, and more to the point, it wouldn't cost me anything because I was on an expense account.

"Okay," I said. "For old times' sake."

Lefty Feep grinned happily, his face in striking contrast to that of the dour waiter's as he came to collect his bill. Feep handed him the proper amount with a lordly gesture, then beckoned me to rise. "Do not wait, gate. First the curry, now the hurry. There is a plane to catch."

As we moved around the table, the waiter counted the money, then intercepted Feep with a scowl.

"What about my tip?" he demanded.

"I got one for you," Feep told him. "Fifth race at Hialeah. The horse's name is Indigestion, which is what I will probably get from eating at this ptomaine-palace."

We stepped outside. Apparently there had been some rain, but now the problem was hailing taxis. Finally we found one and whizzed off to our destination at a steady five miles per hour, not counting stops for traffic signals, jaywalkers, and detours to avoid the bodies of mugger victims lying in the street—which, the cab driver told us, were really bad for the tires.

Once at the terminal Feep was visibly impressed by its size. "Where are we?" he asked.

"La Guardia."

He shook his head. "Do not tell me the mayor of New York now runs an airport?"

"No, it's just a name. Like John F. Kennedy."

"Who?"

"Never mind." I pushed my way to the ticket counter. "Got to get you a seat on this flight."

The ticket-clerk glanced at Lefty Feep's attire with dubious eyes. "Any luggage?"

"Fifty-three pieces," Feep said.

"Fifty-three?"

"A deck of cards and a corkscrew."

She waved us on and I grinned. It was just like old times; I hadn't heard that gag in years.

As we reached the security checkpoint, the guard issued his order. "Please remove all metal objects and place them on the conveyor."

Following my example, Feep emptied keys and change from his pockets, then strode through the detector-gate. A buzz of warning rose and the guard glared at him.

"What else you got?" he demanded. "I said to remove all metal objects from your person."

Feep shook his head. "If you think I'm taking off my truss here in public, you're crazy."

But the guard insisted on leading Feep to a curtained booth where he confirmed his claim, and we lost a good three minutes before getting clearance.

"Why doesn't he take my word for it?" Feep grumbled. "Don't I look truss-worthy?"

"Never mind," I said. "We've got one minute left to catch our plane."

Luck was on our side, because we made it. And luck

continued to hold, because we actually departed less than forty-five minutes late.

The flight was smooth and my seat-mate seemed pleased. It wasn't until somewhere between our third cocktail and Nebraska that the thought hit me.

"Hey!" I said. "What about your time machine?"

Feep shrugged. "Do not get into a fret. I hide it in a safe place. Hiding is the best way of concealing things you do not wish anyone to find."

"It's too bad I forgot," I said. "Otherwise we could have used your machine for this trip and saved time too."

"Just as well," he told me. "The time machine does not serve cocktails." Winking, he raised his glass. "Here's mud in your eye."

THERE WAS no mud in my eye when we arrived at L.A. International Airport—only smog.

Feep blinked as we emerged from the terminal, then started to wheeze.

"What is there in the air?" he demanded.

"Smog."

"This stuff is rough." He coughed. "Do you mention a new invention?"

"Smog is air-pollution. It comes from car exhaust, factory fumes. Haven't you ever heard of toxic waste?"

"No, I do not," Feep said. "But it makes sense. Who wants to save toxics?"

Locating my car in the parking area, I paid its ransom to the attendant, then headed out and onto the freeway.

My companion was visibly impressed. "The traffic here is even worse than New York," he said. "Why is there no leeway on the freeway?"

"This is nothing," I assured him. "You ought to see it during rush-hours."

"How come there are so many more drivers now?"

"Population explosion," I said.

Feep frowned. "I know there are a lot of changes but this is ridiculous. Don't tell me people now get exploded instead of born?" He shook his head. "Personally, I like the old way better. What happens to the birds and the bees?"

"They haven't changed, and neither have people. We do have a birth-control pill, but even so, since nineteen-fifty the population of earth has almost doubled."

"I forget nobody gets killed in wars anymore, since World War II brings peace to the world."

"Wrong," I said. "Right now there are wars in Africa, Asia, Afghanistan, the Middle East and Central America, among other places. We ourselves fought in Korea and Vietnam, though war was not officially declared and people were just killed unofficially."

"What happens to all this progress they promise us?"

"Oh, there's progress," I assured him. "We have nuclear power plants everywhere, even if sometimes they leak a little. And we have enough nuclear weapons to blow up the earth a hundred times over."

"Once is enough," Feep said. "Why do they make more?"

"Armaments are big business. And big business means more jobs for more people."

"Which means they have more money to buy this birth-control pill only they keep on having more children instead." Feep frowned. "Skeetch and Meetch will not like to hear such things because they always say science solves our problems."

"Science isn't all bad," I assured him. "We're into space technology now. Back in nineteen sixty-nine men went to the moon."

"The way things are here on earth, I don't blame them," Feep said. "I am surprised everybody doesn't go."

"Too expensive. You're forgetting about inflation."

"I don't forget. All I want is to find a job and make enough to take care of my list."

"Right now all I want is some rest," I told him. We left the freeway and zigzagged our way to my little mortgage-covered home in the Valley.

Once inside I made up a bed in the spare room and bid Feep goodnight. "Sleep fast," I suggested. "I've got to be at the studio at nine o'clock tomorrow morning."

How fast he slept I don't know. As for me, I conked out immediately and barely rose in time to hear the news as we ate a hasty breakfast, devouring radio reports of rape, murder, race riots, epidemics and other ordinary events, along with our eggs and bacon.

Then we were off to my appointment. "It won't take long," I promised. "And as soon as I'm finished I'll drive you around to some employment agencies."

Arriving at the studio gate, I flashed my pass to the security officer.

"Hold it!" he said, staring at my passenger. "Who's the flake in the funny outfit?"

Being used to Feep, I took his outlandish attire for granted, but obviously others did not. I groped for a logical explanation, and found it.

"He's my psychiatrist," I said.

The guard nodded. "That figures," he said, waving us on.

Reaching my parking space, I climbed out. "You sit here and wait," I told Feep. "I won't be long."

"Can't I walk around a little? I never beat my feet in a real Hollywood studio before and this is my chance to take a glance."

"Stay put," I cautioned. "I have to take this meeting, but you don't have to take chances."

Feep nodded and I raced off. Entering the office, I spent the usual half-hour waiting until the receptionist got through to my producer's secretary. But my meeting was a great success because it turned out the producer had forgotten about it and gone off to Bermuda to make some shorts.

Then I returned to the car. "Let's go!" I said, but I was talking to myself.

Lefty Feep had vanished.

Anxiously I scanned the studio street. It was filled with the usual assortment of bearded young directors, still-younger producers in ragged Gucci jeans, and well-dressed messengers on motor carts, hurrying to their coffee breaks. But the street was Feepless.

In mounting panic, I headed past a row of sound stages, then rounded the corner before the imposing executive offices. And it was there that I spotted my lanky, long-lost friend.

"Hey!" he shouted. "I am looking for you!"

"Why did you leave the car?"

Feep smiled. "I see a gorgeous ginch passing by who looks like Ava Gardner, so I chase into her space and ask for her autograph, only she turns out to be a cleaning lady."

"What's that in your hand?" I asked.

Feep's grin broadened. "I make a contact for a contract."

"Contract? For what?"

"Twenty grand," he told me. "Four weeks guaranteed, play-or-pay, plus two thou per diem for production overrun."

"Where did you pick up all that language?"

"From my agent."

I gulped. "Since when do you have an agent?"

"Since I am on my way back to the car and I run into this character who rushes up to me and makes with the grab-and-gab. It turns out he is casting a horror flick called *Thanksgiving VII* on account it's a sequel to six other turkeys."

"You in a horror picture?" I blinked. "What are you playing—some new kind of monster?"

Feep shook his head. "It turns out they already have a monster. But the story is set in the Forties and they are still looking for somebody to fill the part of a racetrack character. The way I spot the plot, there is some fruitcake who kills off all the other jockeys so his horse will have the only rider left in the big race. Then there is this werewolf—"

"Your agent?"

"My agent is not a werewolf," Feep protested. "At least I do not think so, since he looks more like a barracuda."

"Then just where does he come in?"

"He comes in when he passes by and hears me doing a deal with this casting director. In fact, I am ready to sign for a hundred bucks and a free lunch when he runs over and announces he represents me. And in five minutes he sets this deal."

"Incredible," I muttered. "Who is this agent of yours?"

"Nifty Bizarre."

My jaw dropped. "Now I believe it. Bizarre is one of the top names in the business."

"Then I'm in like Flynn!" Feep exulted. "With twenty Gs to start with, I can lease a Mercedes, rent a lair in Bel Air—"

"What about Skeetch and Meetch?" I asked.

"Who needs them? I'm gonna be a movie star."

I shook my head. "All right, if you say so. Now let's get back to the car."

"Thanks but no thanks," Feep told me. "Bizarre will drive me to the Mercedes showroom in his limo. He says if I want to be a star it is not a good idea to hang out with the little people, such as writers."

AND THAT'S HOW it is. In less than twenty-four hours, Lefty Feep had gone Hollywood.

I couldn't comprehend it, but there was no choice. And in the weeks to come all I saw of Feep was his name in the trades. He had indeed been cast in the picture—it was definitely in production—his part was being enlarged—the studio was touting him as a new media personality—his name was creeping into the columns—it was rumored he might even appear on *The Phil Donahue Show*.

I had my own problems. My producer came back from his long stay in Bermuda shorts and put me to work changing the rewrite of my revision of my altered script so that it would read more like my original first draft.

Lefty Feep was the least of my worries. Until the evening he showed up unexpectedly at my front door. I use the term "unexpectedly" advisably, because he began knocking promptly at two a.m.

I blinked at the familiar figure in the familiar attire, but seeing is believing and this was Feep, in the flesh. All that was lacking was his grin as he spoke.

"Greetings, gate—let's navigate."

"What brings you here?" I mumbled.

"The Mercedes. But it goes back to the showroom tomorrow—as soon as I gad from my pad."

"Don't tell me you lost your job?"

Feep shook his head. "I finish my part and they are so happy they offer me an even better contract for the next sequel. Bizarre says he can get me a quarter mil upfront plus five percent of the gross. And he thinks the picture will be very gross indeed."

"Then why this nocturnal mission, if you'll pardon the expression?"

"I turn down the deal," Feep told me. "On account I am through with Hollywood."

"I don't understand."

"That makes two of us." Feep sighed. "Movies turn out to be a big drag, and I am not referring to the way some of the actors dress offscreen. Instead of four weeks I work thirteen, which is not my lucky number. We shoot overtime night and day, but what they end up with is awful. They show me a preview of the picture, and I can produce a better film from my teeth."

"There'll be others," I assured him. "One swallow doesn't make a Capistrano."

"I cannot swallow any more of this gunk," Feep declared.

LEFTY FEEP

"Hollywood is not like it is in the old days. All I see in the new movies is sex and violence, or just violent sex. They are doing things on the screen that I will not do behind my own back."

"But it's a good life," I said. "Didn't you want to meet the stars?"

Feep sighed again. "I get to know them but they do not know me, on account most of them are freaked out of their beaks. Where I come from you offer friends a drink. Here they hand you cocaine."

"And you refused?"

He nodded. "I tell them to shove it up their nose."

"But what about your Mercedes and that big house in Bel Air?"

"I find it does not matter what kind of car you drive. You still have to fight the traffic, inhale the exhaust and go barking for parking. Also there are too many car thieves and too many traffic cops, and I do not know which is worse."

"And the house?"

"Do you ever try living in a fourteen-room split-level rat-trap? If I hire full-time help it costs more than I make. If I try keeping it up myself I spend two hours a day just turning on all the security alarms. I do not wish to bring strife to my life manicuring the front lawn or figuring out how to cook a hotdog in one of those newfangled electronic gadgets. And believe it or not, there is not one decent hamburger stand anywhere in Bel Air." He shook his head. "Not for me, pal. I am perfectly happy to stay my day in a nice six-buck hotel room with just a cold beer and a hot chambermaid."

"Then what do you intend to do?"

"What I am sent here for. With all the money I get for those extra weeks I have close to forty G's left in cash. This will buy the items Skeetch and Meetch ask me to get. And still leave enough to pay your way roundtrip to New York and back."

"You expect me to go with you?"

"I know it is a big favor, but I need help. How else can I find all this stuff?"

For a moment I thought it over. As it so happened, my work here was finished until my producer found somebody who could read the last draft of my script without moving his lips. And this wouldn't happen tomorrow. Besides, I was curious about one thing.

"If I come with you, will you let me see the time machine?" I asked.

Feep nodded quickly. "You got a promise."

"Then you have a deal," I said.

MORNING CAME, and we went.

At the airport Feep bought our tickets and we hurried to the security-check. His only luggage was a small tote-bag and this time, to my surprise, he went through the detector-gate without setting off a warning buzz.

"What happened to your truss?" I asked.

Before he could reply the answer came in a burst of sound as his tote-bag slid along the conveyor. At the guard's insistence, Feep opened it and pulled out a gleaming metallic object.

"I remember when we go through security before you are annoyed because I wear it," Feep told me. "So this time I take it off. I rather go without a truss than rupture our friendship."

Once aboard the plane, we settled into our seats for take-off. "What is all this security check for?" he asked. "We do not have such a thing in my time."

"You didn't have terrorists then," I said.

"Terrorists?"

As we taxied down the runway and lifted off, I tried to explain terrorism and the hijacking of planes.

"In the old days all we hijack is alcohol," Feep murmured. "Who are these terrorist personalities and what do they look like?"

"Hard to tell. Usually they wear ski-masks."

"You mean people are now ashamed to be recognized when they go skiing?"

"Terrorists don't ski. They plant bombs. They take hostages. They kill passengers and crew members."

Feep sighed. "I guess you can't stop progress," he said.

"Cheer up," I advised. "You won't be around here much longer so enjoy the trip. We're in first-class, the drinks are free, and we have distinguished company." I glanced ahead at the imposing figure occupying the front seat in the cabin. "Do you know him?"

"Isn't that the guy I see in all those violent war pictures?"

I nodded. "It's Stanislaus Steroid."

Feep grinned. "That's right—the Polish Sausage! I do not recognize him at first because he has a shirt on." He stared at Steroid admiringly. "This guy is a bigger hambo than Rambo. He fills up more body bags than all the rest of them put together. Now I can stop worrying about terrorists."

As the seat-belt warning flicked off, Feep rose, clutching his tote-bag.

"Where are you going?" I asked.

"To the washroom. I will take more delight in the flight if I put my truss on again."

I watched him move down the aisle toward the lavatory upfront, pausing briefly to cast an appreciative glance at Stanislaus Steroid's hunklike presence. Then he opened the lavatory door, stepped inside—and jumped backwards, the gleaming truss dangling from his hand.

Turning, he waved the truss at Steroid.

"There is a character in the washroom!" he shouted. "Putting on a ski-mask!"

But his warning came too late.

The character was already stepping out behind Feep, the ski mask covering his face. Standing in the aisle, he leveled an Uzi at the first-class passengers.

"Freeze!" he yelled.

"Never mind the weather report," Feep said. He waved his truss at Steroid. "Quick—go get him!"

Steroid stared at the terrorist and rose to the challenge. Then, turning, he bent down and made a frantic effort to hide under his seat.

As he did so, one of his lumbering legs thrust out into the aisle. It collided with Feep's knees, knocking him back. Flailing to regain balance, Lefty Feep crashed into the masked man behind him and the two men went down in a flurry of writhing limbs.

When the limbs untangled the Uzi was skidding down the aisle, Feep was sitting on top of the terrorist, and his truss was twisted around the ski-masked neck in a choking grip.

"Hold it, buddy!" Feep advised. "Before this truss gives you a strangulated hernia!"

I noted the Uzi as it slid past. "Plastic," I murmured. "So that's how it got through security—"

Then the cabin attendants burst out of the tourist-class section and took over.

By the time we landed in New York, order had been restored. I didn't notice where the weapon disappeared to, but the terrorist was in custody and Feep was wearing his truss and a smile of satisfaction. And at the terminal, reporters were already waiting to interview Stanislaus Steroid about his heroic capture of the armed assailant.

"It was nothing," Steroid declared with characteristic modesty. "I woulda got him even sooner if I woulda had time to take my shirt off."

"I'll say it was nothing," I whispered to my companion. "You deserve the credit. Don't let him get away with this!"

Feep shrugged. "It is more important we get away," he said. "I do not wish publicity about my plans. Let us scram out of here, friend—I got to get hopping with the shopping."

WE HOPPED and we shopped, and we stopped only after the stores were vacant for the night and our arms were full.

"Where is your time machine?" I asked.

Feep stopped a cab and we piled in, lugging packages and shopping bags. "Public Library," he said.

The cabbie frowned. "It's closed," he growled.

"Like your mouth should be," Feep told him. "Don't jive—just drive!"

As we rolled forward I shook my head. "You left your time machine at the Library?"

"Why not? It is the best place in town because nobody goes to borrow books anymore—they just watch television."

We emerged from the cab directly before the stone lions at the Library entrance. Gripping my share of the bundles, I glanced at Feep. "Now where? Don't tell me you checked the time machine at the counter."

"It's up on the roof," he told me. "I figure it is the safest place there."

Safest it might be, but easiest it wasn't. We had to lug our purchases around to the back of the building and it was there I discovered why Feep had bought a huge coil of stout rope and a grappling hook.

By the time we hauled ourselves and our packages up to the roof I was winded, but still curious. Glancing across the rooftop, I shook my head. "The time machine," I wheezed. "Where is it?"

Feep pointed at an object deep in shadow behind the chimney.

I shook my head. "Time machine? It looks more like one of those taxicabs they used to have forty years ago." Then I stared at him. "You mean you're really using a taxi for a time machine?"

Feep shrugged. "Why not? The meter isn't running."

I shrugged back at him. "If you ask me, your friends

Skeetch and Meetch aren't in operating-order either. Imagine using a cab for time travel—"

"It works," Feep said. "And there is plenty of room in one of these babies for all the packages. Come on, let's go with the stow."

Dragging our parcels over to the cab, we filled the back seat as Feep ticked off the purchase items on his list.

Typical items of clothing and adornment went first—baseball caps, T-shirts emblazoned with pictures of rock stars and porno graphics, men's earrings, women's see-through bras, and the plastic pink curlers they wear when shopping for items in high-fashion stores; jogging outfits; and the neckbraces worn by broken-down joggers. Then came the portable radios, the portable telephones and the wrist-band buzzers timed to remind people of their appointments whenever they take off for the wide open spaces to get away from the cares of civilization. There were insurance-claim forms and medical forms and federal and state and city income-tax forms, along with forms to fill out when reporting car accidents, muggings and robberies.

Nor had Feep forgotten about the books. He'd bought one about crooked politicians, one about crooked law-enforcement officers, another about crooked labor leaders, others about crooked business practices and crooked rest homes for the aged. His sixth volume was a health book telling how to avoid stress.

"We do a good job," he murmured. "Skeetch and Meetch will be happy. Here is the plastic stuff to make bombs with, and this here computerized enema-bag—those whips and chains and dildoes from the sex-shop—I fill this can with toxic chemical waste from the water-tap—and here is the LSD I purchase from that guy on the street outside school.

"We got just about everything new and up-to-date in the world today! It is a pity we do not have time to contact a spy in the government and make a deal for a nuclear warhead."

He peered into the front seat of the cab. I noted the

complex array of instruments on the gleaming panel which had replaced its old dashboard. Now, for the first time, I fully realized that this was not a hoax; what I saw could indeed constitute the working mechanism of a time-traveling device. It didn't matter if the controls were installed in an old taxicab or a converted garbage can; the vehicle was merely a convenient conveyance which would whisk its way through time and space at a speed which defied gravity, entropy and all known laws of physics.

It made no sense, but then neither did Lefty Feep. Yet he was here, and in a moment he would be gone. Strangely enough, I knew I was going to miss him.

"All set?" I asked. "Then it's time to say goodbye. But before you go, just one question, something I've wanted to ask ever since I met you. When you talk, why do you always speak in the present tense?"

"Why not?" Feep shrugged. "The present *is* pretty tense, if you ask me."

In a way, it made a strange sort of sense. Even coming into the future like this to find out how fouled-up life had become made sense of a sort—and going back to the past made even more.

"I think I understand," I said. "And now that you're ready to go—"

"Almost."

"Almost?"

He nodded. "There is just one other thing Skeetch and Meetch ask me to get. They tell me they wish to study a citizen from the future. So I am putting the snitch on somebody to take back with me."

"But where will you find one?"

"I already snitch him." Feep grinned, then produced the terrorist's missing weapon from his jacket pocket and leveled it at me. "The citizen I take back in time is you."

And he did.

AFTER WORDS

STANLEY: *Placing Lefty Feep in modern society allowed you to make some poignant and satirical comments on the many things that are wrong in today's world.*

BLOCH: Not too many. If I'd tried to put them all in, I'd end up with an encyclopedia.

JS: *The human race sounds pretty deplorable. Do you have hopes for it in the future?*

BLOCH: Yes—granted they don't goof things up so there won't be any future.

JS: *You especially have fun poking at Hollywood. Have you become bitter about the way the industry is run, and the depths to which many movies have bubbled?*

BLOCH: In view of the cow-flops they turn out, I can only hope the future will be better than the pasture.

JS: *Now that we've reviewed the first eight Lefty Feep stories, and you've had a chance to write a brand-new one, what do you enjoy most about the stories?*

BLOCH: The fact that both they and I are still around.

JS: *What is your over-all reaction to the return of Lefty Feep?*

BLOCH: If Norman Bates can come back, then why not Lefty? It's nice to see one's children grow up. Some day I might even try it myself . . .

BLOCH RESEARCHES

The Next Book
In This Extraordinary Series:

"FURTHER MISADVENTURES OF LEFTY FEEP"

Coming Sooner Than You Had Feared

COLOPHON

Lefty Feep once remarked "If Ma Bell ever installs a new extension in my place, tell her I want a red colophon." Hence, it seems appropriate that this collection of stories ends on a colophon that can indeed be read.

The ripe type is 11-pt. Sabon set on a 13-pt. slug, a caliber that will never fit into a pearl-handled .45 automatic. Sabon is an easy-on-the-eyes type designed by a cheerful Frenchman who used to stroll along the Left Bank singing "Sa-bon Sa-bon, dee dottety dottety dottety dah, Sa-bon Sa-bon . . . "

Assisting the editor (who is himself lost in time and space, and needs all the assistance available to him) was a gentleman whose high-buttoned shoes are firmly implanted in the 20th Century, Paul de Fremery, the West Coast representative for Braun-Brumfield, a company that printed and bound this book in Ann Arbor. (What Ann was doing there at the time was never made clear.) Somehow, Mr. de Fremery managed to keep a straight face through the entire Lefty Feep project.

Approximately five thousand copies were bound as a quality paperback, with an additional 250 copies bound in an expensive deluxe hardcover dust-jacketed boxed edition. Lefty Feep has never had it so good in his life. Remarked Robert Bloch at press time, "Old Lefty would be pleased to see himself in color on the front cover after a lifetime of obscurity in black-and-white interior illos."

Life can be a dream, sweetheart . . .